Heidi's Hope

a novel by

Stephen Goss

ISBN-13: 978-1-4637-2052-0
ISBN-10: 1-4637-2052-1

csR1000-130702

To

Mom and Dad,
my grandparents,
my aunts and uncles,
for their love and encouragement.

And to

Tom, Gary, Heidi, and Don,
for their examples.

Heidi's Hope

The Story In Brief:

As World War II draws to a close, attorney John Richards attends a prominent church solely to rub shoulders with its influential members. Then he meets Lydia, a minister's daughter, and becomes so infatuated he spends hours looking for her name in the Bible.

When John tells Lydia he read Matthew, Mark, Luke, and John in one sitting, she assumes he's a man of faith and their relationship blossoms. By the time she realizes his ship of faith is in shallow waters, she's too deep in love to turn down his proposal.

They raise two daughters through the 1950s and 60s: Katie, the rebel; and Heidi, who wakens to faith at an early age and whose hope, in a surprising way, carries her father through heartbreaking tragedy.

With short chapters and down-home storytelling, HEIDI'S HOPE is an adventure in life that begins with a love story and ends with a two-hanky tug at the heart, an adventure you can warm up to, again and again.

Prologue

Is there life after death? And will I see her again?

According to her diary, she is just asleep and her grave is only a passing reminder of something better to come:

> *The trumpet shall sound,*
> *and I will rise to meet Him in the air…*
> *I will have a new body: Immortal,*
> *imperishable, no longer subject*
> *to sickness or mishap or torments of time…*

She spoke through her diary at the crowded funeral. The faithful nodded in agreement and whispered *Amen,* assured she was in a better place. I sat and wept, assured of nothing, haunted by questions that went unanswered.

But years have passed and she still appears out of the corner of my eye—in a pile of clothes on the bed, riding next to me in the car, or when a gentle breeze ruffles the curtains. And in the ongoing surprise of these moments, I'm reminded again of the power of hope…

John Richards

Oak Park, Illinois
May 12, 1983

The Adventure of a Lifetime

1

I landed in Chicago in the spring of '45, just days before the war in Europe ended. A mild case of asthma kept me out of the Army, much to my father's delight. He had shipped me off to Harvard to study business and law, saying I'd be the better for it when the world returned to its senses. As the battle raged through the streets of Berlin, I fought traffic on Michigan Avenue, twenty minutes late for a job interview with Tom Becker of Braxton-Becker International.

I can still picture Tom poring over my application and rummaging through a dozen others while I stood at the window staring twenty-nine floors down at bathers running in and out of the chilly waters of Oak Street Beach, imagining myself at the water's edge, searching endless blue on blue and listening to shrieking gulls and canvas sails flapping in the wind.

By the time Tom invited me to sit, the applications were sorted into two piles, mine on top of the shorter one. And after reciting the obligatory company spiel, Tom cleared his throat and pressed the black button on the intercom.

"We're ready, Ginger."

Seconds later, a smartly-dressed strawberry blonde rolled in a cart and unloaded a plate of sandwiches, two cokes and a bowl of pretzels.

"I hope you're hungry, Mr. Richards," she purred in a Tennessee drawl that reminded me of home.

I nodded, smiled, and struggled to stay focused above her neckline—a struggle Tom didn't seem to share, judging by the wily grin on his face as his eyes followed Ginger to the door.

We spent less than five minutes between bites talking about the job and *hypothetical salaries*, as Tom called them. With plenty left to eat, we went on to talk about the war, baseball, and schools.

We were bragging about our fraternities when Ginger walked in with two more cokes and the delicate scent of blossoms—reminding me of Hattie Nelson, the prettiest girl at Whittier High, whom I never had the courage to ask out.

Watching Ginger sway back and forth to the door inspired Tom and me onto the subject of Rita Hayworth movies. A half-hour and four sandwiches later, in the midst of our raving over *Cover Girl*, Tom gasped at his watch and leaned into the desk.

"John, do you have any offers?"

"Of course," I said, much to my surprise.

In truth, it was my first interview. I had no offers and no idea how those words got out of my mouth. My parents were not big on religion, but they were firm believers in raising children of strong moral fiber. Lying was not tolerated back home, as my occasionally-spanked bottom could testify. I hadn't lied since seventh grade, and I wondered if my moral slip had anything to do with my having attended law school.

I was about to own up to the truth when Tom jumped to his feet and extended his hand.

"John, I hope to see you again."

He called me that night with an offer.

It was a *great* offer. Seven hundred dollars more than anything mentioned during the interview. An annual salary of sixty-seven hundred dollars might not sound like much now, but it was big money back in 1945 when you could drive away in a well-appointed Chevrolet Fleetmaster for seventeen hundred.

I leased an apartment in Oak Park, west of *The Windy City*. Oak Park boasts of Ernest Hemingway, Frank Lloyd Wright, Cliff and Luella Johnson, and a parade of other notables. But I settled there because Mom said she'd fear for my life if I lived in *Gangsterville*, as she called Chicago. I didn't find out until after moving in that Oak Park borders the town of Cicero, the one-time operations center of Al Capone.

Of course, I never told Mom.

When my boss heard I lived in Oak Park, he suggested I attend Gonner Memorial Church. "It's a good place to meet people," he said as he handed me his *Giants List*—a list of Gonner's most influential members, a virtual "Who's Who" of the area's leading residents.

Over the years, I've enjoyed the friendship of everyone on that list. But there was another giant, not on the list, who led me on the adventure of a lifetime. She was a giant in her own right, though she had neither fame nor fortune and she stood only five-feet, two-inches tall.

Her name was Lydia Rachel Bowman.

And she was even prettier than Hattie Nelson.

Love at First Sight, Twelve Rows Away

2

Lydia was the only child of Horatio and Leah Bowman. If actions reflect who we are, Leah was a saint (as I understand the word) and Horatio was an overbearing Baptist minister. I shudder to think how Lydia might have turned out had it not been for her mother. But I'm getting ahead of myself.

Lydia was twenty-one when she arrived in Oak Park in the early spring of 1946 with a single suitcase and $35 that had to last until her first paycheck.

She landed a job at a private music school set up in the basement of Gonner Church. At first, her father forbade her to take the position, since Gonner was not a Baptist church. Even worse, the church was non-denominational, making its members harder for Lydia's father to pigeon-hole than those "wine-bibbing Methodists" or "head-splashing Lutherans."

Lydia explained to her father that the school was merely housed in the church, not operated by it.

True enough. But she didn't explain that in exchange for the rooms, the school (and therefore Lydia) gave free music lessons to Gonner church members and their children.

Her father would have frowned on such collaboration.

She also didn't mention that she sang and directed music on special occasions at Gonner—which led to the first time I saw her, on the morning of Sunday, April 7th, 1946...

I had just woken up from a nap back in the twelfth row when I lifted my eyes and saw her standing on the platform, her back to the congregation, her arms poised and ready to direct the pre-school choir.

Her upswept hair and long, bustled dress were those of a turn-of-the-century Gibson Girl, leading me to think she was an older, experienced woman—drafted in a desperate effort to work a miracle with the kiddie-choir, whose previous attempts to sing were screeched in keys never screeched-in before.

At the end of the piano introduction, Lydia swept up her arms like an angel about to take flight, and in the two minutes that followed, a miracle *did* occur: those kids actually sang... together... in the same key.

Afterward, Lydia turned around to watch the children stampede down the center aisle on their way to Sunday School. I had not expected to see someone so young (or beautiful, for that matter) and my heart skipped when our eyes connected for the *briefest of moments*, just before one of the pre-schoolers stumbled in the aisle next to me. By the time I helped the little guy up and looked back to the platform, the angel had already flown away, leaving only that briefest of moments to play over and over again in my mind for the rest of the service.

3

I didn't know her name at the time or that she ran up the street to her church, Cornerstone Baptist, shortly after the miracle with the kiddie-choir. When my efforts to find her after the service failed, I cornered an usher and asked if he had seen the children's choir director.

"I didn't know we had one," he said.

"Then who led the kids this morning?"

He thought for a moment, then his face brightened. "Oh, that was Lydia Bowman."

Lydia, I thought, *what a beautiful name.*

The usher went on to explain about Lydia attending Cornerstone Baptist and about the arrangement between Gonner Memorial and the music school. I asked, but the usher had no idea when Lydia would be back for another service.

"You can ask Mrs. Turner," he said, pointing across the sanctuary to a tiny woman standing by the piano. "Just be careful of what you say; she can be cranky."

I clip-clopped across the wood floor and stopped behind Hazel Turner as she was removing bookmarks from hymnals.

"Wonderful music today, Mrs. Turner," I said.

"Thank you," she droned without turning around, sorting books into three piles, then two, then back into three again, waiting for me to go away.

"And Lydia did a great job with the children," I added.

Mrs. Turner's hands curled into fists. And when she started shaking, I figured I was about to find out what *cranky* meant. But when she spun around, she flashed a wide grin, surprised eyes, and a squeaky voice filled with anticipation.

"Oh, are you Lydia's boyfriend?"

My heart sank at the thought of Lydia already having a boyfriend, though it made perfect sense, she being so beautiful and all.

"Well, uh, no… But I *wish*…"

As Mrs. Turner studied my face, a look of sympathy settled on hers.

"Now, now, young man," she said. "I didn't say she *has* a boyfriend. I was just thinking out loud, that's all, wondering if you were that lucky man." Then she leaned in all wide-eyed and whispered, "Lydia is a *wonderful* young lady.

I sighed in agreement.

"And sings like an angel, she does!" Mrs. Turner added, patting my arm like Mom always did just before giving me advice. "You should come hear her sing next week."

An adrenaline rush like I hadn't felt since passing the bar exam had me gasping for air. "Next week…? But I thought… I mean… the usher said she sang only on special occasions."

"It's a special occasion *whenever* Lydia sings," Mrs. Turner said.

I'm not sure what goofy look hijacked my face, but Mrs. Turner winked and the corners of her mouth quivered trying to suppress a smirk before she turned, gathered her music, and headed for the foyer. Halfway there, without turning around, she shouted: "See you next week!"

7

Her words echoed throughout the empty church, as if to remind me again.

Not that I needed reminding.

4

That afternoon, I called my parents and told them what little I knew about the wonderful girl who had taken over my thoughts.

"Son, don't rush into anything," my father warned. "Enjoy your youth."

"Dad, I'm 26."

"Are you that old?" he said in genuine disbelief. "Well, it don't matter no how. You're still young. And remember, Son, you'll be married for most your life. You'd do best *now* to invest your time and energy in your work. Then, when the right time comes, you'll be in a better position to enjoy a nice wife and family *later*."

Mom was more understanding.

"Oh, John... how wonderful!" she said, crying over the phone. "What's her name? Where did you meet her?"

"Her name is Lydia," I said, enjoying the feel of her name as it rolled off my tongue. "I saw her at church today."

"Oh, what a pretty name," Mom said. "It sounds so regal! Come to think of it, isn't there a *Lydia* in the Bible?"

I pressed the phone hard against my ear.

"*Where* in the Bible?"

"I'm not sure," Mom said. "Somewhere in the New Testament, I think."

After the call, the desire to see her name in print had me frantically searching the apartment for a Bible. I knew I hadn't packed one in the half-dozen boxes I brought up from Memphis, but I rummaged through them anyway, hoping Mom had slipped one in. No such luck, and the urge to find her name grew even stronger.

It was mid-afternoon and the church with its platform Bible was locked, so I scurried up and down Lake Street in a futile attempt to find an open store that carried books.

Where's a Bible when you need one, I thought as I plodded empty-handed back to my apartment.

It didn't take long to find out.

While climbing the stairs in the entryway, I heard keys jingling and an older couple trying to catch their breath on the second floor. They turned and smiled when I reached the landing.

The woman had on a long, blue cotton dress and a blue hat with one of those fishnet doohickeys rolled up in front. The man sported a dark suit and tie, but what caught my attention was *the Bible* under his arm.

"You must be John Richards," the man said. "I saw your name on the mailbox."

I extended my hand. "Yes, and you folks must be the Robinsons."

"I see you read mailboxes, too!" the man said with a chuckle. "I'm Vernon, and this is my wife, Ada."

The three of us shook hands and exchanged pleasantries, then I pointed to Vernon's Bible with my eyes.

"You folks just getting home from church?" I asked.

"No," Ada said with a smile in her voice. "We celebrated at a restaurant after the service. Our great-grandson was baptized this morning."

"And he's only nine years old," Vernon added with an air of pride.

Hmmm, I thought. *Nine years old? My folks had me baptized less than two months out of the gate! I wonder if these folks are Baptists...*

"Where do you go to church?" I asked.

"Cornerstone Baptist," Vernon said, tapping his fingers on his Bible.

Bingo!

"You're always welcome to visit us," Ada said.

"Thank you. I may do just that. I know someone who attends your church."

Ada's eyes widened. "Oh, really?" she said. "Who?"

"Lydia Bo—"

"THANK YOU, JESUS!" Ada shouted, throwing her hands in the air. And she and Vernon lit up in smiles.

I watched as they celebrated for the second time that day. Then I chuckled and said, "I take it you know her too."

"Oh, yes!" Ada sighed. "She's a *wonderful* girl! And sings like an angel, she does!"

"You're the second person to tell me that today."

"Well, it's true!" Vernon insisted. "Lydia sang this morning at the baptism. She was out of breath when she arrived—she had an obligation at that big church up the street and she ran all the way—but even so, she was marvelous!"

Ada glared at her husband. "She didn't *run*; she's a lady. A *refined*, young *lady!*"

Vernon rolled his eyes. "Yes, but she's *modern*, My Dear. And I still don't know why you insisted she dress in that silly, old-fashioned outfit and put her hair up like that!"

Ada ignored him, choosing instead to size me up and down and nod her head, as if I were the answer to some problem she was working on. Then she patted my arm and leaned toward me.

"Lydia is a *wonderful, modern, refined,* young lady," Ada said, emphasizing each word slowly and carefully. "She will *surely* be the pride of some *fortunate* man."

"True enough," Vernon muttered, "but let the man be, Ada."

She begrudgingly did so, and we chatted a few more minutes before I motioned to Vernon's Bible again and said, "In the rush of moving to Oak Park, I left my Bible in Memphis. May I borrow yours? Just for the afternoon?"

Vernon handed me The Book without hesitation.

"Here, my friend," he said. "Use it as long as you like. I have another in the apartment."

I turned and flew up the stairs, saying thanks and goodbye along the way, and wondering whether I should feel proud or ashamed that, for the first time in my life, I was excited to have a Bible in my hands.

5

In what seemed to take longer than a root canal, I reached the third floor, unlocked the door, and ran to the kitchen—the only room in the apartment with a table and chair.

As I paged through The Book, still warm from being under Vernon's arm, I remembered bits and pieces of Sunday School stories I had heard long ago: *Noah's Ark, David and Goliath, Jesus Walking on the Water.* And I remembered terms like *Old Testament* and *New Testament* and *Books of the Bible*.

But I had no idea where the testaments were or what books they contained. Only after checking the Table of Contents was I able to open to the New Testament on page 893 and begin reading chapter one in The Book of Matthew.

Lydia was not mentioned in that chapter—or anywhere else in Matthew, as I learned after struggling for over an hour with the THEEs and THOUs of King James English.

The second book, Mark, was shorter and went quicker. Still, no mention of Lydia.

The next book was Luke. Somewhere in the middle, I took a quick supper break. I finished Luke, and was on the last page of The Book of John when the phone rang.

"Hey, Honey," Mom whispered, "Your father is sleeping so I need to keep this short. I called Pastor Barnes this afternoon and asked about Lydia being in the Bible."

I gasped. "And?"

"He said Lydia appears in The Acts of the Apostles. Some folks call it: The Book of Acts. Good luck. We love you."

Click.

I raced back to the Bible and was about to turn to the Table of Contents when I saw the words "The Book of Acts" staring at me from the top of the opposite page.

I was rounding the turn, heading into the stretch, approaching the finish line. But the sun had long set and my eyes grew heavy somewhere in the twelfth chapter, and by chapter fifteen I was weaving in and out of sleep.

After taking another break to splash water on my face, I walked back to the table and flipped through the chapters to see how many pages were left. That's when my eyes came across Acts, Chapter 16, beginning with the 14th verse:

14 And a certain woman named Lydia, a seller of purple, of the city of Thyatira, which worshipped God, heard us: whose heart the Lord opened, that she attended unto the things which were spoken of Paul.

15 And when she was baptized, and her household, she besought us, saying, if ye have judged me to be faithful to the Lord, come into my house, and abide there. And she constrained us.

I had no idea what the verses were talking about. All I knew was I had fallen hard for a girl I had never met. I was in a trance, the proverbial deer caught in the headlights.

But on the following Sunday, I was a man with a plan...

Game Plan

6

Like all great plans, mine called for sacrifice. As much as I wanted to sit in the front row as close to that crown jewel as possible, the plan called for trading a *good seat* for a *good chance* to meet her afterward. That meant sitting in the back pew, next to the aisle, two steps from the door.

Knowing she would leave right after her number, I figured she would either walk down an aisle through the congregation or, more likely, take one of the platform exits. Either way, I'd be in position to slip out the door and "incidentally bump into her" before she left the building.

I think even Dad would have liked the plan, and Mom would have appreciated my last-minute decision to leave the binoculars back at the apartment.

When the time came for the offertory, Lydia rose from the front row and ascended the three steps to the platform.

My heart pounded when she turned around. Gone was the Gibson Girl look. She was smartly dressed in a patterned waistcoat, white blouse, and dark skirt that stopped at her knees. Her ebony hair was swept up and back, and cascading curls brushed against her shoulders. She was a movie star waiting to be discovered—a five-star, blue ribbon head-turner.

I could have kicked myself about the binoculars.

Lydia nodded to Mrs. Turner, and the introduction to "Abide With Me" flowed from the piano.

All rustling in the pews ceased as Lydia's operatic voice filled the sanctuary, lifting the congregation higher and higher with each verse. Softly, gently, her arms and shoulders swayed as if she was leading us through an unseen crowd of angels on our way up to heaven.

On her last note, as her head bowed and her arms lowered gently to her sides, a glorious shaft of light poured through the stained-glass window and showered her in a rainbow of colors. To this day, I don't know if the timing was a coincidence or a higher power showing appreciation. You could hear people gasp before the church fell into absolute silence.

A few moments later, I clapped, just once, before catching myself. I had never heard anyone clap in the church before and I feared I had broken some sacred protocol. But a moment later, there was another clap. And then another, and another, until the whole congregation joined in.

I wiped a runaway tear from my cheek and swallowed hard to jar the lump out of my throat—all while keeping my eyes on Lydia to see which exit she'd take.

The applause seemed to catch her off guard. She hesitated, then curtseyed before exiting through the north platform door. That meant only one thing: she was heading to the basement.

I stood up and calmly stepped into the aisle and through the door to the foyer two steps away, then *dashed* to the stairway and *flew* down the steps, undoubtedly setting an Olympic record in the process.

16

The basement hallway was empty and still, making it easy to hear the footsteps and voices of two women in the stairwell at the far end.

My heart turned to pudding at the sound of the younger voice. Then suddenly, to my horror, I realized I had left one small detail out of my plan.

What do I actually say to her?

I would have turned back, but that *briefest of moments* flashed through my mind again, filling me with resolve.

You can do this, John !!!

As I reached the men's room across from the stairwell, I heard Lydia say goodbye, and the sound of her approaching footsteps told me that in less than ten seconds, she would reach the basement and I would be face-to-face with my destiny…

The Best-laid Plans...

7

I gave in to panic and burst into the men's room, gasping for breath as if I had just run the four-minute mile.

"Coward!" I cried, glaring at the man in the mirror. "You can't just let her go!"

At the sound of her passing footsteps, I summoned up the last of my reserves. And in a full-throttled burst of resolve, I knew exactly what I had to do.

But first I had to pee...

And wash my hands...

And rinse the sink with damp tissue...

Then wash my hands again...

And wipe a smudge off the mirror...

By the time I opened the door, Lydia was nowhere in sight.

So go the best-laid plans of mice and men, and I pretty much knew which of those two categories I belonged in at the time.

I was disappointed, yet relieved. Drained, yet energized. I didn't even know this girl, yet she had me acting like some starry-eyed, high school freshman.

I chuckled under my breath and shook my head.

There will be another day, another chance, I thought as I headed toward the front stairway.

But halfway there, a door opened a few steps ahead and I heard her unmistakable voice softly singing:

♪ *A-bide with me, fast falls the eve-ning tide…*

She backed out of the room, taking one last look inside before flipping the light and turning around no more than an arm's length away from where I stood, frozen to the floor.

She gasped when she saw me, then leaned against the doorframe and began to giggle.

"I thought I was the only one down here," she said.

Maybe it was the warmth in her voice, or the welcoming look in her eyes; maybe it was that wholesome, girl-next-door familiarity about her that put me at ease. Whatever it was, the next thing I knew, I was chuckling out an apology.

"I'm sorry. I didn't mean to startle you."

She took on a blush and cleared her throat. "Actually, I'm glad we ran into each other," she said. "I wanted to thank you for helping Andrew last week."

"Andrew?"

"Yes, the little boy who fell in the aisle."

"Ahh, yes, the little boy…"

"He's one of my students," Lydia said. And after glancing at my arms, she took on a deeper blush. "He told me you're strong."

My knees buckled, yet somehow I remained on my feet, and even managed to roll out a compliment of my own:

"He told me you're the best teacher in the world."

Lydia straightened up, and I was surprised to see caution in her eyes.

"He did?"

"Well, not in those words," I said, feeling the need to back off a bit. "Not then and there. But certainly when he sang. When they *all* sang. It was a miracle! Have you ever heard those kids sing before?"

Though she tried, Lydia could not suppress a grin. "Well, I suppose they've improved."

"Oh, yeah," I said, "and we have you to thank for that. And I have Mrs. Turner to thank for telling me to come hear you sing today."

Lydia broke into a laugh. "*Mrs. Turner* told you to come?"

"Yeah, she said you sing like an angel. And you do! What's so funny?"

"Oh, nothing," Lydia said, still laughing. "It's just that Mrs. Turner and Ada Robinson from my church have been trying to set me up with someone ever since I arrived in town."

I struck a solemn pose and raised my right hand. "I must confess: I ran into Ada last week too."

That got us both laughing, quite hard. And afterward, we stood in the doorway and smiled at each other for a few awkward yet wonderful moments.

"Well," I finally said, "I hope they didn't go to all that trouble for nothing. May I take you to lunch today?"

The sound of the pipe organ and hundreds of voices rolled into the basement as Lydia leaned against the doorframe and softly hummed along with the music from above. That mysterious caution took hold of her eyes again, and didn't let go until the end of the verse, when I got the answer I had hoped for.

8

We discussed time and place quickly because Lydia was due to sing at her church again. I walked her out to the sidewalk and watched her run up the street, certain that my heart was beating faster than hers.

Too excited to return to the service, I snuck over to Scoville Park to burn off nervous energy.

Lydia had told me her church usually lets out at 12:15, but that I shouldn't worry if I got there and they were still in session. "12:30 dismissals are not uncommon," she had told me. "And every now and then, a visiting revival preacher holds everyone until past one o'clock."

Shortly after noon, I headed back up the street. As I was passing Gonner Memorial, Mrs. Turner flew out the door, her left arm loaded with music and her right arm waving frantically at me.

"Hello!" she shouted. "Did you hear Lydia sing?"

"Yes!" I shouted back without breaking pace. "I'm on my way to pick her up for lunch."

It was the only time I ever saw Hazel Turner dance.

The sound of soulful singing grew louder as I approached Cornerstone Baptist, and by the time I reached the steps, a deep voice cried above the music: "Do not leave this house of the Lord if you're not right with Jesus. He's calling you today. Won't you come? Come, as we stand and sing the last stanza."

It sounded like a revival thing to me, and I feared not seeing Lydia until after one o'clock, but when the singing stopped, the same voice cried, "The Grace of God be with you all. You are dismissed."

Within fifteen seconds, two young boys raced out the front door and almost knocked me down. A moment later, a woman yelled from the doorway, "Nathan! Elijah! Don't you go running off now!"

The rest of the congregation trickled out like a slow-dripping faucet, and each time someone opened the door, I caught a glimpse of the wide-eyed, chattering crowd.

But no sign of Lydia.

Fifteen minutes later, I decided to go in.

9

I opened the door just as Lydia was backing out, her arms laden with books. She lost her balance and let out a shriek as her load began to topple. I leaned in and caught her, extending my hands under her arms. The surprise on her face turned to laughter when she looked up and saw me.

"Here we go again!" she said.

I chuckled with her. "And I'm so-o-o-o sorry again."

"I'm the one who should apologize," she said, balancing her books as I lifted her. "I didn't mean to keep you waiting, but I had to talk with the pastor about tonight's service."

"Are you having a revival meeting?"

"No, just our regular Sunday evening fellowship."

I had forgotten that some churches held services on Sunday evenings. The church my family occasionally attended back home was one of the few in Memphis that didn't. My father, a lawyer, joined the church for business reasons. He figured he'd attract more clients if people thought he belonged to a church. Technically, he didn't lie when he pointed to the family portrait hanging in his office and told folks about his church-attending family in an effort to win their trust and business. But he didn't mention our spotty attendance, or that he picked our church only because it took up the least of his time.

Dad once told me, "Son, most folks make up their own religion, taking a little of this and a little of that from what's out there, be it from books or the say-so of others."

I remember asking Dad if he believed in God.

"Some days I do, Son," he confided. "But a man's religion has more to do with the way he lives than with the church he attends or the God he says he serves. I know too many church-goers who, if arrested for believing in God, would be acquitted for lack of evidence."

When I asked Dad about our neighbors, the Hadleys, he conceded they'd be found guilty and sent straight to the gallows. The Hadleys attended one of those *serious churches*. But more important to my dad, the Hadleys were true to their word: yes meant yes, and no meant no; they didn't weasel around with words. With few exceptions, it was the same way with my dad. Telling the truth was his religion, if he had one.

Again, I extended my hands to Lydia.

"May I carry your books?"

As she loaded my arms, four things about her church and its members came to mind, four things that told me Cornerstone Baptist was one of those *serious churches*:

> 1 – The Robinsons' invitation to visit their church,
> 2 – The pastor's plea to come to Jesus,
> 3 – They had Sunday evening services, and
> 4 – Everyone in that place carried a Bible.

I fully expected Lydia to invite me to church that night. But she did not, nor was the subject raised anytime that afternoon.

We dropped off her books at Gonner Memorial, then walked to the Cozy Corner Restaurant just up the street from the Lake Theatre.

As luck would have it, we got a booth by the window. After ordering the Sunday Chicken Special and handing our menus back to the waitress, I looked across the table and said,

"So, you're *Lydia*... like in the Bible."

She sat up straight, and I couldn't tell whether the pleased look on her face was one of surprise or relief.

"Oh, you know my namesake!" she said. "Have you read the Bible?"

Her question caught me off guard. It was blunt, hard to answer without a yes or a no. I couldn't lie to her, but I didn't want to say *no* either, so I fiddled with my napkin until I could think of some other answer, something that was true and yet made me look good at the same time. Finally, it hit me. I stretched my arm over the back of the booth and said,

"Last Sunday, I read Matthew, Mark, Luke, John, and half the Book of Acts."

Lydia's eyes widened.

"You read the Gospels in one sitting?"

I didn't know what she meant by *the Gospels*, but I nodded and smiled anyway, which seemed to please her even more, judging by the way her face lit up.

I knew her religion meant a lot to her, and that it would play a key role in who she'd date and who she'd marry, which had become the two foremost things on my mind.

10

After lunch, we walked to the war memorial at Scoville Park and sat under the frozen gaze of three bronze soldiers and an angel of stone.

The scent of burning leaves hung in the air, reminding Lydia of her childhood. From what she told me about growing up in Atlanta, I could tell she had a close and wonderful relationship with her mother. But she volunteered nothing about her father. And when I asked about him, her answers were short, and whispered, as if he might otherwise hear.

As the shadows grew long and the mercury dropped, Lydia buried her chin in her overcoat and I found myself fighting the urge to wrap my arm around her. But Dad once told me, "Son, someday a special woman will come into your life. And you might be tempted, as many young men are, to go about things too fast. Don't. Take time to become friends first. Building a solid relationship is like building a house. Start with a good foundation of friendship, then build on from there."

I knew, to the core of my being, Lydia was that special woman. I also knew that building a foundation of friendship would take time, and paradoxically require that I not see her as much as I wanted, which was pretty much every waking moment.

I thought I could hold out for a week and then arrange to "bump into her" on the street after church. But a week proved too long to wait, so I took Thursday afternoon off, knowing she would be at Gonner Memorial giving music lessons.

I stood out of view in the church hallway, listening to a little boy desperately trying to sing a scale: *Be-flat*, if you know what I mean. But with more patience than I'll ever have, Lydia consoled and encouraged that little guy until he got it just right.

And wow, did he get excited.

"I can do it!" he squeaked. "I can sing!"

"Yes, you can!" I heard Lydia say. "You're a good singer!"

The boy kept laughing and shouting, "I can sing! I can sing!"

I remember thinking: *she's going to be a great mother.* And as I turned around and snuck out of the church, I knew Lydia would be worth any suffering I'd have to endure in taking things slow.

It took three Sunday walks together before I could muster the courage to ask if I could hold her hand.

"I'd like that," she said, pulling her hand from her pocket and easing it into mine.

Two Sundays after that, I asked if I could walk her up to her apartment. She blushed, but said yes.

I remember the entrance door slamming behind us, sending thunder up and down the staircase and stirring the smell of old, varnished wood. And I can still hear the creaking floors and stairs that announced every step of our ascent.

She turned around when we reached the third landing and a window passed the warm glow of the setting sun onto her face. I came to a stop, just inches away, leaving only our breathing and the pounding of our hearts to fill the silence.

I realize now that all of time had led to that moment, and that the aftermath will ripple into eternity. But on that day in 1946, when our lips first met, nothing else mattered.

A Bump Along the Way

11

After that first kiss, there was no way I could wait another Sunday to see her. So I "just happened" to run into her on the street two more times that week, and three times the week after that. She knew what was going on, and my bumping into her became our little inside joke:

"Oh, it's you again," I'd say, feigning surprise.

"Oh, fancy that!" she'd reply.

Then we'd laugh and walk hand-in-hand to the park or to Petersen's Ice Cream Shop for a treat.

Three months after we first met, we sat down to a root beer float at Petersen's.

"A toast..." I said, raising my straw in the air. "To Hazel Turner and Ada Robinson."

Lydia lifted her straw and threw me a side glance.

"Hazel and Ada?"

"Yes!" I said, inching my straw toward hers. "For their tireless matchmaking efforts. I'm indebted to them."

Lydia dissolved into a smile, then tapped my straw.

"Me too," she said.

I sighed in relief, taking her words as a sign we had gotten past the huge mistake I apparently made a week earlier, when I told Lydia I loved her.

We were standing outside her apartment at the time. We had just kissed, and I drew my head back to see her face in the soft light. The time seemed right to say it, so I did, hoping she'd do the same. But she lowered her eyes instead, and I could see tension building on her face.

I felt sick about it all week, and almost didn't call to ask her out for our quarter-year anniversary. But I did, and she accepted, and there we were in *our booth* at Petersen's, both of us grateful for the efforts of Hazel and Ada, both of us happy to be an item.

After our celebration at Petersen's that night, I walked Lydia up to her apartment. And after we kissed in front of her door and whispered *Happy Anniversary* to each other, I turned around to go down the stairs. But she pulled me back and kissed me again, and whispered what I wanted to hear more than anything else in the world:

"John... I love you, too."

On our walk the next day, Lydia explained her reaction to my telling her I loved her. She explained how her father's temperament kept her and her mother constantly on edge.

"He'd be kind to us one minute and belittle us the next," she said, her eyes filled with the same mysterious caution I had seen in the basement of Gonner Church three months earlier. "I've had to keep my guard up around men... not knowing if I could trust them."

I hesitated before asking, "Not even me?"

The corners of her mouth trembled.

"Not at first," she admitted, breaking into a nervous smile. "But I've enjoyed your company from the start..."

She paused to wipe a tear from her cheek. I brought her hand to my mouth and kissed it, knowing she had more to say.

"When you said 'I love you,' I remembered my father always saying that to my mom after his tirades. Mom always cried afterward, not out of relief, but because she… she…"

Lydia couldn't, or wouldn't, finish.

I gently stroked her hair until she stopped crying.

"I'm not your dad," I whispered.

She looked up at me. "I know," she said. "I know."

A drop fell from her nose onto my shirt. We broke into nervous smiles and giggled until she buried her face in my shoulder and started weeping again.

A minute later she looked up and said,

"I do love you, John. I just struggle with the past…"

Her head returned to my shoulder, and I cried with her.

"We'll work through this together," I said.

Surprise Invitation

12

The tears did us good, and we were both in high spirits when we talked on the phone the next day.

"Last night," Lydia said, "I talked with my mom for over a half-hour. And this morning, I spent another half-hour talking with my mom and *father*."

"Wow, your father?"

"Yes! Can you believe it?" She paused to clear a frog from her throat. "I'm going to have to take out a loan when the phone bill comes."

"Me too!" I said, laughing. "I just got off the phone with my folks—by the way, do your parents know about me?"

"Of course!" Lydia squealed. "And my mom is so happy for us!"

"What about your father?"

"Well, Mom says he'll warm up… eventually."

"Ha, they sound like my folks," I said. "Maybe we should go for a walk and compare notes."

"I was hoping we could talk over supper," Lydia said.

"Sure! Where do you want to go?"

She paused for a moment, and cleared her throat again.

"I was hoping we could eat here, at my apartment."

I almost dropped the phone. I had never stepped into her place. Nor had she ever seen mine.

"Your place?"

"Why not?" she said. "I can cook. And it will give us a quiet place to talk for a change."

I was too stunned to think of anything to say.

"Six o'clock?" she asked.

"Uh, sure… Can I bring anything?"

Lydia laughed. "My mom said if you asked that, I was to tell you to *bring your best behavior*."

"I think I can manage that," I said, chuckling with her. "And what did your dad say?"

"He doesn't know about it. But we can talk about that tonight if you want. Can you wait until six?"

Yes would have been the polite thing to say. But I couldn't say that without lying, so I gave her a big smooch over the phone instead.

Then I waited the longest eight hours of my life.

A Wife of Noble Character

13

I arrived at Lydia's apartment building fifteen minutes early and waited outside for twelve more before stealing into the hallway, only to have the front door slam behind me and announce my arrival to everyone in the building and the northern half of Illinois.

To help calm my nerves, I focused on the stairs, taking each step gingerly to see if I could get to the third floor without making any of them squeak. I could not, but at least the trick worked off some of my jitters.

At six o'clock sharp, I hid the bouquet of flowers behind my back and knocked on her door.

Half an eternity later, she stood in the opened doorway with her right hand on her hip.

"Oh, fancy that," she said.

I was too stunned by her appearance to recognize our little inside joke. Somehow in the previous 24 hours, she had become even more beautiful: starlet face, perfect smile, curled tresses that touched her shoulders—and all dressed up in a belted black skirt and striking red blouse.

"Are you coming in," she teased, "or are we eating out in the hall?"

I brought out the flowers and held them up to her. She drew them to her face and inhaled. "Thank you," she said. Then she stood on her toes and gave me a soft kiss that I wanted to go on forever.

"Come in and make yourself at home," she said after sniffing the flowers again. "I'm going to put these in a vase and check on supper." With that, she was off to the kitchen.

Lydia's apartment was smaller than mine, but unlike my bare Spartan living room, Lydia's had all the touches of home. The scent of potpourri filled the air. The wood floor was shiny and dust free. There were figurines on the tables, embroidered doilies under the lamps, and a tea set on the coffee table. A radio stood against the south wall, beneath three small paintings. And two framed embroideries hung side-by-side on the north wall above the couch.

On the left, it said:

A Wife of
Noble Character
Is Worth
Far More
Than Rubies

And on the right:

Charm is Deceitful
And Beauty is Vain
But A Woman That
Feareth The LORD
Shall Be Praised

Centered between the embroideries was a portrait of Lydia with her parents, Leah and Horatio. One glance at Leah was all it took to see where Lydia got her good looks.

The portrait showed Leah and Lydia wearing long black dresses and standing next to Horatio, who was portly and sitting in a chair, his arms folded at the chest. He wore a dark suit, dark tie, and an exceptionally long frown. Below the portrait were their names:

Jonathan Horatio Bowman

Leah Constance   Lydia Rachel

Lydia always referred to her dad as *Father* or *Horatio*, and I was surprised to learn his first name was Jonathan. In an effort to determine which name fit him best, I looked him square in the eye and said in a deep voice:

"Uh, Jonathan? I love your daughter."

He remained motionless in his chair, still frowning.

I cleared my throat and tried his middle name.

"Excuse me, Horatio? I'd like to marry your daughter."

Again, there was no change in his demeanor.

With these inconclusive results, I leaned in closer to study his likeness further. That's when a new name came to mind:

"Frownathon!" I announced with a chuckle.

I had been so caught up in my investigation, I didn't notice that Lydia had slipped into the room and was standing right behind me when the new name flew out of my mouth. She slipped her arms around my waist and said,

"Who are you talking to?"

I about jumped through the ceiling.

She stepped back and cupped her hands over her mouth. "Oh, I'm sorry," she said. "I didn't mean to embarrass you. Were you talking to yourself?"

"Of course not... well, I mean... uh... yeah."

I gave her more time to laugh before I turned back to the portrait and pointed to her father's name.

"Your father's first name is *Jonathan*?"

Lydia wrapped her arms around my waist again and gently swayed me from side to side.

"Yes, but he prefers *Horatio*."

"Why?" I asked, not nearly as interested in the answer as I was in her gentle swaying.

"*Jonathan* sounds too common to my father," Lydia said. "At least that's what Mom thinks."

We swayed a few more moments before she asked,

"Are you hungry?"

I turned around in her arms and nibbled on her lips.

"Yes," I said, not thinking of food.

She stepped back and held out her hand.

"Let's eat."

She turned off the living room light as we walked into the hallway toward the flickering light in the kitchen. The flames of two candles danced above the table as she stood to the side of the closest chair, which I pulled out for her before taking my seat across from hers.

We sat a few moments in silence as the pleasing aroma and steam rose from our plates. I fiddled with my napkin, waiting for her to start, but she just sat there.

"This looks and smells wonderful," I said.

"Thank you," she said in a voice as soft as the candlelight that graced her face. Her hands remained at the sides of her plate. And as silence took over the kitchen, her mouth trembled ever so slightly.

I was about to find out why.

OK, Now What?

14

When the silence grew too loud to bear, Lydia slid her hand across the table, lowered her head, and closed her eyes.

"John, will you ask the blessing?"

Ummmm… Uhhhhhh…

In a desperate attempt to buy time and ward off panic, I picked up her hand and caressed it until a prayer came to mind that Mom had us say when we were young: *Now I lay me down to sleep*—no, wait, that was for bedtime.

I vaguely recalled a prayer from a Sunday School picnic: *Come, Lord Jesus, be our guest,* but I couldn't remember the second line.

My mind raced through past holiday dinners and other gatherings—and even holiday movies.

Nothing.

Then I remembered something I heard long ago:

The best prayers are from the heart.

I gave Lydia's hand a tender squeeze.

"Thanks for inviting me, " I said, "and for this wonderful time together."

I looked up and smiled. Lydia's head was still bowed.

After a few moments, I remembered to say *Amen*.

When Lydia lifted her head, there was a puzzled look on her face. But she thanked me, and quickly handed me a basket of warm, sliced bread. I could feel her studying my face as I transferred a slice onto my plate.

We began eating in silence, and I tried to avoid Lydia's eyes while I wondered what she thought of my prayer. A minute or so later, she cleared her throat.

"One of the reasons I wanted to have supper here," she said, "is so we could pray together. I noticed you never pray when we go out to eat. "

"Well, I..."

"Oh, you don't have to explain," she said. "My father won't pray in a restaurant either."

"Really?"

"Yeah, he says crowded, noisy places aren't conducive to prayer."

"Well, I never looked at it that way," I said.

And that's all that was said about the matter.

We spent the rest of the evening at the table, talking and laughing and holding hands, letting go only to light new candles. We lost track of time until Lydia turned in the middle of a laugh and caught a glimpse of the clock.

"Oh, my goodness," she said, cupping her hands over her mouth. "It's 1:30 in the morning!"

She leaned over the table and flashed a big grin.

"What will the neighbors think?" she whispered.

She laughed as she stood up and shook her finger at me like an indignant grade school principal.

"You need to leave right now, young man," she said.

We giggled like a couple of sixth-graders as we tiptoed through the hallway to the living room.

I was pleasantly surprised that Lydia did not flip the hall light on, leaving us to stand at the front door in just the dim light from the kitchen.

I rested my forehead against hers and put my hands on her waist. She eased her arms around me and drew me closer. The soft whooshing of our breath took on a deep resonance. Her mouth opened slightly as I lowered my lips to meet hers.

As our noses wheezed, my hands slid up and over the back of her blouse, into a cascade of curls. A moan rose from her throat. My moaning made it a duet. And the room became very, very warm.

Suddenly she buried her face in my shoulder and reached around to open the door. "Thanks for coming over," she said, shaking and gasping for air.

"Thanks for supper," I said, gasping with her.

We held each other for a few moments, trying to settle down, then I kissed her forehead before I turned and slipped out the door.

A few steps later, I heard her whisper, "John…"

I tiptoed back and leaned toward her silhouette until I could feel the warmth of her breath.

"I love you," she whispered.

I still get Goosebumps whenever I close my eyes and imagine being in that doorway with her again, and hearing those words that never grow old.

Going on Six Months

15

Three months later, I was in New York at a conference, brainstorming with executive managers and affiliates from around the world. Working on four projects spread across Europe, China, and Japan, I was too exhausted to work "second shift," as my co-workers called their evening escapades out on the town.

I even shied away from the company-sponsored socials, preferring instead to go to my room, call Lydia, and relax in quiet conversation for hours on end.

The only social event I attended was the annual gala at the end of the week, when all the affiliates gathered to celebrate the accomplishments of the year.

They threw the party in the Hotel's largest ballroom. It was an extravagant affair. Two waiters stood at every table. Champagne flowed like water. A 22-piece orchestra played while affiliates swept the floor with fashion models, hired on as dance hostesses.

The good food, music, and energy in the room had me wishing Lydia was there—and gave me an idea for our half-year anniversary.

I flew out of New York in the wee hours of the morning and landed in Chicago ahead of the sun on the Saturday before Thanksgiving. I drove straight to Lydia's apartment, hoping to surprise her, and tapped on her door while she was still in bed.

A minute passed, and when she didn't answer, I hesitated, then knocked again. I didn't want to wake her, but I ached to see her.

I was about to leave when I heard the patter of feet, followed a few moments later by the sweetest voice in the world.

"Who is it?" she asked through the door.

"A secret admirer," I said.

"Johnny!" she squealed.

I heard her fumble with the chain and rush to slide it off the rail.

"Come in! Come in!" she said in a loud whisper, hopping up and down like she always did when she was excited.

She looked like the Princess of Antarctica—her hair was wrapped in a towel and she had on a fluffy pink robe and oversized slippers—even so, I could think of nothing on earth more beautiful.

She pulled me into the apartment and closed the door behind us. We plunged in each other's arms, swam in each other's kisses—clichés perhaps, but that's how I remember it. Then I took her hand and twirled her 'round and 'round until the towel flew off her head and her hair bounced around in a frenzied dance.

"I missed you so much," I said.

She started hopping up and down again. "I'm so glad you're here. What a surprise!"

"Well, then don't get upset when I leave in a couple minutes."

"What?"

"I have to write three letters and have them in the mailbox by four this afternoon."

"You're teasing me." she said, sticking out her tongue and crossing her eyes. Not her funniest look, but one that always got me laughing.

"Who, me?" I said. "*You're* the big teaser, Lady."

She sunk her face in my chest and growled. For some reason, that always made me laugh uncontrollably, almost to the point of pain, and she took advantage of it.

"OK, stop!" I said. "Stop!"

She looked up, grinning.

"Then give me two good reasons why you think you can just traipse over here and then leave right away," she said, her eyes filled with joy and laughter.

"Well first," I said, "I'm madly in love with you."

She pecked me on the lips.

"That's a good start," she said. "And?..."

"And second..." I paused for effect, until she growled in my chest again.

"OK! STOP! STOP!" I pleaded. "Second, I wanted to ask you out to dinner for our six-month anniversary."

She fiddled with my collar, then reached up and pinched my cheeks.

"I guess I can forgive you," she said in a sultry voice.

"May I pick you up at five?" I asked.

She answered with a nod and five little kisses.

A Puzzling Request

16

I drove the two blocks home and parked on the street. And flying up the stairs with two suitcases, I shot past Vernon and Ada Robinson as they struggled to take up their groceries.

"Put 'em down," I said. "I'll be back in a minute and give you a hand."

After throwing the suitcases in my apartment, I dove back down to the grateful couple still trying to catch their breath. Then I ran their two bags up the flight of stairs and waited outside their door.

"You're in great shape," Vernon said when he and Ada finally arrived at the landing.

"Or else in love," Ada suggested, with twinkling eyes.

"In love," I said, grinning.

"And may I ask who the young lady is?"

"Lydia Bow—"

"Oh yes, Lord!" Ada cried, looking up. Then she grabbed my arm and said, "We have been praying for the longest time that Lydia would meet some nice, young man."

Vernon turned to me after unlocking the door.

"How long have you two been an item?" he asked.

"Going on six months now," I said.

Ada gasped. "Six months? Whenever I asked Lydia if she was seeing anyone, all she'd say was 'keep praying for me.'"

Vernon motioned for me to take the bags inside.

On the way to the kitchen, I wondered why Lydia hadn't mentioned me to Ada, and why she asked for prayer. And when I saw the cross hanging in the Robinson's kitchen, I wondered if Lydia was on to the fact I was somewhat lacking in the spiritual department.

But I pushed the questions and doubt out of my mind. After all, I was back in Oak Park with Lydia again, and excited about the surprise I had for her that night. So after helping the Robinsons put their groceries away, I raced upstairs to type the three letters.

The purpose of the letters was to convince three relief agencies to end their stupid, petty bickering (I used different wording) and pool their resources to help Europeans rebuild their lives after the war.

I volunteered to write the letters as a favor for my boss, who, in turn, was returning a favor to the head of the New York office and, as I found out later, was trying to advertise my work in New York.

My imagination is my writing partner. In this case, I pictured myself and the three agency heads sitting at a round table, having it out. I played the agency heads against each other in a way that led them to agreement on logistical issues that had driven them apart.

I typed the three letters accordingly, on Mom's beloved Remington. And because my grandmother was born in Germany and mom had cousins there, I added a handwritten note, in German, to the letter for the agency in Berlin.

After mailing the letters and running over to Gilmore's Department Store to buy a new tie, I got home in plenty of time to get ready for the big date that night, and to mull over Lydia's puzzling request for prayer.

Oops…

17

"Aren't we walking to the restaurant?" Lydia said when she saw my car parked at the curb. She figured we'd be going to the Cozy Corner, just blocks away. But you don't have six-month anniversaries every day, and I wanted to take Lydia out for a big night on the town.

"Let's try something different tonight," I said.

We drove to the fanciest club on Austin Avenue, and I pulled over to the curb by the door.

"Surprise!" I said.

Lydia stared out the window at the flashing neon lights, then turned to me with a troubled look on her face.

"What's wrong?" I asked.

She mumbled something about the *Cocktails* sign, then spoke in fragments so disjointed I knew she was confused, upset, and maybe even a bit frightened.

Man! What was I thinking?

"Lydia," I said, "I understand… and I'm sorry. Where would you like to go?"

She answered in a soft, distant voice:

"I thought we were going to the Cozy Corner…"

I turned the car around and we drove in silence, giving me a chance to reflect on what a big idiot I was. And when we got to the restaurant, we just sat in our booth by the window, avoiding each other's eyes and not saying a word until I could stand the silence no longer.

"Lydia…" I said. "I'm sorry."

She looked up, her eyes red from crying.

I reached over and touched her hand.

"Please…" I said, "tell me what you're thinking."

She looked back down at the table, grabbed a napkin and wiped her nose. I scooted around the booth and sat beside her, kissed the palm of her hand, then held it to my cheek.

"Princess?" I said.

A tear ran down her face. "Do you go to nightclubs when you travel?" she asked, without raising her head.

"I was in a nightclub only once in my life," I said. "Last month, and only because the head of the New York office insisted everyone from Chicago join him for a drink."

Lydia looked at me.

"Did you drink alcohol?"

"I had a ginger ale."

Her mouth quivered, as if trying to wake up a smile.

"Lydia, I'm not a big boozer," I said. "There's a grand total of one glass of beer on my lifelong liquor ledger. And I didn't even finish the beer! Tastes yucky! Have you ever had a beer?"

She broke into something between a sniffle and a chuckle.

"Johnny!"

She was smiling! Almost laughing!

"OK, rhetorical question," I said. "Anyway, I think beer tastes terrible. Why would anyone—"

"Do you smoke?" she asked, with a bit more confidence and hope in her eyes.

"No," I said. "I have a mild case of asthma. And that's another reason I don't go to nightclubs. To avoid smoke."

I went on to tell her about all the "second shift" opportunities I *avoided*. Her jaw dropped when I told her about the dance hostesses in New York—until I explained that I went to my room after dinner so I could wake up in time to catch the red-eye and surprise her.

I stopped talking, and Lydia blew her nose into her napkin so loud that we both chuckled. Then she blew me a kiss and brought my hand to her cheek.

The waitress came with our plates and asked if we were going to share the same side of the table.

Lydia nodded.

"Most definitely," I said.

Lydia had taken the rough edges off an evening that was about to get even better. As we finished dessert, I motioned out the window to the Lake Theatre.

"Would you like to catch a show?"

She looked pensively at the marquee.

"I've never been to a movie before."

"We don't have to go," I said.

"Well, I guess I'd feel funny if someone from church saw us there."

"Then we won't go," I said. "What do *you* want to do?"

She thought for a moment, then said,

"Can we just go to my apartment and listen to the radio?" And as if that wasn't enough to persuade me, she added in a pleading voice, "Jack Benny's on tonight."

Oh, she was just full of surprises!

18

The first thing Lydia did when we got to her apartment was have me sit on the couch while she turned on *every* light in the living room and hallway. Then she walked over to the radio and tuned to the Jack Benny Show. Finally she joined me, lifting her legs onto the couch and leaning over to snuggle against my side. There, we laughed along with the radio audience as we sat beneath the family portrait and the glaring stare of Frownathon.

After Jack Benny wished us goodnight, Lydia got up, tuned the radio to a big band station, and swayed to the Champagne Music on her way back to the couch.

She sat further over and spun up her feet. And as she leaned back, she asked if she could rest her head on my lap.

"Are you tired?" I asked.

"I just want to rest my eyes and listen to the music."

And there she lay, eyes closed, face relaxed. I gently combed my hand through her hair, and within a few minutes her mouth opened slightly and her breathing grew shallow and spaced.

My heart melted.

Even after the mess I made of the evening, the girl who once kept her guard up around men was now comfortably asleep on my lap. My eyes pooled as I looked at her face. And I dared to imagine waking up next to her someday and telling her how happy I was that she married me.

Static sputtered from the radio after the station signed off. My right foot had fallen asleep, and I begrudgingly gave in to its pain and woke Lydia.

She sat up and gave me a kiss.

"I must have dozed off," she said.

"You did, Sleeping Beauty."

She got up and walked to the bathroom down the hall. "I'll be right back," she said.

I stood to bring back the circulation to my leg, and felt self-conscious when I turned around and saw Frownathon staring at me from the portrait on the wall.

"What?" I said. "You saw me, I was a perfect gentleman!"

"Are you talking to yourself again?" Lydia asked from behind.

This time I wasn't startled. I reached back, took her arms, and wrapped them around my waist.

"I was just telling your dad how well I treat you."

"Oh, really? And does my father approve of you?"

I leaned closer to the portrait.

"Judging from the look on his face, I think he wants to know my intentions toward his daughter."

Lydia rested her chin against my back.

"And what *are* your intentions toward his daughter?"

I turned around in her arms and gave her a soft kiss. "Right now, it's to tell her that I love her. And to let her get some sleep."

Lydia looked at her father in the portrait, then back at me.

"Don't you have any other intentions?" she said.

I donned a playful smile.

"Maybe. But that's between me and your dad."

She nestled closer and nibbled on my lower lip.

"That sounds interesting," she said. Then she turned and looked at her father. "Do you think he saw me kiss you?"

"Maybe," I answered. "After all…"

"He's still frowning," we said in unison.

Dad once told me the hottest passion was no match for a cold shower. I put his words to the test that night when I got home and stood under the cold stream to cool down.

As usual, Dad was right.

I shivered so much, I could hardly dry off. And like a rusty tin man, I jerked my way to the bedroom, grappled with flannel pajamas, and rattled under a mountain of blankets until my body loosened up.

I was just about to doze off when the phone rang. I woke with a jerk, wondering who would call so late, hoping it wasn't Mom with bad news. But when I picked up the phone, there was silence on the other end, followed by a soft voice.

"Is this my Johnny?"

"Oh, Princess," I said. "What a relief. It's late and I thought—"

"I called earlier, but you didn't pick up."

"I was in the shower."

There was a pause, then her soft voice again.

"And now you're all clean and fresh, and all snug in your little bed?"

"Yes… and listening to my princess. "

"Well, I just wanted to thank you for tonight… And for being such a gentleman."

"Mmmm," I said.

I'll let you sleep now," she whispered. "I love you…"

After hearing the gentle *click*, I cradled the phone in my hands as if it were her face and softly kissed the mouthpiece. Then I got out of bed and headed back to the shower, grateful that there was plenty of cold water left.

19

Proclamation 2709 - Thanksgiving Day, 1946

BY THE PRESIDENT OF
THE UNITED STATES OF AMERICA
A PROCLAMATION

At this season, when the year is drawing to a close, tradition suggests and our hearts require that we render humble devotion to Almighty God for the mercies bestowed upon us by His goodness.

Devoutly grateful to Divine Providence for the richness of our endowment and the many blessings received, may we continue to give a good account of our stewardship by utilizing our resources in the service of mankind. May we have the vision and courage to accept and discharge honorably the responsibilities inherent in our strength by consecrating ourselves to the attainment of a better world.

NOW, THEREFORE, I, HARRY S. TRUMAN, President of the United States of America, in consonance with the joint resolution of Congress approved December 26, 1941, do hereby proclaim Thursday, November 28, 1946, as a day of national thanksgiving; and I call upon the people of this Nation to observe that day by offering thanks to God for the bounties vouchsafed us, and by rededicating ourselves to the preservation of the "Blessings of Liberty" envisaged by our forefathers in the preamble to the Constitution.

IN WITNESS WHEREOF, I have hereunto set my hand and caused the seal of the United States of America to be affixed.

DONE at the City of Washington this 28th day of October in the year of our Lord nineteen hundred and forty-six and of the Independence of the United States of America the one hundred and seventy-first.

HARRY S. TRUMAN

The music school closed for the week of Thanksgiving, and I drove Lydia to the airport so she could fly home and spend the Holiday with her parents, whom she hadn't seen in eight months.

As much as I missed her when *I* traveled, being in Oak Park without *her* was worse. Walking past the Cozy Corner reminded me of the simple joy of looking across the table and watching her eat. The fragrance of burning leaves drifting through Scoville Park reminded me of that first date, when I hungered to learn everything about her. And while the smell of varnished wood in the lobby of her building greeted me like an old friend, it also reminded me that my closest friend was away, leaving me to walk up three flights of stairs alone and stand outside her door in silence, eyes closed, so I could relive our first kiss and the supper we ate by candlelight.

The telephone became my lifeline: quiet conversations every evening going late into the night, and quick calls every morning to say *I love you* and to be stirred by her voice.

Lydia told me her parents were beginning to think that I liked her or something.

"Or *something*…" I said.

I knew she had plans to go home again for Christmas, and I asked if she thought her parents would mind if I tagged along. I could hear her hopping up and down over the crackling of the line. And after she picked up the phone again she said, "But aren't you going home to see *your* parents?"

"I have a meeting in Memphis a week and a half before Christmas," I said. "I'll see them then."

When I called Lydia on Thanksgiving Day, she told me her mother's reaction to my hope of coming to Atlanta:

"Mom's eyes lit up; she can hardly wait to meet you!"

"And what about your dad?" I asked

"Well…" she said, "he's still frowning!"

We laughed for a solid half-minute.

"But don't worry," Lydia added. "If you're serious about coming for a visit, Mom and I will take care of my father."

I was encouraged.

"Oh, I'm *very* serious," I said.

20

That night, I called my folks and told them my plan. Mom was disappointed that I wouldn't be home Christmas Day—until I told her, "This is the girl I want to wake up to for the rest of my life. I'm going to ask her to marry me."

Mom gasped, then laughed and cried at the same time. "Oh, John, what a wonderful girl she must be."

Dad's response was more objective, as usual.

"Son, when you weighed the pros and cons of this proposition, did you use your heart or your head?"

Mom must have worked behind the scenes, because Dad had softened by the time I arrived home in December. He even approached me the first night I was in town and invited me into his study for what he apparently thought was a long overdue talk:

"Son, perhaps you've noticed a strange feeling come over you when you're alone with your young lady friend."

"Strange feeling?" I said.

"Well, maybe not strange. But, you know... *different*."

"Different?"

"Sure. Different. Um, that is to say, different from how you might feel when you're talking about, uh, *sports*, for example, with your best friend."

"Dad… Lydia *is* my best friend!"

"Well, yes… Yes! Of course she is, Son. Just like me and your mother!"

Dad put both hands in his pockets, and a puzzled look grew across his face while he stared at his knees, as if he was trying to figure out why they swayed nervously from side to side. Finally, he lifted his head and looked me straight in the eye.

"Son, let me just come out and be frank about this: When a man is with a woman, his body… it, it… reacts, uh… to her presence."

I figured I'd have to help Dad in order to get through our little facts-of-life chat before the end of the decade.

"You mean, like when we kiss?" I said.

"Yes, Son! When you kiss," Dad said with a sigh of relief. "Think about how that *feels*."

"It's feels wonderful!"

"And that's what I've been trying to tell you for all these years. And now you, uh… now you know! It's wonderful! Enough said!" He reached out and took hold of my shoulders. "I'm so glad we had this talk. Do you have any questions?"

"No, Dad. I think you covered it. Thanks!"

"That's all right, Son. That's what fathers are for."

I spent two more days in Memphis, and the whole family gathered together in the home we grew up in. Mom gave each of her two youngest grandchildren a new toy to keep them busy while the meal was being prepared. "This is an early gift from Santa," she told them, "in celebration of your Uncle John's visit." Then she and my sister headed for the kitchen.

The rest of us stayed in the living room and brought each other up to date on our lives. I had just been promoted and Dad wanted to know how the job was going. Everyone else wanted to hear about Lydia. Maggie, the younger of my two nieces, grew especially interested after I said Lydia sang like an angel.

Mom called us to the dining room when the table was ready. Everyone was seated and about to dig in when I said, "This visit is long overdue. I had almost forgotten how much you all mean to me. Would it be alright if I say a prayer?"

Dad looked surprised, as if I had just invented the idea of praying before a meal. "That sounds wonderful, Son."

I was genuinely thankful for too many blessings to count. But that's how I usually felt, without ever having felt the urge to pray. I wanted to pray that night only because that's what Lydia would have wanted me to do, and I thought I could use the occasion to practice for what I hoped would be many Thanksgiving Day prayers with Lydia and our children.

The room grew quiet and we all bowed our heads.

"Thank you for everyone at this table. And for the love you give us, one for another. Amen."

"Amen," Dad said, just before plopping a mountain of mashed potatoes on his plate. "Son, sometimes you do us all proud."

Mom leaned over and said in a whisper that everyone heard anyway, "I think your Lydia is a good influence, John."

"She's an angel!" Maggie shouted, raising chuckles around the table.

"Amen again!" Dad said as he passed the gravy.

And so we ate, laughed, talked, and shared in all the blessings that families too often take for granted. The pleasing aroma and steam rising from the plates reminded me of that first dinner at Lydia's apartment. Everyone at the table wanted to know more about her. And though I was happy to oblige, I didn't want our story to monopolize the gathering—especially since I didn't know what our story would be after our upcoming visit with Lydia's parents in Georgia.

Sensible Things

21

Early the next morning, Mom walked into my room and shook the bed.

"Get up, John. We're going downtown."

"What?..." I said, half asleep. "Why?"

"You may be a whiz when it comes to business," she said, "but today, you're going to learn about sensible things, things husbands should know—just in case the need should soon arise."

I knew what she really had in mind: *shopping*! "Mom, I've got a plane to catch!" I said, trying to get out of it.

"Your plane doesn't leave until four," she countered. "Meanwhile, I'm going to introduce you to sensibilities that I'm sure you—if you're anything like your father—know nothing about."

"Hey," I said. "If you saw my apartment—"

"What, I'd have a heart attack?"

"Of course not. I— "

"Just tell me this, John. Would Lydia feel at home in your apartment?"

"Uhhhhhh..."

Real men don't lie to their mothers. So I spent the rest of the morning and a good part of the afternoon with Mom, learning about the sensibilities of furniture, pictures, linens, figurines, tableware, small appliances, and something that actually interested me: engagement and wedding rings.

"And what about ladies nighties?" I quipped as we walked through the women's department.

It was the first time I saw Mom blush. "We should let Lydia take care of that herself," she said.

As reluctant as I had been that morning, I'm glad Mom dragged me downtown that day. I got to see a side of my mother I had never seen before, and what she taught me in those few hours would serve me well for many years to come.

It Was A Dark and Stormy Night...

22

My parents drove me to the airport and we had just walked into the terminal when a bag handler told us all flights in and out of Chicago were delayed due to bad weather.

"Did you bring a coat?" Mom said.

"No, just this sweater. It was warm when I left Chicago."

"How about your suit jacket, Son?" Dad asked.

"It's in the suitcase."

"Son, you'd be wise to take it out before you get on the plane."

We found a restaurant and ate a light supper. Before we headed back to the airport, I unpacked the suit jacket and draped it over my arm.

"That's my boy," Dad said.

The plane departed two hours late and a blizzard swept down on the Midwest while we were in the air. We had to fly in circles over Lake Michigan for almost an hour waiting for the runways to be cleared.

I knew Lydia would be worried, so I called when I got in the terminal and told her I'd be over as soon as I could.

Of course, I also called Mom and told her I got in fine, and that I loved her, and that I was thankful she was my mom.

And yes, I told her I had my jacket on, after she asked.

The storm was worse than it had looked from the air. It took ten minutes just to clear the snow off the car. Traffic on Harlem Avenue inched along like a caterpillar. Snow plows struggled in vain against torrents of snow and gusty winds that fashioned miniature mountain ranges along the streets and sidewalks. It took over two hours to get to Oak Park, and I was cold and wet from having to get in and out of the car a half-dozen times to clear off the back window.

The streets surrounding Lydia's place were impassible, so I drove home and plowed into my assigned parking spot. Then against brutal winds and snow, I ran the four hundred and forty-four steps to her apartment building.

After the front door slammed to announce my arrival, I stood in the hallway, shivering uncontrollably, trying to catch my breath and bend the arms encased in my ice-covered jacket. My hands and cheeks burned, and I was walking toward the stairway doing my Tin Man routine when a door opened overhead and a frantic, yet heartwarming voice kissed my frozen ears.

"Johnny?!!"

"L-L-Lydia?"

Before I could reach the first landing, the Princess of Antarctica flew down two flights of stairs in her fluffy pink robe and oversized slippers, her hair wrapped in a towel.

"Oh, my precious Johnny," she said in tears. "Are you OK?"

My teeth chattered too much to answer. She helped me up the stairs and into her apartment.

"Oh, you are soaked to the bone," she said after prying off my jacket. "We need to get you dry before you go into shock!"

She led me to her bedroom and sat me on the bed. I was too cold to object, and even too cold to be excited about being where I had never been before.

Her latent, motherly instincts set her in motion with uncanny precision and resolve. She stepped over to the closet and pulled out another fluffy robe and pair of slippers. After throwing them on the bed beside me, she ran and grabbed three towels from the bathroom.

Within seconds, as I shivered helplessly, she blotted melted ice water from my hair using the edges of the first towel, which she refolded, damp side out, and wrapped around my head.

She held up the second towel. "Take off your sweater and shirt," she said.

"W-w-w-what?"

"You heard me," she said in an urgent, no nonsense tone. "We've got to get you dry before you freeze to death."

Her eyes watered as she watched my frozen fingers fumble with the buttons.

"Oh, Johnny," she whimpered. "Here, let me help you."

She lifted the sweater over my head, creating a draft that sent a strong shiver through my body.

"Hold on, My Love," she said. "Just a little longer." A tear ran down her cheek as she unbuttoned my shirt and pealed it off my back.

My teeth chattered louder as she dried my arms, chest, and back. Then she flipped the towel over and wrapped me up like a mummy.

I started warming up right away.

She went back to the closet and pulled out a large Eskimo parka and draped it over my shoulders.

"It's my stadium jacket," she explained, seeing the surprise on my face. Then she sat on the bed next to me and rubbed my back in quick circular motions as we waited about a minute or so for my teeth to quiet down.

"Is that better?" she asked.

I nodded.

She kissed my cheek and said, with the same in-charge manner as before, "Good. Now get out of those wet trousers."

"What?!!"

She laughed as she hopped off the bed and threw the third towel in my face.

"Don't get too excited," she said as she walked away. "I'll be in the kitchen heating some water."

She turned around with final instructions before she closed the door: "Make sure you dry yourself off *completely*, then get into that robe and under those covers."

After her footsteps faded down the hall, I slipped off my trousers and soaked underpants, tucked the latter into the former, and hid the result under the shirt and sweater Lydia had already draped over the chair next to the bed. And after throwing off her jacket and tying myself into her robe, I slipped under her blankets and looked up at the embroidery that greeted her each morning and tucked her in bed each night:

A Wife of Noble Character

Brings Her Husband Good

All The Days of Her Life

I was warming up fast. In more ways than one. It was hard not to think about her having slept under the same blankets the night before. And it was impossible to ignore her unmistakable, baby fresh scent that lingered on the sheets and pillowcase. A few more minutes of that torture and I would have to take a *long* cold shower, or go out and lie in the snow. And how could I explain *that* to Lydia?

Fortunately, I didn't have to. She tapped on the door a few moments later, ending my torment of bliss.

"Are you decent?" she asked from out in the hall.

"Yes," I answered, since she was referring only to my being appropriately covered.

She walked in and made no attempt to hide her grin when she saw my towel-wrapped head poking out from under the blankets.

"The water's on," she said. "Do you want tea or cocoa?"

"Cocoa sounds good, with marshmallows if you have them."

"Of course," she said, walking to the chair to gather my wet clothes. She studied each piece as she picked it up and draped it over her arm. And, of course, the underpants fell from the trousers to the floor. She picked them up and held them out as if displaying a trophy fish she had just caught.

"Oh, I guess you really were soaked," she said.

She chuckled all the way to the door.

"Come join me in the kitchen when you're ready," she said, just before she left.

Fortunately, I had followed my mother's advice: "Always wear clean underpants when you leave the house. You never know if you might have an accident and end up in the hospital or something."

Or *something*, I thought, chuckling under my breath.

Though not totally warmed up, I got out from under the covers and sat on the edge of the bed. Being a bit chilled was better than being tortured lying in her bed thinking about her.

Looking down on the nightstand, I was surprised to see another temptation—a book titled: *My Diary*. I picked it up and opened to the bookmarked page, then slammed it shut after seeing my name. As much as I wanted to read her thoughts, I valued her trust even more. I looked back and forth between her pillow and her diary, and figured there was just too much temptation in the room to handle.

I had to get out of there.

The Princess and Prince of Antarctica

23

I could hear the wind rattle the back door and whistle through the window casings as I shuffled along the hallway in those goofy-looking slippers.

When I reached the kitchen, Lydia was standing at the window, watching snow race in and out of the porch light. My clothes were drying next to the radiator. The kettle spouted a column of steam, and two mugs readied with cocoa and marshmallows stood tall on the table, waiting for a drink.

"Hey there," I said.

Lydia turned and laughed when she saw me in her fluffy robe and slippers and wearing the towel around my head. She laughed even louder after she shuffled up and gave me a peck on the lips.

"Why are *you* laughing?" I said. "You look just like me."

"Trust me," she said. "I don't look *anything* like you."

We chuckled and wrapped our arms around each other, the Princess and Prince of Antarctica, dressed in our royal attire, swaying to the music of the storm as snowflakes danced outside in jubilant celebration of our reunion.

Lydia raised her hands and cupped my face.

"I love you," she said.

"And I, you, Dearest Princess."

We sat down to conversation and frothy cups of hot cocoa. She asked, and I told her everything about my visit back home. Well, almost everything. I left out the part about telling Mom that Lydia was the girl I wanted to wake up to for the rest of my life, and the part about Mom teaching me "sensible things" husbands should know.

I didn't tell her about the diamond ring I bought either.

"Are you ready to meet my parents?" Lydia asked.

"I can hardly wait," I said, trying to bolster her courage. We were scheduled to fly to Georgia in two days, and Lydia was growing increasingly nervous about the visit. She could still hear her father mumbling after she and her mom dropped the news over Thanksgiving. "This can mean only one thing," her father said, without further elaboration.

"Father, " Lydia told him, "John just wants to meet you and Mother."

"He's not a Baptist," her father snapped, having not heard a word Lydia said. "He's a non-denominationalist, whatever that means! My word, Daughter! Is he even a Believer?"

"Father, the week before I met John, he had read all the Gospels and half of Acts in one sitting—"

"Is that supposed to mean something?"

"And he has a good heart," Lydia went on to say. "He works for a mission that helps people around the world."

To call Braxton-Becker a mission was a stretch. But even so, her dad wasn't swayed, and Lydia had given up hope we'd be together in Atlanta for Christmas.

But her mom cornered her dad for a half-hour "discussion" that got loud, Lydia told me. And afterward, her mom went up to Lydia's room, wearing a big grin. "Can you help me prepare the guest room?"

"Father agreed?" Lydia said, practically in shock.

"*Agreed* might not be the right word," her mom said, laughing. "But Sweetheart, John's coming for Christmas!"

All this was playing in Lydia's mind when the wind forced its way under the back door, droning like a bagpipe.

"Whoa! What'd you have for supper?" I said with a wink.

Lydia turned as red as my cheeks had been.

"Johnny?!"

She walked over and bumped her bottom against the door. "It was the wind!"

"Oh, *that* wind," I said. "Right…"

She gasped after glancing at the clock on her way back to the table.

"Oh dear," she said. It's almost 11:30! We have to come up with a plan to get you out of here."

"A plan?"

"Yes. Mrs. Alison downstairs is asking a lot of questions about my late-night visitors—"

"You have others?" I said with a smirk.

"Of course not!"

"Well, then? We're on the up and up."

"Yeah, and I don't need Mrs. Alison thinking anything else."

Twenty minutes later, Lydia and I left the apartment and tiptoed downstairs. Her stadium jacket was draped over my shoulders and a large scarf she fashioned from a tablecloth was pulled over my head and tied under my chin. The scarf hung out over my face as we walked down the creaking steps.

Mrs. Alison opened her door as we were sneaking by on the second floor landing.

"Oh, Lydia?" she said in her overly-sweet-I-caught-you voice. "The pilot light went out on my stove. Can you help me, Dear?"

I froze on the spot. Lydia turned around and said in her usual, cheerful voice, "Of course, Mrs. Alison." Then she turned to me, laid her hand on my back and said, "Can you make your way home, Patty?"

I paused, nodded, and continued along the landing, lowering my head so the scarf would cover my face as I turned to go down the stairs.

"Call me so I know you got home safely, OK?"

I nodded again, without stopping.

The wind had died down, but the endless horde of giant snowflakes continued their invasion of the earth. I walked into my apartment seven minutes later and called Lydia first thing.

"Hi, it's Patty," I said.

She laughed. "Well, isn't your middle name *Patrick*?"

Snowbound in Chicago at Christmas

24

Rattling windows woke me the next morning.

An opposing front had blown in from the northeast, picking up moisture from the lake and dropping mountains of the white stuff all over the city and suburbs. The man on the radio said another twelve to eighteen inches was expected on top of the twenty that had already fallen.

The phone rang, and when I picked up I heard the same radio station at the other end.

"Did you hear about the airport?" Lydia asked.

"No, I just got up."

"It's closed. They canceled all flights for twenty-four hours. And if we get the snow they're predicting, it could be closed even longer."

The snow stopped mid-afternoon the next day, leaving thirty-four inches on the ground and drifts towering six feet and higher in some areas. Abandoned cars were sprinkled along the streets like pepper on mashed potatoes.

I called Tony Stiller, who handled travel arrangements for our office. He said there was no way I'd be flying out of

Chicago any time soon. "But John," he added, "now you can come to the office Christmas party. All the married fuddy-duddies will be at home with their families. We'll have a swell time with all the ladies! Or bring your own girl, if you want."

I seldom talked about Lydia at work, because I missed her when I did. But everyone at the office knew about her, especially Tony and the other *Flying Conquistadors* (as they liked to call themselves) who couldn't figure out why, when we were out of town on business, I always went to my room after work to call Lydia rather than party with them.

"Write this down, John," Tony ordered over the phone. "Christmas Eve… Four o'clock… Food, Drink… Party!"

"I'll be in Atlanta," I told him.

He laughed and hung up the phone.

But Tony was right; our flight was cancelled. And the radio said the airport would be closed for at least two more days.

The streets were cleared by the twenty-third of December and the airport opened that night. But we couldn't book a flight to Atlanta, not even with Tony's help. It looked like Lydia and I would spend our first Christmas together alone.

Not that that was bad.

In exchange for Tony's reluctant help to get us on a plane, I had agreed to ask Lydia to the party if Tony was unable to work his magic with the airlines. I think he purposely left out a few of his magic words. But true to *my* word, I invited Lydia to the party, and was surprised when she agreed to go.

Another surprise met me when I picked Lydia up at her apartment. My legs buckled when she answered the door in her red blouse and belted black skirt; her hair was lush with curls and she was wearing *makeup*—not a lot, but enough to nudge her natural beauty a notch or so higher on the marquee.

She held the door open with one hand, and her moist, red lipstick creased when she pursed her lips and blew me a kiss.

I could have died. She was drop-dead gorgeous.

I leaned in to kiss her, but she backed away.

"No, no! Not now," she said. "You'll ruin my lipstick."

"But I—"

"But nothing," she said with a laugh. "If I have to suffer with this stuff, so do you."

"Why wear it then?"

She playfully ran her finger over my lips.

"I know your work is important to you," she said, "and I want to help in what ways I can."

She blew me another kiss and jiggled her head from side to side, which she knew drove me crazy.

I stood speechless in the doorway as she grabbed the coat draped over the chair.

"Don't worry," she said with a wink. "The lipstick will wear off eventually."

25

When we walked into the office at 4:30, the guys seemed even more stunned at the sight of Lydia than I had been. Or maybe they just weren't as shy about showing it, already on the sauce as they were.

"Now THAT explains it all!" Tony shouted as he teetered and sized Lydia up and down, his eyes popped out like organ stops.

"Explains what?" I said, trying to deflect attention off Lydia, who was flush and holding onto my arm so tight I could feel my blood pulsing.

"Explains you going back to your room... calling your girl... OH, YEAH !"

By this time, all eyes in the room had fastened on Lydia. Bob Pieters, the regional director, came out of his office with his coat on, just in time to rescue us from the wolves.

"You must be Lydia," he said with a cordial smile. "John told us so many wonderful things about you." He turned to me and added, "But you didn't tell us how beautiful she is, John!"

Lydia blushed.

"You make a stunning couple," Bob said in a loud voice, as if to tell everyone in the room to *lay off*. Then he leaned in and smiled again. "Now, if you'll excuse me, I need to get home to my own stunning lady."

As soon as Bob was out the door, Tony made the official announcement: "It appears all the fuddy-duddies have gone home, so LET THE PARTY BEGIN!"

I had traveled on business with nearly everyone who cheered at Tony's announcement, and had heard about their countless conquests, and about all the women who couldn't keep their hands off them. So I couldn't help but notice that none of them brought a date. In fact, Lydia was the only woman there. Even the secretaries left early, or should I say, *escaped*. Lydia was the lone sheep among the wolves—not counting me, of course, on whom she clung tighter than a lamb's fleece.

"Let's get some punch," I suggested. Lydia walked in step with me, holding onto my arm for dear life. I poured her a glass and raised it up to her lips. She relaxed a bit, we being the only two at the bowl. She even smiled before she took a sip. But her expression turned to shock and she began to gag as soon as she swallowed. I sipped from her glass. The punch had been spiked.

I gently slapped her on the back a few times.

"Thank you," she said, coughing. "But I think I've had enough punch."

I knew she was determined to stay as long as I wanted, *to help in what ways she could*. But I wanted nothing more than to get her out of that place.

"Princess, I'm sorry," I said. "This party was a bad idea. Let's go."

"Are you sure?" she asked, her eyes hoping I'd say *yes*.

I kissed her forehead. "Oh, yeah," I said.

"Hey, where are you going?" Tony asked in surprise when he saw us in our coats at the door. "The party's just starting!" His speech was slurred, and his eyes were even freer with Lydia than they had been before.

"Big plan tonight, Tony," I said, in truth.

He teetered and leaned in my ear. "I understand," he whispered with an impish grin.

No, he didn't understand, but I smiled and shook his hand anyway. "Merry Christmas, Tony!"

He opened the door and bowed as if he were our butler. "And a Merry Christmas to you, John." Then he gingerly took Lydia's hand and kissed it. "And to you… *Lady* Lydia."

I turned around, waved, and wished everyone a Merry Christmas before we left. Lydia waited for the door to close behind us before she let out a deep sigh.

We could hear them carrying on as we walked down the hall. When we reached the ladies room, Lydia paused. "Can you give me a moment?" she said. "I need to wash my hand."

She came out a few minutes later, looking relieved.

"Please forgive Tony," I said. "He can be crude at times—especially when he's had too much to drink—but he really has a soft heart."

Lydia pinched my cheek.

"And you have a good one," she said.

We joined the stop-and-go parade on North Avenue all the way back to Oak Park. And just as I turned south onto Oak Park Avenue, my growling stomach reminded me that we had not eaten yet.

"Oh no… dinner!"

"What?" Lydia asked.

"Dinner," I said, feeling like an idiot. "I figured we'd eat at the party."

"Are you hungry?"

"I haven't eaten since breakfast. You?"

"I had a peanut butter toast this morning."

"So we're both hungry. And there are no restaurants open."

"We could fix something at my apartment," Lydia said, "if there's anything to fix. I didn't go shopping; I figured we'd be in Atlanta.

"I have a tin of meat at my place," I said.

"I have two potatoes," she chuckled. "And maybe a jar of peas."

Out of the corner of my eye, I could see her soft smile in the light of oncoming traffic. I reached over and took her hand and brought it to my lips. "With you, it will be a feast."

She leaned over and pressed her lips hard against my right cheek. Schmooooooch! Then she leaned back, looked at me, and laughed.

"It's a date then," she said.

I pulled over to the curb in front of the Oak Park Manor.

"Can I leave you here a few minutes?"

She nodded.

I left the engine running, then shot across the street and up to my apartment, straight to the cupboard where a half-dozen tins of meat were waiting for an invitation to dinner.

"Who wants to go to Lydia's?" I said, grabbing one of the tins and putting it in my coat pocket without waiting for a response. Then I reached way back on the top shelf and pulled down the jewelry box. I flipped it open and watched light explode off the diamond that I had hoped to give to Lydia that night in Atlanta.

Snow was dancing under the streetlights when I returned to the car. Lydia chuckled and blew me kisses as I cleared the windows with my hand.

"That was quick," she said a few moments later when we pulled away from the curb and headed toward her place around the corner.

"Well… I don't want to be late for *this* dinner."

An Unforgettable Night

26

As we climbed the steps to Lydia's apartment, we saw notes taped to some of the doors. One was taped to Lydia's as well. She took it down and I read it over her shoulder.

> *Trouble with one boiler.*
> *Full heat not expected until Friday.*
> *Sorry for any inconvenience.*

"Looks like I won't need to hang your coat," Lydia said.

A door opened one floor below and we heard Mrs. Alison's voice. "Lydia?"

Lydia leaned over the railing.

"Yes, Mrs. Alison?"

"It's cold in my apartment. May I borrow a coat or a blanket?"

"Sure, I'll be right down."

Lydia unlocked the door and led me in. "Leave it open," she whispered. She went to her bedroom and returned a few seconds later with her stadium jacket. "I'll be right back."

A few moments later, I heard Mrs. Alison say, "Oh, you are such an angel!"

I smiled and nodded in agreement.

"And this coat looks just like the one your friend Patty wore the other night," Mrs. Alison added.

I was still chuckling in the open doorway when Lydia returned, pushed me into the apartment, and closed the door behind us. She stood on her toes and kissed my chin, nose, and forehead. Then she stepped back, looked at my face, and broke out laughing.

"What's so funny?" I asked.

She kissed me hard on the left cheek. "You'll see soon enough."

She took my hand and led me to the bathroom.

"You can wash up in there," she said, giving me a gentle shove. "And thanks for helping me remove my lipstick."

Even with the bathroom door closed and the water running, I could hear Lydia laughing down the hall. Five minutes later, after discovering you can't just wipe lipstick off with tissue, I joined Lydia in the kitchen where diced potatoes and onions were sizzling in a pan.

Lydia was opening a jar of peas and singing "O Little Town of Bethlehem". Her coat lay draped over a chair while she stood in front of the stove, wearing a white apron tied behind her neck and back.

I walked up from behind, put my arms around her waist and planted little kisses on her shoulders. "Mmmmm, what smells so good?"

"Potatoes and onions," she said, "sautéed in butter."

"Oh, are you cooking? I was talking about you!"

She tilted her head back and smiled. I gave her a kiss and pulled the tin of meat from my pocket.

"Hier ist das Fleisch, meine Liebe."

"Merci, mon amour."

She poured the peas into a small pot, and after a flick of her wrist, a soft blue flame rose from the burner. Then she turned around in my arms.

"Do you want me to take your coat?" she asked.

Not with the surprise I'm packing, I thought.

"Maybe later," I said.

She leaned in and kissed me. I felt her cascading tresses brush against my neck.

"Suit yourself," she said. "Now run off while I mind supper."

I walked straight to the family portrait in the living room and whispered in Frownathon's ear,

"May I have your daughter's hand in marriage?"

27

Twenty minutes later, Lydia lowered her head and slid her hand across the table under soft, flickering candlelight. I stumbled through some top-of-the-head prayer, something along the lines of: *Thank you for the snow and the way it gave us this time together. Amen.*

Lydia's head was still bowed when I raised mine, and her lips moved in silence, bringing to my mind her mysterious prayer request to the Robinsons. After she looked up and wiped her cheek, she squeezed my hand. "Merry Christmas, John."

I told myself the concern in her voice was only my imagination.

Fortunately, the rest of the meal flowed into our usual, comforting routine of unending conversation seasoned with laughs—flashbacks of Tony and the office party providing much of the latter.

After supper, we went to the living room where Mary and Joseph, wise men and shepherds, and a stable full of animals had gathered on top of the radio, around the Baby Jesus.

Lydia tuned to a station playing Christmas music.

It was chilly in the apartment, and on her way to join me on the couch, she took off her coat and shivered in front of me.

"Let's share," she said.

I opened my coat and she eased down and snuggled beside me, curled her legs onto the couch, and rested her head under my chin. I closed my coat around her with one hand and used the other to pull her coat over us like a blanket. She took my arm and held it tight. Her soft curls and warm, gentle breath brushed against my shoulder.

We held each other as orchestras played and choirs sang like Heralds from on high. Every few minutes or so, Lydia would say something about what we'd be doing if we were in Atlanta.

"We would've just gotten up from the table," she said, "so stuffed, we'd barely be able to walk to the parlor."

"I can't imagine a tiny girl like you eating that much."

"You've never tasted my mom's cooking."

"Ahhhh, so that's why yours is so good."

Lydia squeezed my arm.

A few minutes passed.

"You, Mom, and I would be sitting by the fireplace now."

"What about your dad?"

"Father would be in his chair, next to the radio, reading the paper until he dozed off."

A vibrant orchestration of "Joy to the World" trumpeted from the speaker.

"Would we be listening to the radio in Atlanta?" I asked.

"Oh yes. As long as my father approved of the music."

"Surely, he'd like this!"

"I think so. It's about Christmas, not about snowmen or reindeer or trees."

A commercial came on, and when the announcer talked about looking your best, I felt Lydia giggle.

"What's so funny?" I asked.

"I just pictured Mom looking at us and saying what a lovely couple we make."

"Did she try to set you up with someone back home?"

"Not really. But she was always telling me how a nice young man would sweep me off my feet some day and love me for the rest of my life." She paused before she went on. "Although we never talked about it, Mom knew my fear of ending up with someone like my father."

"Wouldn't someone like that be easy to spot?"

"My father wasn't," Lydia said right away. "My father can be really inspiring. Mom fell in love with a gifted preacher, and married him before she knew the man inside."

A change came over her voice, like she just remembered something.

"It's funny," she said. "I got homesick after I arrived in Oak Park. I remember thinking how strange that was because I was so glad to get away from my father. But now I realize how much I missed my mom… her encouragement…"

Lydia's body grew tense, and her voice tightened.

"I was so lonely after I moved in," she said, "and afraid that my only options were to be alone or married to someone like my father for the rest of my life."

I groaned inside, not knowing what to say, and decided silence would be better. I kissed her head and slowly ran my hand in little circles on her shoulder.

A choir was singing "Away in a Manger" and somewhere in the middle Lydia's voice returned to normal.

"If we were in Atlanta now, Father would get up and tune to a different station," she said with a giggle.

"Why? This song is about Christmas."

"Yeah, but it's being sung by Mormons."

"Your dad has something against Mormons?"

"No more than he has against Presbyterians, Lutherans, Catholics, Methodists, and Episcopalians" she said, laughing.

"At least he distains them equally," I said.

"Yes, but he saves the brunt of his distain for his favorite target—"

"Non-denominationalists," we said together.

I looked at the portrait above the couch. "Excuse us, Sir."

We sat and listened to another Christmas carol, and I was glad to feel Lydia's body relaxed against mine again.

"Thank you for being with me tonight, John," she said, stroking my arm gently. "This is my first Christmas away from home."

I slipped my hand into my coat pocket and parked it around the felt-covered jewelry box I had taken from my apartment.

"I hope we'll remember this Christmas for the rest of our lives, " I said.

The Power of One Little Word

28

"Things certainly did not turn out as planned," Lydia mused. "But at least you didn't have to be dragged down to Atlanta."

"What do mean, *dragged*? I wanted to go. I still do."

She lifted her head and looked at me, and hiding in the eyes above her smirk was a hint of hope.

"Why?" she asked.

"I want to meet your wonderful mother, and I want to talk with your dad."

She leaned back. "Talk about what?"

"I want to talk about his wonderful daughter. How her beauty arrested me the first time I saw her gently waving her arms like an angel in flight. How her tender, gentle spirit awakens longings I never knew before. How her selflessness inspires me to be the same. How she's the last thing on my mind when I fall asleep... and the first thing I hope to wake up to for the rest of my life."

Lydia's eyes began to fill, and I fought back my own tears as I pulled the ring out of my pocket and held it up to her.

"Most of all, I want to ask your father for your hand...

"Lydia, will you marry me?"

Tears emptied onto her cheeks and she began to weep. I couldn't tell if she was ecstatic or frightened. I only knew that she was thinking, and that my heart was pounding.

Her eyes volleyed back and forth between mine, then she gasped and put her hand to her mouth.

"Yes," she finally said, in a soft voice that shattered the room.

After Lydia had released the power of that one little word, I asked if she wanted to call her parents, and I volunteered to break the news to her dad. Lydia said she would call her mother later, and that she and her mom would figure out a way to tell her father.

I thought it best not to pursue the matter further—a good decision, judging by the wonderful time we had when Lydia held mistletoe over our heads before I left.

I walked into my apartment a few minutes before midnight and called my folks.

Mom picked up the phone on the first ring.

"John?" she said, barely able to contain herself. "We're all here. Did you ask her?"

"Yes..."

I heard her hand slip over the mouthpiece, and a muffled, "He asked her! HE ASKED HER," followed by a half-dozen voices screaming in the background:

"SO WHAT DID SHE SAY?"

Mom's voice turned clear again. "What did she say?"

She dropped the phone after I told her, and I heard the whole gang down in Memphis shouting and carrying on:

"YES! YES! Shine those wedding bells! She said YES!"

I found out the next day that Lydia's mom was just as thrilled, though she showed it in a different way.

Lydia told me, "Mom and I rejoiced and prayed for over a half-hour on the phone last night after you left. She is so happy for me, so happy for *us*. 'God will surely bless your marriage, Sweetheart,' she assured me. 'Never have second thoughts about that.'"

Her dad wasn't to find out until days later, when I flew to Atlanta with Lydia to meet her parents. As odd as it may sound, Lydia and her mom thought her father would best accept the news from the mouth of a stranger. And what better stranger than the one who wanted to marry his daughter, they reasoned. I don't understand their logic to this day, but who was I to argue? I was certainly up for the job, but had no idea of what was about to happen…

29

Peering over the bobbing heads of other disembarking passengers, I saw an elegant woman with long dark hair standing at the gate, searching expectantly.

"I think I see your mother," I said to Lydia.

Even on her tiptoes, Lydia could not see over the crowd, but someone ahead momentarily swayed and Lydia caught her mother's eye for a brief second.

"Yes, that's her!"

Leah threw up her hands and waved. I told Lydia, whose view was blocked again, and we both waved back, Lydia raising her hand above the crowd. A few moments later, mother and daughter were locked in a warm embrace.

"Oh, Sweetheart," Leah said, "I am so happy for you."

After rocking in her mother's arms, Lydia stepped back, brought out her ring, and put it on for her mother to see.

"It's beautiful," Leah said. Then she turned to me and smiled. "John, I'm so happy to meet you at last."

"Thank you, Mrs. Bowman."

"Mrs. Bowman?" she said, with open arms. "Come here!"

As we hugged she said, "Forgive my informality, but with

all that Lydia has told me about you, I already think of you as my son. And I hope someday you'll feel comfortable enough to call me *Mom*."

It was obvious how Lydia had turned out so well.

"Where's Father?" Lydia asked as she put her ring back in its box.

"Oh, he's out in the car," Leah said, "and that's probably for the best."

It was Friday night, seven o'clock and sixty degrees under starry skies in Atlanta when we reached the idling Hudson Sedan.

"John, why don't you ride up front," Leah suggested. "Lydia and I can sit in back."

I put the suitcases down and opened the back door. Lydia ducked in first, stepped over the hump, and put her hand on her dad's shoulder. "Merry Christmas, Father!" she said in a cheerful voice.

I couldn't make out what he mumbled.

Leah got in after Lydia. "Thank you, John."

"Yes, Ma'am," I said, loud enough for her husband to hear.

With the ladies seated, I opened the front door, leaned in, and extended my hand.

"Pleased to meet you, Reverend Bowman. I'm John Richards."

He just stared at me, with the face of a world champion poker player. After an awkward length of time, just as I was about to withdraw my disregarded hand, he abruptly turned off the engine and handed me the keys.

"Put the bags in the trunk," he said.

While Lydia and Leah talked and laughed as if they were best friends at a reunion, which they were, I struggled to defrost the iceberg who drove the car on that thirty-minute ride that seemed to last forever.

"Is it always warm in Atlanta this time of year?" I asked, trying to get a response out of him.

"No," he said.

"Nice roads," I said a minute later. "Does it snow here?"

"On occasion."

I had him up to two words, and decided to go for broke with an open question. "So how was your Christmas?"

I saw his eyes roll in the dim light of the dashboard.

"What do you mean?" he said.

You've got him up to four words now, John. You're on a roll!

"Well, did you find a good tree?"

"What tree?"

"Your Christmas tree!" I said.

I knew I was in trouble when the back seat suddenly fell into silence. Another indication was the sour look Horatio threw at me before he grunted, shook his head, and turned his attention back to the road. Immediately, an image of Lydia's apartment on Christmas Eve came to mind; I could see the nativity set—but no tree! And I remembered Lydia saying her dad liked *Christmas* music, not music about snowmen or reindeer or *trees*!

"Yes, these are really nice roads," I said, expecting no response, and getting none.

So much for being on a roll.

Horatio parked in front of the house and handed me the keys again. "My wife will show you where to take the bags," he said. Then he got out and walked toward the back of the two-story Colonial, leaving the three of us to watch in bewildered silence until he disappeared behind the house.

30

"You're doing just fine, John," Leah said as I carried the bags through the front door.

"They're really not that heavy," I said.

"No," Leah said. "I meant you're doing fine with my husband. He just needs to warm up to you."

Lydia broke into laughter first, after seeing her mother try to hold hers in. And the three of us laughed all the way up the stairs and into the hall where Leah stopped and motioned to Lydia's room.

"John, if you would be so kind as to put Lydia's bag in there. The bathroom is the next door down, on the left, and the guest room is at the end of the hall. I hope you find it comfortable."

"I'm sure I will, Ma'am."

"Good! Then when you two get settled, come join us downstairs in the parlor."

After helping Lydia unpack, I carried my bag into the small but homey guest room and hung my suit in the cedar-lined closet. As I threw my bag under the bed, I heard light tapping on the door.

"Are you ready, Stranger?" Lydia said.

I opened the door and assumed the stance of a Halfback. "Just point me toward the goal," I said with the look of raw power on my face.

Lydia pointed toward the stairs. "Go get 'em, Red."

Some of that raw power dissipated when I saw a shotgun hanging in the room opposite the bath.

"That's my parents' bedroom," Lydia said as we passed.

On the way downstairs, we saw Leah handing an envelope to a woman at the front door.

"That's Mrs. Freeman," Lydia whispered. "She's been like a second mother to me, and a Godsend for my mom."

"I put some extra in, Esther," we heard Leah say. "It was so kind of you to stay so late. I'll see you Monday afternoon."

Leah closed the door and turned around just as we stepped into the parlor.

"Where's Father?" Lydia asked.

Leah gestured, bringing her hands together as if she were praying. "His sign is up," she whispered.

Lydia interpreted for me. "My father has a sign he puts on his door whenever he's not to be disturbed."

"Perhaps he's working on his sermon or something." Leah offered.

"Or *something*," said Lydia.

Leah motioned to the table in the center of the room. "That doesn't mean we can't enjoy each other's company," she said.

And we did just that. And as I watched and listened, I noticed how much Leah and Lydia looked and acted like twins born twenty years apart—from their petite frames to their facial features to their lush, dark hair. They laughed and smiled alike too, and made the same gestures. Even their voices sounded the same: light, and full of wonder.

At the top of the hour, the grandfather clock chimed and Leah turned to me. "Forgive us, John. We don't mean to leave you out of the conversation."

"I didn't take it as such," I said. "I've enjoyed watching the two of you. You look more like twins than mother and daughter. And I bet you sing, too."

Lydia reached across the table with both hands and picked up her mother's. "She's my teacher," Lydia said with a look of deep gratitude.

Though they made polite attempts to include me, I knew they had a lot to talk about, and I felt my presence only restrained their conversation. Despite their protests, I excused myself to go back to my room.

"I'll walk you up," Lydia offered.

Outside the guest room, she put her arms around my neck and looked up into my eyes.

"Do you know how much I love you?" she asked.

"If it's as much as I love *you*, then I'm the most loved man on the planet."

"You are," she said, and a low hum sounded in her throat as she gave me a long kiss. "I'm afraid that might have to last a while," she said afterward. "I don't how much time we'll have alone here."

"But I'm so hungry," I pleaded.

She closed her eyes and leaned in again. "Well, maybe just another taste," she whispered.

31

After a restless night, I hopped out of bed at six-thirty, threw on my clothes and went downstairs. And following the sound of rustling newspaper to the kitchen, I found Horatio sitting at the table.

"Ahh, Reverend Bowman. I was hoping to find you here. Do you have a moment?"

He tossed the paper aside and guzzled what little coffee was left in his cup. "Now's not a good time," he said. "I've got things to do at the church."

"Perhaps I could help?"

"Perhaps you'd only get in the way," he said, grabbing his coat as he walked out the door.

Later that morning at breakfast, I told Lydia and Leah what happened, except for Horatio's parting words, which I softened considerably. Lydia and Leah invited me to go downtown with them. I *knew* I'd get in *their* way, so I told them I needed to stay behind and rethink my strategy, which was the truth.

That afternoon, I remembered what Dad told me on the day I graduated from law school. "Son, if you ever have something really important to say, something of major consequence that will affect the rest of your life one way or another: write it down and memorize it. It's the only sure way to get the right words out when you're under fire."

So I sat at the kitchen table and wrote out a two-page speech, finishing it just as Lydia and Leah walked in the back door, their arms loaded with packages.

They listened attentively to my strategy and the speech, but when I looked up, the smiles of approval I expected to see were not there.

Their sweet natures made it impossible for them to offer even *constructive* criticism. After prying it out of them, I learned that while my poetic declaration of love and promise had a swooning effect on them, swaying Horatio would require an entirely different approach—a shorter one, one with a little butter on it, and based on scripture to make it harder for him to dismiss.

Rather than reveal my near-total ignorance of the Bible, I asked for their suggestions. Leah brought a King James to the table, and within an hour we penned a short imploration based on the writings of Peter and Paul:

Reverend Bowman: Being well-versed in the Bible, you know Peter's admonition that a husband honor his wife as heirs together of the gracious gift of life. And you know Paul's admonition that a husband love his wife as he loves himself.

Sir, that's how I love and honor your daughter, and I have asked her to marry me. She said yes, but her joy can be complete only with your blessing, which I entreat of you now.

By the time we wrote the final draft, I knew it by heart and I recited it in front of them. When Lydia saw my tears and heard the crack in my voice, she leaned over and kissed my cheek right in front of her mom.

"Please excuse me, Mother."

Leah nodded in approval. "That's alright, Sweetheart. If you hadn't kissed him, I would've done it myself."

Unfortunately, it was the only recitation of the day. Horatio came home at eight o'clock, ate a light supper, and went straight to bed. "We need to be at the church tomorrow by seven," he barked before retiring for the night beneath his shotgun.

32

I sat in the front row inside Graceland Baptist Church as Lydia and Leah sang during the offertory. Their interweaving harmonies produced a chorus effect that had me wanting to stand up in applause. But Lydia had told me that clapping for performers at her church was considered diverting due praise from God, so I held my peace and wasn't surprised when the sanctuary was silent at the end of their duet.

What *did* surprise me was the stirring I felt when Lydia's father delivered the sermon a few minutes later. His insight into the deceitfulness of the heart and the squandering of life led me to tears twice, and I wondered how he could be the same man whose picture led me to call him *Frownathon*, for which I felt deeply ashamed as he spoke.

But after the service, in the car, when I tried to express my sincere gratitude and compliments, it was clear that the man who had been in the pulpit was not the man driving us back to the house.

He dropped us off and muttered that he had members to visit in the hospital. And when he finally returned after nine o'clock that night, he went straight to bed.

I had trouble sleeping that night, on two accounts: first, I was concerned I wouldn't be able to talk to Lydia's father at all during the trip. And second, I couldn't get the image of Lydia—lying in bed less than thirty feet away—out of my mind. A cold shower was out of the question; they didn't have a shower. So I got up and walked to the bathroom and splashed cold water on my face.

Looking in the mirror as water dripped off my chin, I tried to find solace in Dad's words:

"Long-suffering leads to great rewards."

As I was thinking, the door cracked open slightly and I heard Lydia whisper, "Are you decent?"

"Yes," I whispered back.

She tiptoed in quickly and softly closed the door. She had on her Antarctica outfit—fluffy pink robe, oversized slippers, towel around her hair—and there was yearning in her eyes.

"What's the matter?" I said.

Her mouth drew to my lips.

"Now *I'm* hungry," she whispered.

33

Leah knocked on my door to wake me at six the next morning, as I had asked. I rehearsed my speech as I got dressed, then hurried down to the kitchen to talk with Horatio before he left.

He was already gone. I saw his note, taped to the icebox:

I'm at the church. We leave
for the airport when I return.
—H.

Our plane was scheduled to leave Atlanta at 3:30. Lydia and I enjoyed a wonderful lunch with Leah, whom we thanked from the bottom of our hearts for all her love and support and encouragement.

The only dark cloud hanging over us was the unspoken speech. We knew it would have to be delivered in the car, with the four of us present, on the way to the airport.

Lydia squeezed my hand and Leah gave me two thumbs up before they ducked into the back seat of the sedan. I loaded the bags into the trunk and took my place in the front seat.

Just as I sat down, Horatio turned on the radio.

I was hoping we could talk, Sir," I said.

"Not now," he mumbled.

He turned the radio up too loud for me to compete, especially when you consider what I had to say. We spent the next thirty minutes listening to long-since forgotten news. But I don't forget how miserable I felt, especially after seeing the long faces on Lydia and Leah in the back seat.

Horatio parked the car in view of the runway and turned off the ignition, which thankfully shut off the radio. Then, while looking straight out the front window, he handed me the keys and said, "My wife will walk you to the gate."

I took the keys and held them in midair until I could feel the weight of Lydia's and Leah's eyes on me.

I took a deep breath.

"Sir, I have been trying to talk with you since we arrived."

He said nothing as he continued to stare out the window.

I drew another breath, then went for broke: *"Reverend Bowman: being well-versed in the Bible, you know—"*

"STOP!" Horatio shouted, "STOP!" Then he scrunched his shoulders, lifted his hands to his face, and began to shake. "Please," he pleaded, "just stop." He leaned forward and wept into the steering wheel as the rest of us looked on, not knowing what to do, say, or even think.

When he was finally able to speak again, he leaned back in the seat and dropped his hands to his lap. "You can save the speech," he said. "I already know what you have to say. Does my opinion even matter?"

I looked at Lydia and then at her father.

"I've asked your daughter to marry me. She said yes. She knows I'll love and cherish her more than anything on earth. But she wants—she *needs*—your blessing."

Horatio wept softly until a look of resignation came over his face, like that of a man hanging over the edge, unable to hold on any longer.

He looked at Lydia in the rear-view mirror.

"I am not a monster," he whimpered.

Lydia placed her hand on his shoulder, and he placed his hand on top of hers. Then he addressed her in a way he hadn't done in years.

"My precious little one," he said as tears freely washed over his cheeks. "Do you want this man, to have and to hold all the days of your life?"

"Yes, Father," Lydia said, weeping with him.

He took her hand and kissed it, then held it to his cheek, unable to say another word. And after nodding his head, he got out, walked to the front of the car, and leaned against the hood.

A few moments later, I got out and opened the door for Leah. Before I could walk over to Lydia's side, she let herself out and walked up to her father. She put her arms around him and rested her head on his shoulder.

And I heard her say, "I love you, Daddy."

All Aboard

34

Leah, Lydia, and I stood at the gate crying and laughing and hugging when the stewardess announced the final boarding call. Before turning to walk on the plane, I bent down and kissed Leah on the cheek.

"Thanks, Mom," I said. "For everything."

We set the date for Saturday, May 3, 1947.

The first four months of that year are now a blur. I vaguely remember Lydia rushing about, making all sorts of arrangements for no apparent reason. I also remember our moms flying into Chicago, and the shocked look on their faces (and Lydia's) when they saw my apartment. They dragged me along on the subsequent shopping spree for furniture, wall coverings, throw rugs, *real* curtains, pots, pans, silverware, small appliances, towels, and too many other things to mention, including toilet cleaner.

Pastor Davidson at Cornerstone Baptist led us through premarital counseling. He was a practical, gracious man who readily agreed to perform the service even after we told him we'd be attending Gonner Memorial after we got married.

On the Wednesday prior to the wedding, both sets of parents flew to Chicago and stayed at the Oak Park Manor, across the street from my apartment.

Lydia and the moms went busily about, tying loose ends. The dads and I mostly just sat around, scratching our heads and other parts of our anatomies.

The Day of a Lifetime

35

At the appointed time, 4:30 in the afternoon, ten thousand one hundred and fifty-two days after my birth, Mrs. Turner took over the organ and played, "Sheep May Safely Graze". A few minutes later, I walked in from the alcove and stood next to the railing in the front of the platform. The best man escorted the maid of honor, my sister, to the front before taking his place beside me.

"We're all proud of you, Son," he whispered.

I stood tall and strong as the other couples in the wedding party marched in a solemn succession. Then we faced the entrance and the church fell into silence. My legs weakened when I saw Lydia step out of the shadows of the entryway in her flowing white gown.

The organ and trumpets began the processional: "Jesu, Joy of Man's Desiring", and at the minister's gesture, the congregation stood in honor of the bride. Arm-in-arm with her father and holding two white roses, Lydia walked toward the altar, her gown waving in cadence. She offered each mother a rose, and stopped a few steps in front of me, just as the music ended.

"Who gives this woman in Holy Matrimony?" Pastor Davidson said in a deep, solemn voice.

"Her mother and I," Lydia's father said, which finally put an end to my worrying about him changing his mind.

Lydia walked two steps forward and looked up at me, her smile through the veil renewing my strength.

Pastor Davidson spoke about the sanctity of marriage, the joy of the bride and bridegroom, and facing the uncertainties of tomorrow in the certainties of Christ.

My emotions held up fine, and I thought I would make it through the whole ceremony like a man—until Lydia's mom got up to sing. Her voice reminded me of Lydia's, ringing with purity. And as I imagined Lydia someday singing at *our* daughter's wedding, my tears of gratitude wouldn't stop, and flowed even freer throughout the vows, although no one seemed to mind.

After the ceremony, everyone gathered in the fellowship hall, and I beamed as Lydia walked among the guests.

There goes Mrs. Lydia Richards.

Then I noticed her dad and Pastor Davidson talking in the corner. Horatio had a scowl on his face. His arms were folded, his foot tapping. It looked like Pastor Davidson was trying to calm him down, but Horatio suddenly turned away and hurried over to where our moms sat, talking.

He interrupted Leah mid-sentence. I couldn't make out his words from across the room, but I could hear his tone, and it wasn't pleasant. Leah looked shocked, then stood up and handed her cup to my mom in an apologetic manner. Then she turned around, threaded her arm through her husband's, and proceeded to walk him briskly out of the room.

Five minutes later, Leah returned and sat down with my mom, smiling, as if nothing had happened.

Horatio walked in a few minutes later, looking grumpier than ever but not saying a word to anyone.

(We found out later what happened. While everyone else celebrated at the reception, Horatio and Pastor Davidson discussed doctrine. Before he flew into a rage, Horatio said something to the effect of "Please don't be offended by all my questions, I just want to be sure my daughter and son-in-law are properly fed here."

"Oh, they won't be attending here," Pastor Davidson said in surprise. "They'll be at John's church: Gonner Memorial."

We practically had to force Lydia's mother to tell us what happened next.

"Well," Leah said to me, "after my husband came over and interrupted me and your mother, I knew he was about to lose all civility. So I handed my cup to your mother and politely asked to be excused."

Leah turned to Lydia. "Then I grabbed your father's arm and dragged him out of the room before he could make a complete jackass of himself and spoil your wedding day."

After she blushed and apologized for the rough language, Leah went on to say,

"Of course, this angered your father even more. When we got out of the room he said, 'Did you know your son-in-law intends to turn our daughter into a non-denominationalist?'

"I told him, 'You will not say a word about this now and ruin their day! Do you understand?' He turned beet red. I rarely stood up to him, and never with such resolve.

"Then he shouted, 'I *will* say something! What would my congregation say if they found out about this?'

"I shouted back, 'What would they say if they found out we were divorced?'

"He pointed his finger at me and said, 'How dare you!'

"And for the first time in my life, I pointed back and told him with a firmness that even surprised me, 'And how dare *you* say anything to spoil this day for our children!'")

After the reception as we got ready to leave the church, Leah walked up to us, towing Horatio. With joyful tears in their eyes, Leah and Lydia clung onto each other for over a minute, whispering into each other's ear. Then Leah stepped over and planted a big kiss on my cheek.

"I am so proud to call you my son," she said in her sweet drawl.

Apparently Horatio was not as proud. After pecking Lydia on the cheek, he looked at me and shook his head in disbelief. Leah wrapped her arm in his and whisked him away, looking back at us to grin and say in a cheery voice:

"Enjoy your honeymoon!"

OH, YEAH!

36

We spent our wedding night in the new, abundantly appointed Bridal Suite of what was formerly my scarcely furnished apartment. Lydia had hoped and dreamed about this night since she was a little girl. She did not want to spend it in a hotel. She wanted to be able to walk into our bedroom in the days, months, and years ahead and be reminded of what she knew would be one of the most memorable nights of her life.

And memorable it was.

Unfortunately, after reading my notes, Lydia asked that I not divulge certain details about our first night together.

"It's our private story!" she said, in dismay and disbelief.

Actually, I was relieved by her request. I remember lying in bed, quivering when she walked into the room in her translucent, flowing nightgown. How could words describe what I felt when she eased into bed beside me, the soft candlelight accentuating the arresting features of her face, and the swell of—uh, I best stop there, except to add (again at Lydia's request) that we were both virgins on our wedding night.

As Dad had said, long-suffering led to great reward. Lydia and I benefited by waiting for intimacy until after we got married. Without the burden of guilt, and downright eager to fulfill her "marital duty" to her husband, Lydia was free to enjoy the gift of intimacy within the sanctity of our marriage.

And I relished in her freedom.

We also benefited from the persistence of an annoying but effective teacher. The squeaky floor beneath our bed taught us to be slow, deliberate lovers. Lydia felt self-conscious about the floor's *complaining*, as she called it, especially since Vernon and Ada Robinson occupied the apartment below.

Although the Robinsons never spoke with us directly on this matter, Lydia wondered what Ada was thinking when they'd meet on occasion in the hallway and Ada asked in her overly-sweet way: "How was your night, Dear? Did you get enough rest?"

Our yearlong courtship of abstinence left Lydia and me with a deep hunger for each other, and there were times when hunger pangs came over us in public places where we could do little about it.

During those times, we expressed our longings to each other with one of three codes: the Short Squeeze, the Short Double-Squeeze, and the *Long* Squeeze.

If we were on a crowded elevator and she gave my hand the Short Squeeze, she was saying *I love you*.

If we were watching a movie at a theatre and I gave her knee the Short Double-Squeeze, I was saying *I wish we were alone, right now*.

Sorry, but details of the *Long* Squeeze are classified.

I did some juggling at work to cut down on travel, against the advice of the regional director who was grooming me to head the Chicago office. I was known throughout the company as a hard-working, versatile manager who got things done on time and on budget. The regional director stressed the importance of my making the rounds to other offices and being seen by top management and key decision makers.

But the carrot they dangled off in the future could not compete with the banquet who welcomed me home every night. Promotion and advancement would have to wait. My top priority was to spend time with Lydia. It was the best investment I ever made, an investment that kept growing as we fell even deeper in love: walking and talking together, laughing and crying, and planning for a family.

Expansion Plans

37

Shortly after our first anniversary, I was sitting in the living room reading the newspaper when Lydia walked in, nestled on the floor between my feet, and rested her head against my knee.

I put the paper aside and gently combed my fingers through her hair. I knew something was troubling her, and that she would tell me in her own good time.

Ten minutes later, she leaned back and looked up.

Her cheeks were wet.

"We've been married a year now," she said, "and..."

She cleared her throat and returned her head to my knee, leaving it there until the grandfather clock counted off another minute.

"And?" I said.

"Still no signs of a baby," she whispered.

"It's not for lack of trying," I said, with immediate regret. But to my relief, she chuckled, then leaned back and looked out the window at the trees slow-dancing in the wind.

"It's just that my mom had trouble conceiving, and I'm wondering if... if something might be wrong."

I scooted off the chair and settled with her on the floor, taking her hands in mine and giving each a soft kiss.

"What did your mom do?" I said.

"She went to a doctor, a specialist."

"Well, we can do that."

The next day at work I overheard one of the accountants talking about a doctor who specialized in fertility testing and treatment.

The doctor must have been good; his earliest opening was four months away. I made an appointment over the phone and waited until I got home to tell Lydia, hoping to see her hopping-up-and-down-like-an-excited-little-bunny routine.

I was not disappointed.

"Four months, huh?" she said, grinning. "What can we do in the meantime?"

"Uh, keep trying?" I suggested.

A playful moan rose from her throat.

"I was thinking the same thing," she said.

38

I had forgotten about the appointment four months later when I got home and found Lydia standing in the doorway, wearing a playful smile and bouncing on her toes like a little girl trying to keep a secret impossible to hold back.

"What?" I asked, knowing I was in for a surprise.

"Remember that appointment you made four months ago?"

"Four months ago?"

She gave me a nudge. "Quit teasing me. You know which appointment. The fertility doctor?"

Oops!

"Oh, yeah, that appointment."

"You *did* forget!" she said.

"No, I didn't... uh, well... OK, yes, I forgot. But now I remember—*that* appointment."

"Yes, *that* appointment," she said, her big grin telling me that I wasn't in the doghouse.

"I'm really sorry, Princess," I said. "I meant to go with you. What did the doctor say? Is everything all right?"

"*That* appointment was scheduled for tomorrow," she

said. "But I cancelled it this afternoon."

"Why?"

"Because I saw Dr. Nichols this morning."

"Dr. Nichols from church? What for?"

There was a slight quiver in her smile and pools formed in her eyes when she took my hand and placed it on her tummy.

I gasped. "Oh, *Dearest Princess*… I LOVE YOU !"

She threw her face into my shoulder and we laughed and cried, *both of us* hopping up and down like excited little bunnies.

Katie Leah Richards was born six and a half months later at West Suburban Hospital.

Tough Delivery

39

It was an exhausting 18-hour delivery, and the doctors were talking C-section. But at the last minute, Lydia asked for one more try.

It worked.

I was pacing the waiting room when the doctor walked in and announced I had a little baby girl. Then he told me Lydia needed to stay in the hospital a few extra days.

"Is anything wrong?" I asked.

"I don't think so," the doctor said. "The labor ran a little longer than expected, and we'd just like to run a few tests to make sure everything's OK."

When he saw the worried look on my face, he smiled and added, "Look, Mr. Richards, it's just a precaution. Your wife's resting comfortably and appears to be fine. I wouldn't worry if I were you."

But I *was* worried—and elated, relieved, and tired. All at the same time. I took a few minutes to recuperate in the phone booth before reaching in my pocket filled with nickels, dimes, and quarters.

The phone at the other end rang only once, and I heard Leah ask in a frantic voice, "Is that you, John?"

"Yes–"

"Oh please... tell me everything's OK."

"Everything's fine," I said. "It was a long delivery, but Lydia did a great job and is resting comfortably now."

"And the baby?"

"A little girl! 7 pounds, 4 ounces, 19 inches long."

I saved the best for last. "We named her Katie Leah."

Beneath the crackle of the long distance line, I heard Leah whisper a prayer. And after she finished, I thought:

Amen, thank you... whoever you are...

Leah cleared her throat and raised her voice. "You realize I'm coming up there, don't you? I'm coming first thing in the morning."

Lydia and I had hoped she would come, but thought it too much to ask. "You don't have to–"

"Oh, yes I do," she said. "I've been looking forward to this for years. And I want to help!"

I could hear Frownathon talking in the background and Leah saying in a muffled voice, "It's a *girl*... Katie Leah."

When Leah's voice became clear again, I asked, "How will Horatio run the ship without you?"

"Oh, he'll manage."

The operator broke in. "You have one minute remaining."

"Give Lydia my love," Leah said. "And squeeze that baby for me. I'll call you in the morning and let you know when my plane comes in."

I hung up the phone and sighed in relief at the thought of Leah coming to help. Then I reached into my pocket for another handful of Jeffersons, Liberties, and Washingtons.

"Hello, Operator. I'd like to place a long distance call to Memphis, Tennessee."

I heard the phone ringing at the other end and thought I would burst with pride if someone didn't answer soon. There was a click, and I choked back tears when I recognized my mother's voice, full of anticipation.

"Hello?" she said.

"Hey, Grandma…"

The Trouble with Katie

40

Lydia spent six days in the hospital. The day before her release, doctors told us Lydia's chances of conceiving again were slim, if that. The news shook us, Lydia to the core.

Lydia's mom was in the room at the time. As soon as the doctors dropped the news, Leah put her hand on Lydia's shoulder. Although Leah's eyes were open and her mouth was still, I knew she was praying.

Even in the daily bustle of life, Leah proved her sainthood day in and day out for the entire month she stayed with us. Cleaning the apartment, cooking, doing the laundry, running a thousand errands. Always pleasant, never condescending. Not once did she mention her workload, or ask me to pitch in, or lecture me about my travel schedule. She was just happy to help. Mother-in-law jokes make no sense to me.

Leah also let *us* raise Katie, which proved to be difficult. I am an optimist. When asked if a glass is half-empty or half-full, I say it's about to overflow. Like my imagination, my optimism served me well at work, but left me blind to realities of childrearing that were obvious to Lydia and Leah.

Katie was strong-willed from the start. Her demanding disposition drained Lydia who, when exasperated, told me how fortunate she was to have only one child. Of course, I didn't believe her. Lydia was born to be a mother; she was just off to a rough start.

I got another promotion and was making more money than I ever thought possible. We talked about buying a house, but Lydia said she was too run down to think about setting up a new home.

My increasingly frequent travel only made matters worse. One day I came home after a short, two-day trip. Katie was throwing a tantrum in her crib. I found Lydia crying in our bedroom. I hugged her and said, "Let me take care of this. I'll be right back."

It took twenty minutes to quiet Katie down, which about drove me crazy and helped me finally realize what my poor wife had to go through day after day. When I returned to our bedroom, Lydia was asleep. I pulled the blanket over her shoulder, then went to open a few cans for supper.

That night, after Katie fell asleep, I sat with Lydia and told her how sorry I was for being so blind to her plight. When I suggested we hire some help, she started weeping and I felt even sorrier, especially when she forced herself to stop and put on the happiest face she could muster.

"No, really, I'm fine," she said. "And I can't just hand over my duties to a stranger."

There were six months left on a project that took me out of town for a full week each month. I wasn't about to let Lydia suffer through another week alone.

"We won't get a stranger," I said. "Let's call your mom. If she's willing to fly up the weeks I'm gone until this project is over, we'll cover the airfare."

I don't know who was happier: Lydia, who ached for her mother's physical and spiritual support, or Leah, who was always willing to help and get a vacation from Frownathon.

But even with Leah there to help, I dreaded having to leave Lydia home. And at a luncheon during the last trip of the project, as colleagues applauded my surprise appointment to the Transatlantic Integration Committee, I sat at the table in shock, trying not to think of all the travel that would entail.

I arranged to fly home two days early, but didn't tell Lydia because I wanted to surprise her. The plane touched down at Midway Airport at eight o'clock on a Saturday night, and I rolled up to the apartment at about half past nine.

After slipping into the building and sneaking upstairs, I opened the door to the apartment, slowly, to keep it from squeaking. The lights were on, but no one was in the living room. And Katie was not crying, meaning she was asleep.

I could hear faint voices drifting from our bedroom as I tiptoed into the entryway. I eased over to the bedroom door, but stopped short at the sound of Lydia weeping and her mother trying to comfort her.

Overheard

41

"Mom," Lydia said, struggling to catch her breath. "How can I go on like this?"

"Sweetheart, you are strong and this will surely pass. John will be home Monday, that awful project will be over, and you two can work through this together. But you need to talk with John; you need to tell him how you feel."

There was crying and the clanging of the radiator, then a period of silence before Lydia continued.

"Sometimes I wonder if he still loves me."

"You're just tired, Sweetheart."

I fought back tears. *Oh, Lydia, of course I love you. If you only knew how much I love you, how much I long for you when I'm away.*

"You still love *him*, don't you Sweetheart?"

"Yes," Lydia said, right away.

I heard a kiss, and Leah say in a soft voice, "Then there's hope."

After the sound of a passing bus faded up the street, Lydia said, "Did I ever tell you it took him five weeks to work up the courage to kiss me?"

"No," Leah said with a chuckle. "Is he a good kisser?"

Lydia's voice lightened. "He's a wonderful kisser... and a passionate lover—"

"OK, OK," Leah said. "Spare me the details!"

They both laughed, giving me opportunity to clear my throat and palm the tears from my cheeks.

Then the room grew quiet, and somber again.

"Have you two prayed about this?" Leah asked.

Lydia said nothing.

"I'm sorry," Leah said a few moments later. "I didn't mean to—"

"It's OK, Mom. You've been around John long enough to know his spiritual state. I'm just glad he and Father never talked in any depth. Father would have seen through him right away, whereas I assumed John was a man of faith when he told me, on our first date, that he had read all four Gospels and half of The Book of Acts in a single sitting."

"That's a good sign," Leah said.

"Well, I thought so too at the time, but later I found out he read them only because he heard my name was in the Bible and he wanted to see it in print."

They both chuckled, at which I took no offense.

Lydia continued. "By the time I realized John's ship of faith was in shallow water, I was head over heels in love with him. I didn't know what to do. I asked everyone at church to pray for me. And even as *I* prayed, thanking the Lord for such a loving and caring man, I wondered what God was thinking in putting us together."

"I wouldn't be surprised if God has good plans for John," Leah said.

"I know," Lydia said. "There's a reason for everything. And I know you're praying for us."

"Of course I am, Sweetheart."

The room fell silent, and I was about to slip out of the apartment when Lydia poured out her heart again in a voice spattering with frustration and doubt.

"Mom, why do I feel so hurt and angry every time John goes out of town? Why does he have to be gone so much? I'm at my wits' end with Katie—"

Lydia gasped for breath and cried again before she continued.

"Sometimes I think it's best to not have another baby... yet I long for another one... and I get depressed thinking I won't be able to have one."

"It's best to leave that in the Lord's hand, Sweetheart."

When Lydia settled down, there was defeat in her voice. "The way things are going, I couldn't get pregnant anyway," she said. "With John so busy and me feeling so overwhelmed, we haven't... you know... been together for a while."

There was a long pause, then Leah said,

"I know we never talked about it. About sex, that is. Perhaps we should have. Sex is important to a husband, more than most folks let on."

"It's important to me too," Lydia said. "And I want to love him that way, but when I feel like this..."

There was weeping again, followed by silence.

Then Leah said, "Let's pray."

42

I stopped trying to hold back tears as I stole out of the building and ran down the block, replaying in my mind what I had heard, weeping out loud at times, and renewing my promise to love and cherish Lydia till death do us part.

After washing my face in the drinking fountain at the park, I returned to the apartment, retrieving my suitcase from the car along the way.

I purposely let the slamming door and creaking steps announce my arrival in the building. And when I reached the door to the apartment, I knocked.

A look of surprise and relief came to Leah's face when she answered the door. "Lydia," she said in a loud whisper, "John's home!"

I heard our bedroom door open. And out of the corner of my eye I saw Lydia run into the bathroom. "Johnny! Johnny!" she cried. "Just a minute!"

I knew she had gone in to wash so she could present her Happy Face. I put the suitcase down, and leaned over and kissed Leah's forehead.

"Thanks for being here, Mom," I said, fighting back tears.

A few moments later, Lydia rushed out of the bathroom and gave me one of those in-front-of-your-mother pecks on the cheek. I reached for her and pulled her in close. Her arms slid under mine and up my back. Our eyes locked, and I was reminded of the longing we shared just before that first kiss in front of her apartment.

"Please excuse me, Leah," I said without turning, "but I love your daughter very, very much."

And I gave Lydia a long, long kiss.

Later that night, I laid in bed and reviewed for the umpteenth time what I had overheard. Leah had retired in Katie's room. Lydia was in the bathroom. The apartment was silent, except for the occasional whooshing of water and clanging of pipes when Lydia turned the faucet on and off.

When Lydia walked out of the bathroom, the outline of her figure peeked through her nightgown in the soft light of the hallway. Katie had always insisted that the hall light be kept on, and that her door and ours be cracked open at night. Lydia walked into the bedroom and closed the door until only a thin blade of light cut into the room.

She shuffled quietly over to where I was lying on my side, holding up the blankets for her. She eased into bed, snuggled her back against my chest, and curled up into a ball.

I slipped my arm around her. "I love you," I whispered.

She pulled my arm in tight. "I love you, too."

We lay in silence for about a minute before I whispered, "I missed you."

She cleared her throat and tightened my arm around herself even more, but said nothing.

Another minute passed. "I missed you... *a lot.*"

A few moments later she whispered, "Johnny, can you... can you just hold me tonight? Hold me close?"

I curled my legs up against hers, and felt more warmth flow between us.

"Sure, Princess," I told her, kissing the top of her head. "I love you."

She lifted my hand and held it to her cheek.

"And I love you," she said, with a quiver in her voice that told me she was holding back tears.

One Again

43

When I woke the next morning, Lydia was already out of bed and in the kitchen helping her mom fix breakfast. Usually, I'm a light sleeper. For Lydia to get up and about without waking me showed how exhausting my traveling had become—which reminded me of my travel-burdened appointment to the Integration Committee, and had me wondering how I was going to break *that* news to Lydia.

As I lay there thinking about it, Lydia peeked around the door, her head wrapped in a towel. Seeing me awake, she put on a big grin, waltzed into the room, and sat on the bed. She unwrapped the towel and her long, ebony hair fell onto her shoulders. Then she leaned over and gave me a moist, passionate kiss. I heard a chuckle in her throat just before she sprang up and threw the towel in my face.

"Hurry up, Mister," she said, "we've got church this morning!"

I smiled, and as she reached for the door, I said, "Oh, and here I was hoping you and I could—"

"You keep hoping, Mister" she said with a laugh. "Now go jump in the shower."

I moaned, then cried out before she closed the door:
"Did you save me any cold water?"

When we walked into the church, Leah reached for Katie
and said, "Let me drop her off this morning."

"Thanks, Mom," Lydia said. "We'll save you a seat."

"No, you two sit alone and catch up on your time
together. I'll pick up Katie after the service and we'll meet you
in the foyer."

(Years later, Leah told us that after she dropped Katie off,
she sat in the balcony and prayed for us during the entire
service.)

Lydia and I sat on the left side of the sanctuary, near the
front, Lydia's favorite spot. I beamed with pride during the
hymns as people within a three-pew radius turned to see and
hear the angel who sang next to me.

When it came time for the first Bible reading, the associate
pastor stood up and began reading from Genesis, Chapter 2,
beginning with the 21st verse. Lydia opened to the passage
and slid her Bible across both our laps.

> *And the LORD God caused a deep sleep to fall upon
> Adam and he slept: and He took one of his ribs, and closed
> up the flesh instead thereof;*
>
> *And the rib, which the LORD God had taken from
> man, made He a woman, and brought her unto the man.*
>
> *And Adam said, This is now bone of my bones, and
> flesh of my flesh: she shall be called Woman, because she
> was taken out of Man.*
>
> *Therefore shall a man leave his father and his mother,
> and shall cleave unto his wife: and they shall be one flesh.*
>
> *And they were both naked, the man and his wife, and
> were not ashamed.*

We followed along in Lydia's Bible as the pastor read. My hand rested on Lydia's knee, and her hand was on top of mine. With my eyes on the page, I gave Lydia's knee the Short Squeeze when the pastor said, "*Therefore shall a man leave his father and his mother, and shall cleave unto his wife.*

And when the pastor said, "*And they shall be one flesh*", Lydia gave my hand the *Long* Squeeze.

Surprised, I turned my head and watched Lydia as the pastor continued. She kept her eyes on the page, but was unable to suppress the smile that slowly dawned on her face.

That night, shortly after Leah retired in Katie's room, Lydia came out of the bathroom and into the bedroom where I lay, waiting in the dim light from the hallway.

I was disappointed when Lydia backed into bed again. I had hoped the day had recharged her more than it apparently had. Perhaps I had misread her playfulness in the morning, and the Long Squeeze at church. Perhaps her spirit was even more crushed than I had thought.

I wrapped one arm around her, and she reached back for my other arm and tightly held on to both. I felt her body gently rise and fall with her breathing, then I planted a single kiss on her shoulder to wish her good night.

A few minutes later, she rolled around in my arms. Her eyes were open, searching mine. In silence we caressed each other's face in the soft light. Then she kissed me and whispered, "*Johnny…*"

We exchanged soft kisses and slipped into a deep embrace. And as time slowed to a crawl, we eased into a rhythm the floor could not complain about.

Someone told me the Bible says that the way of a man with a maiden is too wonderful to understand. And I heard there's a passage that talks about the passion of lovers to explain a deeper, spiritual truth. I may never plumb the depths of those passages, but one thing both Lydia and I knew at the time: Never before had our bodies and souls been more entwined as they were that night.

Elizabeth Heidi Richards was born eight months and twenty-seven days later, on the first day of spring.

The Pink House

44

Whereas Katie's delivery had been long and difficult, Heidi's went quickly and held no surprises. And whereas Katie looked like me, all it took was one look at Heidi's face, dark hair, and blue eyes to know she would take after her mother and grandma.

When we brought the baby home from the hospital, Katie looked at her and said, "I wuv you, Heidi." Maybe Katie found *Heidi* easier to say than *Elizabeth*. Or maybe she was thinking of the little girl in her favorite story. For whatever reason, the name stuck, and everyone called her *Heidi* from that day on.

While Heidi's birth was by far the highlight of 1951, the year would also be remembered for two other momentous events: my promotion to head of the Chicago office, and the move to The Pink House.

Let's get the promotion thing out of the way before we go on to the really good stuff.

To this day, I believe the promotion would not have happened had I not snuck into the apartment and overheard Lydia and Leah nine months earlier. My resulting resolve to cut back on travel led to my development of a certification program that reduced transatlantic integration costs by 26%.

The idea for the program literally flew into my head on the way home from work one day. The train had stopped between stations and I was looking out the window, watching a father and son trying to fly a kite in a park across the street. After two unsuccessful running attempts, the boy picked up the kite and started walking back toward his dad.

"Run toward me!" his dad shouted. "Into the wind!"

A dozen steps later, the kite was soaring overhead.

That got me thinking. We had been "running" affiliates using the conventional wisdom of the day—with the wind, so to speak. Why not run them into the wind, I thought, against conventional wisdom? Get them soaring!

Within a week I had a detailed, three-phase plan.

I knew it would be a tough sell to the committee, especially the certifications component. And sure enough, committee members thought certification would be seen as a ploy and give the affiliates yet another thing to gripe about. But affiliates embraced the certification idea heartily when they saw the extent of their role in its development.

What started out as a self-serving attempt to reduce my travel turned into the company's top story that year. A survey conducted by an outside agency showed a 42% improvement in affiliate satisfaction under the new program, and company morale posted a 23% gain as affiliate relations improved.

All this led to my promotion to the company's top job in Chicago. And as if that weren't enough, I was able to develop and direct the program without *any* travel outside Chicago.

Now, on to the saga of The Pink House…

After Heidi was born, we graduated Katie from the crib, which we left in the room for Heidi. At first, Katie liked the idea of sleeping in a big-girl bed next to her little sister. However, as the room grew smaller through the accumulation of clothes and toys, and as things got even tighter whenever grandma Leah flew up to visit, Katie's graciousness in sharing her room waned.

Things got worse the month after Vernon and Ada Robinson finally got their wish for a 1st floor apartment and vacated the unit beneath ours. We were happy for the Robinsons—and for ourselves, at first; with the apartment below empty, Lydia no longer felt the need to keep the girls quiet in consideration of the Robinsons. But within a month, new tenants moved in, including two teenaged boys who apparently had no idea what "considerate" meant.

One of the brothers practiced his trumpet, of all things, during the girls' naptimes. When Lydia changed the schedule, the would-be Doc Severinsen changed his practice time. We figured he waited for the pitter-pattering of feet to abate before blowing into that screeching chainsaw of tin. His brother was even worse in that he practiced basketball in the apartment, using the ceiling below the girls' room for the hoop. And he took lots of shots!

I talked to their mother, whose reaction added little to the downtrodden look already on her face when she answered the door. Within five minutes, I learned more than I needed to know about that poor lady who had been abandoned by her husband and who had absolutely no control over her sons. I talked it over with Lydia and we ditched our plan to complain to the building superintendent. Instead, we focused our energy on house hunting.

The Oak Park and River Forest area has many large and beautiful family homes. We found our dream home in a three-story Queen Anne Victorian, crowned with a finished attic that the girls would later call the fourth floor.

The girls had their own large bedrooms, which they called castles because of the built-in, three-windowed turrets. A bath, another bedroom, and two other rooms used for storage rounded out the third floor.

The master bedroom (with its own fireplace and adjoining bath) shared the second floor with a guest room, along with another bath and a set of rooms we remodeled into an office and study.

The main floor featured an oversized living room that served us well for entertaining. It also featured a formal dining room; a den with fireplace; a study with library; and a large, well-planned kitchen with two stoves and plenty of cabinets and counter space.

For reasons unknown to the real estate agent who showed us the house, a two-lane bowling alley ran the full length of the basement. We seldom used it, other than for starting conversations.

The only downside, as far as Lydia was concerned, was that the outside of the house was finished in light pink stucco. When the agent saw the concerned look on Lydia's face as we walked up the sidewalk toward the front door, she said the owners were willing to extend a $500 allowance (a decent sum in 1951) to cover "minor remodeling expenses." From that day on, whenever I'd see Lydia with a concerned look on her face, I'd say, "What's with the $500 frown?"

We were glad the agent made the offer before Lydia's expression changed from one of misgiving to one of awe when she walked inside and fell in love with the place. As for the pink stucco, I told Lydia we could have it painted, but we never got around to it.

Heidi was an infant, and it was hard to tell what Katie was thinking, but on moving day, Lydia and I knew we were home, where countless memories would be made.

Spiritual Birth

45

Lydia took great pleasure in reading Bible stories to the girls as soon as Heidi was old enough to sit in one place for more than ten minutes at a time. Katie usually fidgeted and fussed during those times, while Heidi leaned back in her high chair and studied her mom attentively.

Heidi's interest in spiritual matters took a giant leap after she took part in a Sunday School Christmas play. She was only four years old at the time, had no lines, and was on stage less than thirty seconds of the twenty-minute production.

Just after the wise men had offered their gifts to the baby Jesus, Heidi and the other shepherds walked on stage and stood before the manger. "Behold the Christ child!" the head shepherd shouted, just before the curtain closed.

The children were marched backstage, where each child received a small, gift-wrapped box of chocolates. The parents came back a few minutes later to help their sons and daughters out of their costumes.

We found Heidi already out of her shepherd outfit, sitting off by herself in the far corner of the room, her head hanging low, her eyes staring through the unopened box on her lap.

Lydia placed her hand on Heidi's shoulder. "Honey, you were wonderful!"

Heidi looked up. We could see she had been crying.

"What's the matter, Sweetheart?" Lydia asked.

"Mommy, why wasn't Jesus in the play?"

Play organizers had debated over the casting of Jesus. Some could not imagine the play without a live baby in the role. Others argued, "What if he cries while everyone is singing: *but little Lord Jesus, no crying he makes*?" The debate ended a week before thanksgiving, with the birth of Pastor Parker's first grandson.

Lydia bent down and wiped a tear from Heidi's cheek. "Didn't you see Mrs. Parker's new baby in the manger?"

"Yes, I saw Timmy," Heidi said as she started weeping again. "But where was Jesus?"

Lydia looked at me, then back at Heidi.

"Honey," Lydia said, "this was just a play. With actors."

"I know."

"Well… actors just pretend to be other people."

"I know that," Heidi said, clearing her throat. "Just like I pretended to be a shepherd."

"That's right, Honey. You pretended to be a shepherd. And Timmy pretended to be Jesus."

Heidi stopped crying and thought for a few moments about what she had just heard.

"But Jesus wasn't a baby," Heidi said. "He was a man. Remember the stories? He helped people."

Tears gathered in Lydia's eyes. "Yes, he did," she said. "I remember the stories. And I'm sorry if I didn't make it clear that when Jesus first came to earth, he came as a baby."

Heidi blinked a few times and her mouth opened, revealing a missing tooth. She said nothing until her mother stood up, then she softly recited the last line of the play to herself: "Behold the Christ *child*!" And her face lit up when she realized, out loud: "He came as a *baby*... just like Mommy and Daddy and Katie... and *me*!"

As soon as we got home, Heidi ran into the house, threw the unopened box of candy on the table and ran to the living room where the family Bible lay open on the coffee table. She couldn't read yet, but she knew where the pictures were, and she frantically turned to the section of religious art. Her eyes scanned the masterpieces as fast as she could flip the pages until she came to the one that showed the baby Jesus lying in the manger with outstretched arms, solemn face, and a halo around his head.

Heidi leaned in closer and whispered, in wonder:

"There he is... and he's *glowing*..."

From that innocent start, Heidi's hunger to learn about God grew in ways I could not have imagined. She wanted every bedtime story to be a Bible story, to which Katie strongly objected.

And so it was Bible stories on Mondays, Wednesdays, and Fridays, while Katie got her pick of other stories on Tuesdays, Thursdays, and Saturdays. On Sundays, Mom took a break and the girls were on their own. Heidi spent those times teaching Bible stories to her stuffed animals and answering their questions, which only she could hear.

"If your ancestors weren't on the ark, you wouldn't be here to ask the question... Of course God could have finished in five days, but he wanted to take six... No, Jesus did not wear wings under his robe."

Heidi had her own questions for us—or should I say, for Lydia, since I was no help at all.

I remember one question she asked: "Does God know what we are thinking?" I remember that question because I was amazed when Lydia answered it off the top of her head, citing a half-dozen Bible passages, and saying there were more.

At Heidi's pleading, Lydia spent an hour each day teaching her how to read while Katie was at school. By the time Heidi entered Kindergarten late that summer, she could sound out all the words in the children's Bible we gave her on her 5th birthday. And by the time she entered first grade, she could read and study out of the big Bible.

And study she did.

She knew the names and order of all the books in the Bible, and the names of the patriarchs and the twelve disciples.

She could recite the Ten Commandments, the Beatitudes, and the third chapter of John in its entirety.

By the time she was seven, she had memorized over 200 verses, which she printed neatly on paper and hung on the walls of her room. Moreover, she did more than recite; she understood and could summarize passages in her own words.

It was as if a light had turned on inside Heidi, a light destined to grow brighter with each passing year. But her adventure in faith had barely begun when another adventure came along...

Starting
a
scene
Ch 46-49

Something Amiss

46

Heidi had lots of energy. Actually, *bursts* of energy would be more accurate. She could go non-stop like the wind for a couple of hours, then become tired and have to take a nap. She ate like a horse but never gained weight; she was thin even by a child's standard. Other than that, she appeared to be fine, and neither Lydia nor I suspected anything other than that she was an energetic kid with high metabolism.

But around her sixth birthday, we noticed she got sick more often, and took longer to recover. We attributed it to being around all the kids at school. But during the 1957 cold season, Katie caught only one cold that lasted three days while Heidi caught three colds, each lasting a week.

Our family doctor, Tom Nichols, attended our church. Lydia cornered him one Sunday after the service to talk about Heidi. He told her not to worry, and that colds were just going around, nothing serious. Only because of Lydia's insistence did he agree to see Heidi in his office that week. Of course Heidi was fine by the time the appointment came and went.

When Heidi got sick after the cold season, Lydia marched her into Tom's office again. This time Heidi had symptoms.

Tom examined her and, knowing Lydia would not accept a diagnosis as simple as *a cold*, suggested we take Heidi to see one of the pediatricians at the clinic where Tom worked.

Dr. Downing ruled out allergies, but could not pinpoint any specific problem other than a cold. He suggested we let it run its course and see how Heidi fared over the summer.

Heidi got sick again in July, and talked about being tired and thirsty all the time. Lydia overheard two women at church talking about the pediatrics program at Loyola. Within a week we had Heidi there for an appointment.

I took the afternoon off and caught up with Lydia and Heidi at the clinic. We registered at the front desk, and a nurse called Heidi's name right away and led us down the hall to a small examination room.

The nurse measured Heidi's weight and height on a scale outside the room and wrote the results—37 pounds, 42 inches—on a clipboard. Then she led us into the room, which was sparsely furnished. I offered Lydia the lone chair next to a desk against the wall. Heidi climbed up and sat on the examination table.

A lump formed in Lydia's throat when she looked on the desk and saw neatly arranged brochures on various childhood diseases. "I didn't need to see those," she said under her breath.

The nurse took Heidi's blood pressure and temperature, and recorded them on the clipboard. "The doctor will be in shortly," she said, smiling as she left the room, closing the door behind her.

I saw Lydia struggling to ignore the brochures. And out of the corner of my eye, I saw Heidi shiver. I took my suit jacket off and draped it over her shoulder. "Are you cold, Little Princess?"

She shivered again and said, "Yes, Daddy. Thank you."

I wrapped my arms around her and planted a loud, extended smo-o-o-och on her forehead.

She started to giggle, and by the time I leaned back to see her face, she was laughing. "What's wrong?" I asked in a cartoon voice, "Don't you like loud kisses?"

"Of course I do," she said.

"So why are you laughing, little girl?"

"Because your coat is so big. I feel like a scarecrow."

She stretched her arms out to the sides, her fingers barely reaching mid-sleeve.

"Boo!" she said. Then she dropped her arms and the coat collapsed like a tent around her tiny shoulders. We all broke out laughing, which pumped a little color into Heidi's cheeks, the sight of which brought another lump to Lydia's throat.

The laughing stopped abruptly when we heard tapping at the door, just before the doctor walked in.

"Don't stop laughing now," the doctor said as he finished reading the notes the nurse had taken. He stood in the center of the room with an infectious grin on his face and took a few moments to study each of us, Heidi last. "Laughing is good medicine, wouldn't you say?"

"Yes, it is!" Heidi said, without hesitation.

"Ahh, an agreeable patient!" the doctor said. He raised the clipboard and spoke in a cartoon voice while pretending to write: "Patient... looks... great... in... suit... coat."

Heidi giggled again, and even more color flowed into her cheeks. In the midst of her chuckles, the doctor extended his hand to her. "I'm Dr. Adler," he said.

47

The examination took less than ten minutes. When he had finished, Dr. Adler jotted a note on a small piece of paper attached to the clipboard. Then he stood at attention in front of Heidi, bowed slightly and said, "Thank you for being such a wonderful patient."

Heidi hunched over in a giggle. "My pleasure."

Dr. Adler straightened up and turned to Lydia and me. I reached over and took Lydia's hand. "Well," I said. "Can you tell us anything?"

The doctor's smile softened as he put on his adult face. "I think I can. But first I'd like to run a few simple tests." He tore off the piece of paper he had written on and handed it to me. "Give this to the young lady at the registration desk. She'll have someone show you to the lab."

Before leaving, Dr. Adler turned to Heidi again. His infectious grin was back. "Nice coat!" he said.

The doctor's office called late Friday afternoon. For two days, Lydia had dreaded every time the phone rang. She hoped the weekend would come without a word from the doctor. *No news was good news*, she thought. And as the afternoon wore on, she grew more confident she would get what she hoped for. But when the phone rang at 4:30, somehow she knew her weekend would be shattered.

Lydia picked up the phone with both hands. "Hello?"

"Good Afternoon," a young woman's voice said at the other end. "I'm calling from Loyola Medical Center. Is this Mrs. Richards?"

Lydia tightened her grip on the handset, as if it was trying to get away. "Yes," she said in a small voice.

"We have the results of the tests Dr. Adler ordered for your daughter, Heidi." Lydia's mind raced, making the voice over the phone sound like a record played at half speed as the woman continued, "Can you come in next Friday at 4 PM to meet with the doctor?"

Lydia swallowed hard. She looked out the kitchen window and tried to quell her fear by watching the neighbor's dog sort through the contents of a tipped-over garbage can. The trick worked—until the woman on the other end said in a somewhat louder voice: "Mrs. Richards?"

"Yes?" Lydia said. "That is… yes, I'm here. Couldn't we— me and my husband—just talk with the doctor over the phone, when my husband comes home?"

"Dr. Adler prefers discussing results in person," the woman answered.

"OK," Lydia finally said. "Next Friday then, 4 PM.

Lydia gave me the message as soon as I got home, and we both agreed to play it low-key around Heidi. No need to worry her, we figured.

The following Tuesday, Heidi took a two-hour nap after she came home from school. When she woke, she walked into the living room and asked, "Mom, did the doctor ever call?"

Lydia turned off the iron and walked over to the couch. As she sat down, she opened her arms wide and said, "Come here, Sweetheart."

I had come home early and was working in the dining room, putting finishing touches on a conference speech. When I heard Heidi's question, I got up and joined Heidi and Lydia in the living room, sitting across from them in the low-back chair.

Heidi climbed up on her mother's lap. Lydia rocked her gently back and forth, searching for the right words to say. She gave up her search a few moments later and simply said,

"Yes, the doctor called. And we're going to see him again, on Friday."

"Does he know why I get sick?"

"All I know is that he wants to talk with us."

Heidi looked at me. "Are you coming, Daddy?"

I leaned over, took her hand. "Of course, Little Princess."

Lydia kissed Heidi's forehead and continued to rock her gently back and forth. I ran my other hand through Heidi's long, dark hair.

Heidi closed her eyes, and wrinkles grew on her forehead as she mouthed silent words. Then her face relaxed and she whispered, "OK, I will."

I wondered what she prayed, and what caused her to whisper what she did, but I couldn't bring myself around to ask her. When she opened her eyes, they were bright and clear. She looked assured and at peace, her only wrinkles being the dimples that came with her smile.

I flew to the conference late Wednesday night, gave my speech Thursday morning, then headed straight back to the airport. Lydia was surprised and happy when I arrived home at two in the afternoon.

"How are you holding up?" I asked.

"OK, I guess—better, now that you're home."

"Has Heidi said anything?"

"No, it's as if nothing's going on."

"Well, for all we know, nothing is." I said. "After all, if something drastic was wrong, they wouldn't wait a week to tell us… Would they?"

48

The sun smiled above clear skies and the temperature was mild on Friday. I hoped the weather was a sign of good news to come. I dropped off Lydia and Heidi in front of the clinic, then drove around back to park. By the time I walked into the reception area, a nurse had already taken Lydia and Heidi to an examination room and the weight, temperature, and blood pressure routine was out of the way.

I found the room, opened the door, and peeked in.

"Hello, I'm Dr. Richards."

Lydia's hand flew to her chest. "John," she gasped. "You scared me half to death."

"I'm sorry."

"Oh, it's not your fault," she said, patting her chest as if she were performing CPR on herself. "I just don't feel comfortable in a doctor's office. It's so intimidating."

"It's supposed to be," I said. "It's part of the doctor-patient relationship. We come and wait, fearing the worst, the doctor walks in and we hang on his every word. If he gives us the thumbs up, we're relieved. If he doesn't, we listen in fear to what we need to do because he is the all-knowing doctor

149

and we are just the frightened patients."

Heidi laughed. "If they are all-knowing, why don't they warm the stethoscopes before they use them?"

Several raps on the door interrupted our chuckles. Dr. Adler peeked into the room and said, "Oh, it's the laughing Richards family again. You're amazing! I don't think I could laugh in such a dreary room—let's take a walk to my office."

He led us down the hall and into a larger, carpeted room with wood paneling. An oak desk stood in the middle, with two cushioned chairs on one side and a larger, leather chair on the other. On the way in, Dr. Adler grabbed another chair from along the wall and placed it beside the cushioned chairs. "Come in and have a seat," he said, walking around the desk.

He sat down, opened a manila folder, and skimmed through the notes and chart from the lab.

A group of framed degrees and certifications hung on the wall behind him. To the left of those was a painting of a little girl lying in bed. The little girl's parents and a doctor were at her side, wearing grim faces. And there, leaning over the bed, was Jesus, with his hand on the little girl's head. Inscribed below the painting were the words: *The Great Physician*.

Dr. Adler lowered the folder and leaned back.

"So, Heidi, how are you feeling today?"

"Fine, thank you."

"That's good to hear. You don't get scared coming to the doctor's office?"

"Not as much as my mom."

Lydia blushed. "There goes my secret," she said.

"What's so unsettling about going to the doctor's office?" Dr. Adler asked.

Lydia began tapping her knees. "Well... I find the setting and procedure somewhat intimidating."

"They are supposed to be," Dr. Adler said, winking at me. "It's part of the doctor-patient relationship... You are the frightened patients and we are the all-knowing doctors."

I turned red as a beet.

Lydia chuckled nervously. "Sounds familiar," she said.

Heidi pointed to the painting on the wall. "There is only one doctor who is all-knowing."

"Ahh!" Dr. Adler said, leaning back and spinning his chair toward the painting. "You like that picture?"

"Very much so," Heidi said. "Do you know *The Great Physician*?"

"I do," Dr. Adler said, looking at Jesus' hand and then at his own, "but I don't have his power to heal." He spun his chair back around and smiled. "Fortunately, God gave us amazing bodies that pretty much take care of themselves. When someone gets sick, the best any doctor can do is just help the body heal itself."

A more relaxed Lydia appeared in my peripheral vision.

"How do you know when someone is sick?" Heidi asked.

"Well, our first clue is they show up here," Dr. Adler said with a wink. We all chuckled, and Dr. Adler milked it some more. "People don't usually come in just for the fun of it."

He walked his fingers across the table toward the manila folder. "Actually, people come in and tell us why they came and how they're feeling." He looked down at the scribbled notes. "In your case, we considered what you and your parents said, and what your other doctors said. Then we examined you and made a preliminary diagnosis—a guess, really. Then we took some tests to confirm our guess."

Dr. Adler took a final look at the lab chart, laid the papers down, and leaned back in his chair.

"Heidi, you have a condition called diabetes."

49

We talked with the doctor for another half-hour. He explained there were two types of diabetes. Heidi had juvenile diabetes, commonly called Type 1 diabetes today.

When Heidi was diagnosed in 1957, no one knew what caused diabetes. As I write these notes in 1983, they still don't know the cause, but they have better treatments, and they can slow down and even arrest some complications of the disease. The future holds even more promise.

Back in 1957, we did our best to control Heidi's sugar levels through diet and insulin. Thankfully, Heidi was not afraid of shots. We dreaded to think how Katie would have handled such a regimen.

On the drive home from the doctor's office, Lydia and I heard Heidi whisper "OK, I will" in the back seat, just as she had done a few days earlier in the living room. This time, I asked her what she meant.

"I will trust God," she said. "I will trust the Lord with all my heart, and lean not on my own understanding."

Later that night, Lydia told me Heidi's words came from the Bible. *Even so*, I thought. *She's only six!*

A Tale of Two Sisters

50

When I think about Heidi and Katie, I wonder how two sisters could be so different in their approach to life and in their affect on their mother. As terrible as it may sound, sometimes I think Heidi was given to us to make up for what we got in Katie. Without Heidi's balancing effect, I think Katie would have eventually driven Lydia insane.

I remember one particular Sunday afternoon, in Autumn. After church we went for a drive around River Forest, a town just west of Oak Park. Katie was eleven, Heidi nine.

We parked the car on Edgewood Place and walked into Thatcher Woods, just north of where we sledded the previous winter. We hiked up the path to the pond behind the Trailside Museum. There, Katie and I floated leaves while Lydia and Heidi went inside the museum to see the animals.

On the way back home, I deliberately drove down Park Avenue to show the girls the big houses. Their little faces pressed against the back windows while Lydia and I acted as tour guides.

I pointed to a house on Heidi's side and said, "Look at that mansion!" Then I turned to Lydia and winked. "Whoever lives there must make at least two dollars an hour."

Lydia smiled in place of a chuckle, then pointed to a larger house across the street. "Katie, what do you think the guy living there makes? Two and a quarter?"

Katie didn't respond.

"Wow, look at that one!" I said, motioning to a house on Katie's side. "That guy must own a bank or something."

Lydia pointed two doors down. "That guy must be a doctor."

I pulled up to the curb and turned off the engine as a gust of wind rattled the windows.

"Someday," I said to Lydia, "our little girls will grow up and meet some nice young men who will sweep them off their feet and marry them. And they'll live happily ever after, all safe and sound in a nice, big house."

We turned around and looked in the back seat. "What do you think, ladies?" Lydia asked. "Do you have a nice, young man in mind?"

Katie rolled her eyes.

"And do you have a house in mind?" I added.

Heidi looked out her window again, glancing back and forth at the two biggest houses on the block. "Those are just temporary," she said innocently. "The houses in heaven will last forever. They will be *mansions*."

Katie rolled her eyes again and pointed to a house on her side of the car. "I'll take *that* one," she said in a snotty tone. "It's real."

"Katie?" Lydia warned, softly.

"It's real only for a little while," Heidi said. "It's the unseen things that last forever."

Katie repeated Heidi's words with dripping sarcasm. "*It's the unseen things that last forever.* Blah, blah, blah."

"OK, Katie," Lydia said in a louder, firmer voice, "that's enough!"

Before Katie and her mother could escalate into another of their famous shouting matches, Heidi continued, unfazed. "That house there?" she said, pointing to the most imposing house on the block. "Probably just a small cottage compared to where Moses lives. And that house?" she said, motioning across the street. "Just a pup tent compared to Peter's place."

"Where do you get this stuff?" Katie asked in a tone carefully calculated to touch, but not pull, her mother's trigger.

Heidi turned her head and looked out her window again. "Jesus said he would prepare a place for us. I believe him. Jesus would never lie."

Katie put on a cynical face and mouthed the words *Jesus would never lie.* Lydia's eyes became slits, and I knew another war would have broken out had Heidi's face not been turned away from her sister's taunt.

51

Katie's cold, hard exterior often cracked under pressure or trial, whereas Heidi's faith kept her on a even keel. Their differing abilities to deal with stress surfaced dramatically during the Cuban Missile Crisis in 1962—when Katie was thirteen and Heidi, eleven.

The cold war between the United States and the Soviet Union had peaked, and President John F. Kennedy confronted Soviet Premier Nikita Khrushchev with a blockade of Cuba after surveillance photographs revealed the build up of Soviet missile bases on the island.

For six tense days, uncertainty gripped the nation.

Katie, whose imagination worked against her, was afraid to go to bed at night, fearing she would never wake up again. She regressed to her childhood days of having the door open at night and the hallway light on.

On a positive note, Katie behaved in a civil manner for the duration of the crisis. She even hugged Lydia and told her she loved her. What a surprise *that* was for everyone!

It was also the first time Katie turned to her little sister for comfort and support.

I remember the family sitting down at breakfast on Wednesday, October 24, 1962—the day a showdown was expected at the blockade.

We brought the radio into the kitchen, something we hadn't done since the mid-50s when we used to listen to the *Breakfast with the Johnsons* radio show.

The Johnsons lived in Oak Park, within a mile of our house. We used to pretend we were actually in their home on Kenilworth—eating and talking with Cliff and Luella and their five children—instead of just listening to them on the radio.

How I wished it was the Johnsons on the radio that morning in 1962, talking about garage sales, homework, and favorite ways to enjoy Broadcast Brand Corned Beef Hash. Instead, we were "treated" to a horde of reporters who painted alternating pictures of hope and doom.

I remember Heidi asking for more pancakes and bacon, while Katie wouldn't even look at her food. "How can you eat at a time like this?" Katie asked.

"There's nothing to be afraid of," Heidi said, holding up her plate.

Lydia dished her up another pancake and one of the last two pieces of bacon. "No more syrup," Lydia said, and added for the zillionth time, "You have to watch your sugars."

"Why?" Katie said. "Let her eat all she wants. It could be her last meal! The world could end TODAY!"

Heidi took a bite of bacon. "The world will not end today," she said in a calm voice as she chewed. "Or this week, or this month, or this year for that matter."

Katie's face flared, and she started crying. "How can you be so sure?" she sobbed.

Heidi finished her bacon and wiped her fingers. And reaching across the table she took hold of her sister's hands.

"We can *all* be sure," Heidi said, looking Katie square in the eye, "because the nations are in God's hands, not man's. And nowhere in the Bible does it say that mankind will destroy itself."

Lydia, still holding the frying pan with one hand, gently stroked Katie's hair with the other. To my surprise, Katie didn't flinch or even make a face.

Heidi looked around the table and then up at her mom. "If no one wants that last piece of bacon, I'll take it."

52

One week before her thirteenth birthday, Heidi came into the living room while Lydia and I were trading sections of the *Chicago Tribune.*

"I hope it's all good news," Heidi said.

"If only that were so," her mom replied, taking a final glance at an article on runaways and shaking her head as she handed the section to me. "Ets-lay old-hay our eath-bray."

"Let's hold our breath for what?" Heidi asked.

Lydia gasped.

"Mom, I've understood pig Latin for years. I'm almost a teenager."

"Oh, that's right," Lydia said, grabbing the opportunity to change the subject. "Have you decided on your present yet?"

"Yes, I have," Heidi said with a grin.

I set the paper aside. "Well, well, well," I said. "The Teen Queen has decided!"

Heidi put on a regal flair. "Yes, and the Queen desires materials and assistance in assembling a hand-crafted marker board to hang in her royal bedchamber."

We picked up the materials that afternoon, and it took us less than an hour to assemble the board out in the garage.

"Of course, you don't get this until your birthday," I told Heidi.

"But Dad, I already know what it is."

"Yeah, but isn't there a verse in the Bible that says *Thou shalt not receive thy birthday present early*?"

Heidi laughed. "No, that passage is in the Lunch Meat Guide, in the baloney section."

A week later, the house was decorated with balloons, streamers, and a large banner draped across the dining room:

Happy Birthday, Teen Queen!

It was the same banner we used two years earlier at Katie's coronation into teenhood. Katie wasn't keen on her own party back then, and now that she was fifteen and *way too cool* for a teen party, she left the festivities early to meet with friends as soon as the mandatory ten-minute appearance we agreed on had passed.

Heidi was delighted that all ten girls she invited were able to come to the party. Her best friend, Mary, had called a day earlier and said she wouldn't be able to attend because her uncle's family had just moved to the Chicago area. Mary explained in tears: "We're having a barbeque and I'm supposed to entertain my cousin. He's from out-of-state and has no friends around here."

"Bring him to the party!" Heidi suggested. "We're all friendly!"

Of course, she was right. And of course, Matthew was the only boy there. I took him under my wing when I saw how uncomfortable he looked in the gaggle of giggling girls.

I learned that his family had moved from New Mexico and that his dad was a research scientist sent to the Chicago area to work on a special project he could not talk about.

Matthew's face filled with excitement as we talked about sports. He hoped to be on a team someday, but from the looks of his slight build and below-average height, I thought his only involvement in sports would be in the stands or sitting in front of a TV.

On the other hand, within the first few minutes of talking with him, I knew Matthew was not your typical 12-year-old boy. His vocabulary, sentence structure, and discussion of the physics of football told me he was exceptionally bright.

When the girls asked Matthew to join in the games, I rescued him, saying we had preparations to make. Lydia caught on right away. She winked, motioned to the front door with her head, and raised five fingers. I glanced at my watch and asked Matthew if he could help me out in the garage.

We went out and dusted off the assembled marker board and carried it along with a hammer, two nails and some wire to the front of the house. Exactly five minutes after she had winked, Lydia opened the door. "The coast is clear," she whispered.

53

Lydia, Matthew, and I snuck the board upstairs and into Heidi's room.

"OK, go down and start the record in about two minutes," I told Lydia. "Leave the volume where I set it. Fifteen seconds is all we'll need."

"Good," Lydia whispered. "Fifteen seconds is about all I can stand." She walked out and returned downstairs to the living room where the girls were playing bingo.

Out of the corner of my eye, I saw Matthew swallow. "Your daughter looks a lot like your wife," he said.

"You're right, Matthew. Aren't they both beautiful?"

Matthew turned red, and the look on his face told me he hoped I hadn't noticed.

I rescued him again. "Can you bring me the hammer and nails?"

I walked to the north wall and spotted the two pencil marks I had drawn earlier that morning while Heidi was running an errand for her mother. I took the hammer and one of the nails. "Be ready to hand me the other nail," I said.

I held the first nail to the wall and rested the head of the hammer on top of it. "Now all we need is a little music."

"Uh, Mr. Richards?"

"Yes, Matthew."

"If you're going to run wire around the nails, it would be better to position them at a 45 degree angle to the wall."

"Thank you," I said after making the adjustment.

Two seconds later, the whole house shook from the stereo blasting downstairs, accompanied by the screams of twelve young ladies, counting Lydia.

I timed four blows of the hammer to the driving bass drum, then rushed two steps over and held out my hand. Matthew positioned the nail between my forefinger and thumb before I could even say *Nail!* After four more blows, the critical job was over. Seconds later, the music stopped, leaving the ladies to scream *a cappella*.

We took the wire and made loops at the ends, which we slid over screws on the back of the board. And after hanging the board over the nails and adjusting it this way and that way until it was just right, we stood back to admire our job.

"Well, Matthew, what do you think?"

"It looks good. I might make one for my room."

"What would you use it for?"

"Oh, lots of things… Work out math problems, draw out trajectories, balance chemical equations…"

"Why not just do those on paper?" I asked.

"There's something special about writing on a board," Matthew said. "Perhaps it's the larger writing. Or maybe the vertical orientation—a change from the norm that stirs up creative juices. At any rate, for problems I don't know the answers to, I work better at a board."

He turned his head and looked up at me. "What does your daughter plan to do with hers?"

"At this point, only Heidi knows," I said.

Matthew's eyes widened when I mentioned Heidi's name, just as mine had done eighteen years earlier when I heard Lydia's name for the first time. And in a reenactment of history, Matthew closed his eyes and a slight smile grew on his face. "Heidi," he whispered to himself. Looking up at me, he added, "That's a beautiful name."

We walked downstairs as Chubby Checker sang over the stereo speakers:

♫ *"Come on, Ba-by... Let's do-oo the twist..."*

We spied around the corner and watched the girls twist back and forth, rise up and down, and swing their arms from side to side.

"C'mon, Mrs. Richards," one girl yelled. "Do the twist!"

Lydia's polite decline was met with a chorus of, "Oh, c'mon, it's fun!" and "Yeah, Mrs. Richards, you can do it!"

Lydia finally caved in to their demands. Considering her strict upbringing, I figured she'd have no propensity for dancing. Yet there she was, dancing with the girls in front of us all. Dancing *quite well*, actually. I had never paid much attention when our girls danced in front of the TV during *American Bandstand*. And I didn't understand what older folks were talking about when they spoke despairingly of the younger generation's "sensual dancing". To me, the kids just looked like a bunch of agitated bugs squirming around. But my heart picked up its pace when I saw Lydia's hips sway and her—*uh, let's get back to the party...*

54

The look of surprise and wonder on Matthew's face told me he was in a heightened state of awareness, a look that turned to horror when one of the girls yelled over the music, "We need some boys here," and another shouted, "Where's Matthew?" and a third girl pointed our way and screamed, "THERE HE IS!"

The three of them ran over and grabbed the petrified lad.

"C'MON, MATTHEW, LET'S DANCE."

They dragged him into the center of the room, where he stood like one of the guards outside Buckingham Palace.

Heidi shouted above the music, "Mom, go get Daddy."

Lydia twisted over and reeled me in with her arms, grinning and singing: *"C'mon, Ba-by... Let's do-oo the twist..."*

When I resisted, she yelled back into the room. "I'm going to need a little help here!" A posse of deputies arrived within seconds to assist in the arrest. They marshaled me into the center of the room where the other prisoner remained frozen.

Heidi laughed. "It's easy, Daddy! Just pretend you're drying your back with a towel and squishing grapes under your feet."

I figured I could draw attention off Matthew by making a fool of myself, so I dried with the imaginary towel and squished invisible grapes—to the howls of eleven little girls and one slightly taller one.

Everyone clapped at the end, even Matthew as the shock wore off.

The girls all screamed to play it again, but Lydia had a better idea. "Who wants cake and ice cream?" she shouted above the hullabaloo, resulting in a stampede to the kitchen.

Even though Lydia had put both leaves in the table, we had to stand shoulder-to-shoulder when we sang happy birthday. Heidi closed her eyes for a few moments, then blew out the thirteen candles in one breath.

"What did you wish for?" Mary asked.

"I wished God's rich blessings on everyone here."

"Let that be our prayer then," Lydia said.

I seconded it with a loud "Amen!"

After we ate, we went back to the living room to open presents. Heidi had written on the invitation that any gift had to be imaginative and cost no more than a dollar. We all laughed as she opened the following:

An 8-track tape cartridge—without the tape
Half of a record album
A toy car with gumdrops for wheels
Two cans of soda, labeled Heidi Cola
A stuffed sock for Heidi's animal collection
Paul McCartney's picture from a magazine
An empty perfume bottle
A magazine cover of The Beatles
The volume knob from a radio
and $10,000 in play money.

Then Mary nudged Matthew until he sheepishly handed Heidi a single strand of horsehair from a violin bow.

"Matthew, do you play the violin?" Lydia asked.

Mary jumped up before her cousin could answer. "He has won numerous competitions and has played with professional orchestras!"

I was curious to hear him play. "Heidi, why don't you run upstairs and get your violin," I said.

Panic struck Matthew's face. "Oh, no, I don't want to spoil your party by play—"

Heidi was out of the room before he could finish his sentence. She came back a few minutes later, tuning the instrument as she walked. "Here," she said, smiling as she held out the violin for Matthew. "Play for us."

Matthew turned red again.

"Oh, come on!" Mary said. "You've played in front of *large* audiences."

"Yes," Matthew said, taking the instrument, "but they weren't all sitting this close to the stage."

"And they weren't all girls either, were they?" Mary teased, raising giggles around the room.

Matthew stood up straight and cleared his throat. "So as not to burden you, I'll play just one piece, an adaptation of a song heard earlier today."

He played a mesmerizing montage built around the traditional happy birthday song. He shaped and reshaped the theme—from its usual rendition, to a haunting largo in a minor key, to a lively baroque interpretation—using a variety of bowing, plucking, and harmonic techniques.

When he finished, we all sat in silence, too dumbfounded to even clap. A few moments later, Heidi stood and cupped her hand around Matthew's arm. "God has given you a gift," she said. "Thank you for sharing your gift with us."

I walked to the coat closet and returned with two boxes wrapped for the occasion. "Speaking of gifts," I said as Heidi put her violin away, "you have two more to open."

"Open the gold one first," Lydia said.

Heidi's face lit up when she saw the new Bible. "Yes, Mom! This is the one I wanted! She opened The Book and scanned the index, then turned to the back and flipped through the concordance, map, and note sections.

"Oh, yes! Mom! Dad! Thank you so-o-o-o much!"

"You have the rest of your life to look at it," I said. "Open your other gift."

"Yes, Daddy," Heidi said, smiling and wiggling on her chair as she tore off the wrapping paper, revealing a box of colored markers that she held up for everyone to see.

"Can we go out to the garage and show everyone the board?" Heidi asked.

"The board's not out there," I said, placing my hand on Matthew's shoulder. While your mother was blasting the stereo, Matthew and I were pounding nails into your wall."

Heidi's eyes grew wide and her jaw dropped. "Let's go!" she screamed as she and ten other girls raced out of the room, leaving Lydia, Matthew, and me to follow at our usual pace.

Heidi's Work

55

By the time we reached her room, Heidi was writing in large letters near the top of the board:

HEIDI'S WORK:

When she stepped back, a tear was on her cheek. She put the marker back in the box and wrapped her arms around me and Lydia. "God gave me the best parents on earth," she whispered. "I love you so much."

After the party ended, Heidi took her new Bible and went to her room for over four hours, taking only a half-hour break for supper, and only that long because we insisted that the birthday girl join us.

Long after dark, she came down to the living room again.

"Mom, Dad, I want to show you something."

We followed her upstairs to her room. The party mess had been cleaned up, and the hammer I forgot to take back to the garage was lying next to the door. The stuffed animals were crowded around the open Bible on the bed, as were Heidi's diary and a pad of paper, scribbled with notes.

Heidi stopped in the center of the room and motioned to the board on the north wall. We looked, and knew in an instant that Heidi was about to go public.

In big letters, the board said:

HEIDI'S WORK: (from Matthew 25:31-40)

Feed the Hungry:

Give Drinks to the Thirsty:

Take Strangers In:

Clothe the Naked:

Visit the Sick:

Go Unto the Prisoners:

Hippies

56

The homeless shelter operating out of Gonner Memorial Church was a goldmine for Heidi. There, she was able to exercise at least four of her six directives: *Feed the Hungry, Give Drinks to the Thirsty, Take Strangers In,* and *Clothe the Naked.*

You had to be at least fourteen years old to work at the shelter. We had taken Heidi to visit Pacific Garden Mission in Chicago as part of her research, and on her 14th birthday, Heidi was ready and eager to join Gonner's volunteer staff.

Lydia, Heidi, and I walked out of church earlier that Sunday on our way to the Cozy Corner when one of those *Free-Love Mobiles* pulled up and stopped along the curb. You know what I'm talking about? One of those Volkswagen vans with peace signs, flowers, and the words *Peace* and *Love* painted all over it?

The driver, who couldn't have been over 20 years old, hopped out, walked around the van, and opened the door for a girl on the passenger side. At first I thought it odd that this longhaired, scrawny-bearded, headband-wearing young man would be so chivalrous, but then the door opened and I got a better look at the girl.

She had on a granny dress and looked twelve months pregnant. My jaw dropped, and I heard both Lydia and Heidi gasp as they instinctively rushed over to help. I joined them a few moments later, more out of guilt than instinct.

Of course, with the three of them helping the girl, there was nothing for me to do but look in the back of the van that was strewn with clothes, cookie boxes, cigarette cartons, baby toys, and a dirty mattress. There was a strange, pungent odor too, an odor I had smelled on Katie before. (She said it was incense, but I had my doubts.)

The four of them made it to the sidewalk and the young man hurried back to the van where I remained, gaping inside.

"What's your problem?" he growled.

I stood aside as he closed the door. "Was that incense I smelled?" I asked.

"Yeah, right," he said before adding a crude, two-word colloquial expression that basically meant *mind your own business*.

Potty-mouth followed me back to Lydia and the girls, who were talking and laughing as if they had known each other for years.

Heidi squealed with delight. "Daddy, this is Peggy! "Her baby is due any day now!"

"That's wonderful," I said, not meaning it at all. I was too schooled in reality to hold out much hope for that couple and their kid.

"Maybe they can join us for lunch," Heidi suggested.

You've got to be kidding, was my first thought. But then I tallied the faces around me.

Heidi pleaded with her eyes, and Lydia could not hide the pity she felt for the frail-looking mother-to-be. Peggy's head was hanging low, and there was a yes-vote in her nervous chuckling. It looked like the only no-vote came from the scowling young man. And when an image of the scattered cookie boxes in the van flashed through my mind, I figured Peggy was due for a good meal.

"Why not?" I said, "If they want to join us, that is."

Peggy looked up at her—*oh, I don't know, her boyfriend? Acquaintance? Worst nightmare? All of the above?*

"Andy?" she said.

When he saw the pleading in Peggy's eyes, Andy's scowl softened a bit. Actually, he looked like he was about to cry.

"You go," he said softly, shaking his head. "Just be back by five forty-five."

After he shuffled away, I turned to Heidi.

"Since this was your idea, you pick the place."

Heidi turned to Peggy.

"Have you ever been to the Cozy Corner?"

"No," Peggy said, "but we've driven by it."

Heidi said, "You'll like it. My parents ate there on their first date, back when you could play the jukebox for a nickel. They've got great cheeseburgers."

"Sounds wonderful," said Peggy. "I'm really hungry."

Lydia looked at me. "Maybe you should get the car."

But Peggy said, "Isn't it just a couple blocks away? I've been sitting down so much. I'd like to walk, if you don't mind."

57

Needless to say, we didn't run to the restaurant. The girls chatted along the way, and as Lydia talked about our other daughter, I hoped that Katie would not run into the same situation that now balled and chained Peggy.

Our favorite booth opened up shortly after we walked in the door, and four groups let us cut to the head of the line when they saw Peggy.

Lydia and Peggy sat across from each other, next to the window. Heidi sat on the aisle, next to Peggy.

The usual, warm memories greeted me as I sat next to Lydia in *our* booth. Lydia must have been having similar thoughts. She told Peggy, "This is the very booth where John and I sat on our first date."

"Aw-w-w, how sweet," Peggy said.

Over the next forty-five minutes, Peggy told us more about herself and Andy than I ever wanted to know while Lydia and I ate our usual—the Sunday Chicken Special—and Heidi and Peggy enjoyed cheeseburger platters.

Peggy grew up on Chicago's North Shore, a child of

privilege. She dropped out of high school during her senior year and ran away from home when she found out she was pregnant with Andy's baby.

I listened half-heartedly as Peggy told Andy's story.

Andy was another child of privilege, from River Forest. He had a falling out with his dad when he refused to register for the draft. He had been living in his van for three months when Peggy saw him at an anti-war demonstration in Grant Park. He was painting his van. Peggy offered to help. She probably mistook his guarded insecurity and moodiness for sophistication.

Peggy told us that she and Andy "did it like rabbits" in the van the first day they met. "I was a virgin," she said. She rolled her eyes and added, "I was also very, *very* stoned."

I saw Heidi swallow hard, and I pretended to scratch my ear so I could turn my head and see Lydia's reaction. Her mouth was wide open, frozen like the rest of her face. Later, she told me she didn't know if she should cry *for* Peggy or *at* her.

Peggy counted on her fingers. "I think I got pregnant that night," she said. "And by the way, it's a little girl."

Heidi cleared her throat. "How do you know?"

"For five generations on my mother's side, every firstborn has been a girl."

The three of them talked on as I wondered how kids who had everything could reject it all and just walk away. Then I thought of Katie again. I guess things make more sense when they hit close to home.

Heidi told Peggy about the homeless shelter at Gonner, which Peggy already knew about—that's why she and Andy came to Oak Park that day. And that's why she had to be back by five forty-five; the shelter opened at six o'clock sharp and dinner was served right away.

Peggy looked tired after lunch, and Heidi asked if she would like to come to our house and take a nap. Peggy politely declined, saying it would upset Andy too much.

I could see the disappointment and concern on Heidi's face. And on Lydia's. But I was *relieved* that Peggy wasn't coming over. I didn't mind Heidi *Taking Strangers In* to the shelter at Gonner, but inviting hippies into our home was another matter. I didn't want any hippies even *knowing* where we lived.

"At least let us drive you back to the park," Heidi said before turning to me. "Can we do that, Daddy?"

I felt too guilty to say no. I smiled, stood up, and took the check. "I should be back in a half-hour."

Heidi reached out and touched my arm. "Daddy, can you go in my room and bring back the box with the pink bow on it? It's on the right side of the closet, on the floor."

58

Fifteen minutes later, I was in Heidi's closet, holding the box with the pink bow. Heidi used the right side of her closet as her hope chest. I shook the box and heard the muffled sound of clothes jostling within. I knew they were clothes Heidi had hoped to dress her little girl in someday.

I didn't need to look at her board to know what she was thinking:

Clothe the Naked.

I got back to the restaurant to find Peggy asleep, leaning against Heidi. I slipped quietly into the booth next to Lydia and gently laid the box of clothes on the table.

Heidi smiled and mouthed the words *Thank You.*

"So, what's going on?" I whispered.

With her eyes and a slight nod, Heidi motioned for Lydia to speak.

"She fell asleep a few minutes after you left," Lydia said in a soft voice. "She said to wake her when you came back."

I aligned my head with Peggy's, which rested on Heidi's shoulder. "She looks beat," I said. "I'd hate to wake her."

"That's what we were thinking," Lydia said. "Maybe just a few more min— "

A passing car blasted its horn at a bus pulling away from the corner. Peggy opened her eyes and slowly lifted her head. "How long have I been sleeping?" she asked.

"About twenty minutes," Heidi said as she slid the box with the pink bow toward Peggy. "I want you to have this, for your little girl."

We drove Peggy back to the park at 3:30. The van wasn't there and I suspected the worse, especially when Peggy started crying frantically and screamed, "THAT BASTARD!"

Lydia and Heidi did their best to comfort her, while I imagined Peggy moving into our house, having her baby, and… and… *thank goodness* the horn of Andy's Love Wagon woke me from *that* nightmare!

Peggy saw the van and shouted hysterically:

"ANDY! ANDY!"

The tires squealed. Andy jumped out and ran around the van that he left running in front of a line of honking cars, eliciting a spontaneous hand gesture from the agitated young man before he pointed to us and yelled,

"WHAT DID YOU DO TO HER?"

"Andy! Andy!" Peggy cried, throwing her arms around him. We stood there, not knowing what to say.

"They did nothing wrong," Peggy said in our defense. "They've been real nice to me."

"Then why are you so upset?"

Peggy cried in his shoulder while we looked on.

"I thought you left me," she said.

Andy's eyes grew red and swollen, then he kissed Peggy's hair. "No, Baby" he whimpered. "It's you and me, forever. Remember?"

They took a few moments to wipe each other's tears, then Peggy asked, "Where did you go?"

"I went to see my dad," Andy said. He reached in his pocket and pulled out a wad of twenty-dollar bills. "We got some money, Baby. We're going to be OK."

I saw tears running down the faces of Lydia and Heidi, and I knew they were thinking—or at least hoping—that things actually *would* work out for Andy and Peggy.

Heidi laid her hand on Peggy's head, closed her eyes and said a prayer that was drowned out in the cacophony of honking horns. I took another assessment of the utterly pathetic situation and tried not to think of Katie.

Peggy kissed Heidi's cheek, then Andy helped Peggy to the van. "Thanks for the gift, Heidi," Peggy yelled out the window as they sped off. "And for the prayers!"

"You're welcome," Heidi shouted back. "I'll see you tonight at the church."

The three of us stood and watched the van disappear in traffic. We didn't know it then, but that would be the last time we would ever see Peggy and Andy.

"I feel so blessed," Heidi said.

"Me too," I said as I slipped my arms around the two wonderful girls at my sides. "Me too."

Heidi arrived at the homeless shelter at five o'clock sharp for the orientation training for new volunteers. Then she helped prepare the evening meal of soup, salad, sandwiches and cookies. They prepared enough food for thirty-five guests, which was average for early spring. She also helped make sack lunches for the guests to take with them the next day.

According to her diary, Heidi served thirty-two adults and two children that night, and she played games with the kids until their bedtime.

She came home at nine and gave us an animated account of the evening before going up to her room to write the date and tiny notes next to the first four directives on her board.

And later that night she wrote in her diary,

There's so much to do...

Disconnected

59

On December 2, 1966, after the evening news, Lydia woke from a nap and joined me in the living room, dusting the hardwood floor with her fluffy slippers as she shuffled in.

"Are you feeling better?" I asked, reaching out to her.

She plopped down next to me and curled her legs up on the couch. "A little, I guess. It's not that I feel sick; I just feel a little... disconnected."

"That's what happens when you nap too long," I said, massaging her shoulder. "If I nap for over a half-hour, I'm in a daze for at least an hour afterward. It has something to do with the body waking up in stages, or something."

She gave me a peck on the lips, then snuggled against my side. "Thank you, Doctor, but I felt disconnected before I laid down."

"Still, you could have post-nap syndrome," I said in my doctor voice while slipping my other arm around her.

She lifted her mouth and was planting a bouquet of kisses on my neck, jaw, and ear when the phone rang.

"Let your nurse get it," she said.

Who was I to argue?

The phone stopped after eight rings, and we continued Lydia's therapy until the phone rang again, once.

It could have been a quick hang-up, or it could have been the signal our family and friends used prior to an urgent call. When the phone rang 20 seconds later, Lydia sat up and said, "Something has happened. I've felt it all day."

"It's probably nothing," I said.

She swallowed hard on the next ring. "Can *you* get it?"

I kissed her hand. "Ok, but don't go anywhere; the doctor still needs to see you."

I walked over and picked up on the fourth ring, then turned and faced Lydia standing a dozen feet away.

"Hello?"

Lydia's mother was weeping on the other end.

"John?"

I braced for the worst. "Yes?"

"Is Lydia there? With you now?"

"Yes—"

"John, don't put her on. I don't think I can talk with her yet..." She wept louder, and I turned to hide my concern from Lydia.

"I understand, Mom."

Lydia gasped. I turned back and saw her eyes grow wide and her hands cover her mouth. I motioned for her to stand by, and as Leah told me what happened, I wondered how I'd be able to break the news to Lydia.

"Can you tell her for me, John?" Leah said afterward.

"Of course."

"And when she's ready… have her call."

"I will… We love you, Mom. And we'll all fly down, first thing in the morning."

Lydia was crying when I hung up. She ran up and threw her arms around me. "John," she whimpered. "I'm so sorry."

I knew she was thinking it was *my* dad who died. I figured she'd think that when I called Leah, *Mom*. I hadn't done that for years, not that I didn't think the world of her—I can't imagine having a better mother-in-law—but to avoid confusing Katie and Heidi, I always referred to her as *Leah* or *Grandma*. And *Mom* always meant Lydia.

I guided Lydia back to the couch and continued to search for words as we sat down. My eyes welled at the sight of Lydia pouring out sympathy and love for *me*.

"Princess," I finally said, "that was your mother."

Lydia's gasp was soft, her mouth barely open, her eyes staring through me. Disconnected.

I slipped my arms around her and rocked slowly.

"Your father came home from the church at lunchtime, saying he wasn't feeling well. He sat at the table while your mother heated some soup. She turned away for just a moment to take the pan off the stove. When she turned back, he was slumped over the table."

Lydia sniffled softly and began to tremble. I waited a few moments, then continued.

"He had a pulse, but it was weak and erratic. Your mother couldn't wake him… She called the police, an ambulance was there within minutes… They tried to stabilize him, but he died before they got to the hospital."

Lydia turned her head and stared out the window.

"He didn't suffer," I said. "He just slipped away."

We held each other until we heard Katie and Heidi laughing and walking up the porch steps, and the sound of the swing creaking back and forth.

"Can you tell them?" Lydia said. "I need some time alone."

60

We flew out of O'Hare early the next morning and landed at Atlanta Municipal Airport before noon, local time. I had planned to rent a car, but Leah insisted on picking us up at the airport. I think that worked out best for her and Lydia. Leah met us at the gate, and I watched through tearful eyes as the triplets born 20-some years apart hugged and wept.

Leah handed me the keys and asked if I would drive. Katie rode shotgun while the triplets rode in back—grandma in the middle—taking turns crying, praying and talking in small voices.

When we arrived at the house, people from the church were busy cleaning and preparing food. Katie helped me take the bags upstairs while the triplets, arm-in-arm with grandma still in the middle, walked to the peach trees out back. I watched from the guest room window as they huddled in a circle, their heads lowered. I couldn't tell if they were crying or praying. Probably a little of both. And I wondered what I'd be doing had it been my dad.

The visitation began at two o'clock the next day and went until nine. The funeral was held at the church the day after that. Even with extra chairs set up in back, there weren't seats enough to go around. Reverend Bowman was well-known in Atlanta, practically a celebrity. A television crew shot the procession outside the church, and another crew was at the cemetery when we arrived.

"The trumpet shall sound, and the dead shall be raised incorruptible," the minister said at the gravesite before handing roses to Leah, Lydia, and the rest of the family. We walked Leah to the casket and laid our flowers next to hers.

We relived the day again on the 10 o'clock news.

Death asks many questions and offers few answers. It leaves those left behind to regret things they did and things they left undone, things they said and things they wanted to say but didn't. I often regret having thought of Horatio as Frownathon, and for not looking past the hard shell he wore when he wasn't in the pulpit. My only consolation is a handful of memories, softened by time, that speak well of the impassioned preacher who struggled as a husband and father.

We spent three more days in Atlanta helping Leah transition to the vacuum. For the triplets, it was a time to reach out to one another and, as Heidi put it, "a time to reach *up*, to take hold of that which takes hold of us."

I remember longing for faith like theirs, and wondering if I'd ever be touched as they were.

On the day we left, we invited Leah to live with us in Oak Park. She said she'd only get in the way. That was far from the truth, and we told her so. We reminded her how much she helped with Katie, and what a blessing she had been for Lydia when I was on the road. She said she might reconsider in the future, but for the time being, her place was in Atlanta.

I went upstairs to pack. When I came back out of the guest room Lydia was in the hall, staring into her parents' bedroom. I set the bags down and stood at her side. And when I looked into the room, the shotgun was gone.

On the flight back to Chicago, the girls sat at the windows while Lydia and I took the aisle seats. Heidi sat still as Lydia told her about her grandfather and his ministry. And for the last half-hour of the flight, Heidi turned and stared out the window, deep in thought.

That night, we all retired early. Lydia came to bed just as I was nodding off.

"Are you awake?" she whispered.

I snuggled up and kissed the back of her neck. "Just waiting for you," I said. "How are you doing?"

"OK, I guess," she said, stroking my arm. The sound of the clock filled the room for another thirty ticks. "I guess Heidi and Katie didn't know much about their grandfather."

"I saw you and Heidi talking on the plane."

"She asked me what it was like having a pastor for a father... I told her about his ministry."

"He was a gifted preacher," I said.

"We talked about that. And about his concern for the eternal well-being of others..." A few moments later Lydia added, "He was a good man."

Life Goes On

61

When I got home from work a few days later, the savory smell of curry chicken greeted me at the door, reminding me again that the first Monday of the month was always something to look forward to.

Lydia appeared in the foyer moments later. I couldn't remember how long it had been since I saw her in a ponytail. Nor could I ever remember seeing her outside our bedroom in one of my T-shirts.

A spice-stained apron was hugging her, inviting me to do the same. She reached up and draped her arms over my shoulders. The delicate scent of apples was on her breath as her lips roamed about, pushing and tugging on mine.

"Welcome home," she purred.

My fingers climbed up her back and searched through her curls as our lips played tag. Lydia giggled when my breathing grew deep, and I chuckled along with her.

"Mmmm," she said. "Where's this going, so close to supper?"

I lifted my head and we stood there a minute or so, searching each other's eyes, caressing each other's face.

"Is that a tear?" she whispered.

I kissed her nose.

"We've been married twenty years," I said, "and you still surprise me... What's the secret behind that unfading beauty of yours that runs so deep?"

Lydia cleared her throat. "I hope it's not a secret..."

I searched her eyes again, and nodded.

"Ahh, yes," I said. "Sometimes I look at you and think there *must* be a God. Do you think I'll ever understand? Ever be touched like you and Heidi?"

Before she could answer, we heard the back door open and Heidi calling, "Mom?"

Lydia turned her head and shouted, "In the foyer!"

She turned back to me as a tear ran down my cheek.

"I love you, John," she said. "You're a good man, a good husband and father. I believe God has good plans for you."

Then she kissed me.

"I saw that," Heidi said as she walked around the corner.

The three of us chuckled, and I ducked my head behind Lydia's to hide my tears.

Lydia kissed me again and whispered in my ear, "Oh quit your blubbering and go jump in the shower. Supper's on in fifteen minutes."

Heidi and Lydia were carrying the last of the serving plates to the table when I walked into the dining room.

"Good timing," Lydia said as she sat down.

Heidi and I took our seats. Katie's empty chair meant she was out with her new boyfriend, Brad. As soon as I lowered my forearms to the table, Lydia and Heidi slid their hands across the table toward mine.

"Let's say grace silently tonight," I said. I did this on occasion, usually when I was either tired or distracted. I was neither that night. If anything, I was overwhelmed with gratitude, aware of many blessings: a satisfying job, our home, the smell of my favorite foods... and best of all, the two spiritual giants who sat with me at the table.

Lydia and Heidi bowed their heads. I choked back tears as I thought about Lydia, the most loving and beautiful woman I had ever met, and Heidi, whose beauty was catching up with her mother's and whose faith had gone on ahead. As I was thinking, I realized my gratitude was a prayer in itself. And I whispered, *Amen*.

Lydia and Heidi concurred aloud and squeezed my hands before withdrawing their own.

A tear escaped my eye, but not Lydia's attention. She reached for my hand again.

Heidi turned and asked, "Is something wrong?"

Another tear fell and I started to laugh. "Actually, things are going great," I said, chasing the frog from my throat. "As strange as it sounds, I'm just overly happy."

Heidi smiled as she speared two drumsticks and put them on her plate. "Sounds like you're having a joy attack."

"Could be," I said, not knowing what she meant at the time.

Prayer Walks and Dorks Club

62

After her grandfather's death, Heidi added a seventh directive to her work: *Share God's Love with Others.* She found ample opportunities to do so, both within and outside of Dorks Club.

Dorks Club was not an official organization at Heidi's High School. You won't a find a Dorks Club photo in the 1967 yearbook. There were no dues involved, and no fieldtrips. It was a virtual club whose members found humor in how they were labeled by others. For according to Heidi, who laughed when she told me this, you were a Dork if you weren't a Zombie or a Dooper.

Doopers (pronounced Dew'-pers) might have been called *Socialites* at other schools, while Zombies might have been called *Greasers.* Like their counterparts at other schools, Doopers (short for Dear Old Oak Parkers) had school spirit— which, as you probably already figured out, Zombies were "too cool" to have.

Doopers and Zombies kept their individual ranks small and "elite" to set themselves apart from what they called "the Dorks" who made up the majority of the student body.

Doopers and Zombies thought the Dorks were too dumb or too smart, or too unattractive, or too clumsy, or too weak, or too whatever. Doopers and Zombies knew the dangers (e.g., social ramifications) of being a Dork. They also knew how easy it was to become one. All you had to do was sit at a Dork table in the cafeteria, or be seen talking with a Dork in the hall or anywhere outside of school.

If you find all this confusing, consult a local teenager. The labels may have changed, but the game's still the same.

Heidi found out about Dorks Club through Matthew, who moved to Oak Park during his and Heidi's sophomore year. A few weeks later, Heidi literally bumped into him after school one day.

Here's how it happened:

It was Heidi's custom to pray every day for students and teachers at her school.

Every day she'd write a list of prayer reminders, based on what she saw and heard that day. Then she'd "prayer walk" the empty corridors in the late afternoon, visiting specific rooms, places, and lockers to pray for people on her list.

Even as she walked, she prayed with her eyes closed. Every ten steps or so she would blink them open just long enough to make sure she wasn't about to bump into a wall. Then she'd close them again and continue along her way. When she came to the end of a hallway, she'd look at the list tucked in her Bible to see where to go next.

Sometimes she'd reach one of her destinations and pray with her hand on a classroom door or on a specific student's locker, like she did when Mr. Thornton's wife had her miscarriage, and when Patty Jones flunked her trigonometry midterm, and even when Fred Wallner got suspended for leaving Marty Wilson in his wheelchair between floors in the stairway after school.

And then there were her favorite times. Times when she'd be walking along and rapture would come upon her, and she'd wave her hands over her head and shout, "Yes, Father... Yes, Lord... Oh, thank you, Jesus... Thank you, Lord!"

These were her *Joy Attacks*.

It was during one of these joy attacks that Matthew, having just turned a corner on his way to chemistry lab, saw Heidi coming straight toward him on a collision course. For some reason, which Matthew was at a loss to explain afterwards, he just froze.

Heidi—laughing joyously, eyes closed and hands waving in the air—walked straight up to him and stopped, just as she finished saying, "Thank you, Lord!"

Not knowing what else to say, Matthew peeped:

"Uhh, no. I'm Matthew. Remember? Your birthday party? I played your violin?"

Heidi's face relaxed, and her eyes slowly opened as her spirit returned to earth.

Then she looked up at Matthew and lit up again.

"Matthew! You've grown!"

63

At lunch the next day, Matthew whispered to a girl sitting beside him and pointed with his eyes to Heidi who sat two tables away, preparing her list for that day's prayer walk. After a minute or so of deliberation, the girl stood up and walked over to Heidi's table. Heidi was so deep in thought she didn't even notice the girl standing beside her.

"Hi, I'm Martha," the girl finally said. "Are you Heidi?"

Heidi looked up and smiled. "Yes."

"Can I sit with you for a minute?" Martha asked, with a look that said she had asked that question many times before and had been turned down.

"Of course!" Heidi said, sliding her books and papers over to make room.

Martha sighed and eased into a smile, and even before she stepped over the bench and sat down, both girls knew a connection had been made.

"How did you know my name?" Heidi asked.

Martha turned her head and motioned to Matthew, who waved sheepishly.

"Hi, Matthew!" Heidi yelled above the noisy chatter of

the cafeteria. Matthew hesitated, then nodded.

"Matthew told me about your encounter after school yesterday," Martha said, and added in a whisper, "I guess you freaked him out a bit."

Both girls chuckled.

"Are you Matthew's girlfriend?" Heidi asked.

"Not in any romantic sense," Martha answered. "We're just friends, a couple of Dorks. We eat lunch together and he helps me with my calculus and chemistry. Right now he thinks I'm talking to you about our club, but I've been carrying a problem around for over a year now, and when he told me about your run-in yesterday, I thought you might be able to help me."

Martha swallowed hard before she asked,

"Are you a Christian?"

Matthew saw Heidi nod her head, and watched Martha talk for a few minutes before she broke into tears. He saw Heidi lean in and take hold of Martha's hands, and watched Heidi comfort Martha with words he could not hear above the din. Then Matthew saw Martha sit up straight, still crying, but wearing a rapturous smile, the likes of which Matthew had never seen on her before.

By this time, Matthew had worked up enough courage to join the two girls. "Did you ask her about the club?" he said to Martha.

Martha laughed as she wiped tears from her cheeks.

"Club?" Heidi asked.

"Yeah," Martha said, chuckling and sniffling at the same time. "We call ourselves *the Dorks*."

Heidi's eyes volleyed between Martha and Matthew, as if she was waiting for one of them to deliver the punch line, which neither of them did.

"*Dorks*?" Heidi finally said. "There's a *Dorks Club*?"

Martha chuckled. "Yeah, well, we're not a *real* club. There's no president or anything like that. But according to the Doopers and Zombies, most kids at this school are Dorks, so some of us figured we might as well hang out with our own kind."

"So, I'm a *Dork*?" Heidi said, laughing. Then her eyes widened and she grabbed the list from inside her Bible. She spoke aloud as she wrote, *"Pray... for... all... the... Dorks."* Then she looked at Martha and asked, "Who else did you say? Doopers and Zombies?"

Heidi, Matthew, and Martha ate lunch together from that day on, and over time, Matthew and Martha became deeply involved in Heidi's work. So much so, I called them *Heidi's disciples*, much to Heidi's chagrin. "They're only helpers," she told me. "And I'm only a servant. My work is to believe in the Lord, and to love him, and to show the world I'm *his* disciple."

Despite her efforts to go about her work without fanfare, Heidi's influence and reputation grew among kids from every caste at school, which led to some interesting situations. Like the time when Matthew, Martha, and a dozen other kids were sitting on the grass after school one day, listening to Heidi tell a story from the Bible.

One of Heidi's trademark gestures was to hug the Bible to her chest with the words *Holy Bible* appearing just above her arms as she swayed from side to side. She also liked to raise her Bible overhead when she made an important point. These gestures caught the attention of Katie's Zombie friends, who happened to pass by just as Heidi raised her Bible in the air.

Some of Katie's friends immediately tried their hand at preaching, holding up invisible Bibles and parading back and forth on imaginary stages.

"We want you to be part of this ministry!" one of them pleaded in a southern drawl.

"Yes, so send us your money!" another added.

"Send *all* of it. *Now!*" another barked.

"And when you write, include a carton of cigarettes and some six-packs!"

"And a picture of your girlfriend..."

"Send it all to *Zombie Preachers, Oak Park and River Forest High School.*"

Heidi laughed, to the surprise of her friends and the Zombies alike. Then she turned to Katie, who had been silent and hoping that none of her friends knew Heidi was her sister.

"Oh Katie," Heidi said as if she had just remembered something. "Good thing you came by, I forgot to tell you earlier: Mom wants you to come straight home so the two of you can finish wall-papering your room."

"Well, well, well," one of the Zombies said with a laugh. "Looks like Katie has a little sister—a missionary, no less."

Katie put on a face that could make the front cover of *Sullen Teenage Girl* magazine.

Another Zombie shuffled his feet and pulled on the cuff of his leather jacket. "Hey, maybe *Katie* is a missionary. You know, sent to live among the Zombies, to bring us to salvation."

The Zombies laughed. "Hey Katie," one said. "Are you a Baptist too?

"Cut it out, Jerks," Katie snarled. "No, I'm not a Baptist." Katie motioned toward Heidi. "Neither is she. She goes to Gonner's."

"She's a goner, alright," one of the Zombies quipped. "And now she's preaching to the Dorks. Hey, maybe that's it! Jesus died for Dorks!"

Heidi raised her Bible overhead and shouted:

"That's right, Jesus died for Dorks."

And after the surprised Zombies stopped laughing, Heidi added in a softer voice: "And we're *all* Dorks."

That story raised quite a few chuckles around the supper table that night as Heidi mimicked the Zombie preachers.

Too bad Katie wasn't there to hear it, but she was out with Brad, up to who knows what.

God Works in Mysterious Ways

64

As Heidi traveled along the high road, Katie continued her downward slide.

I came home one night and found Lydia crying in Katie's room, sitting on the bed, holding her head in her hands.

I kneeled at her side. "What's the matter?" I said.

She stood up and walked over to Katie's dresser, pulled out a small metal pipe from the top drawer, and held it out for me to see.

"Katie smokes?" I said.

Lydia jiggled the pipe. "Smell the bowl."

I had been around pipe smokers before, but I didn't recognize the scent. "Smells different from other tobaccos I've smelled."

Lydia swallowed hard.

"I wish it was tobacco," she said. "As bad as *that* sounds."

"What do you mean?"

Lydia pressed her other hand against her forehead, as if it were about to explode.

"Karen—Jennifer's mother—came over today. She told me they found a bag of marijuana in Jennifer's room.

Jennifer's dad suspected she got it at school and threatened to take her down there and create a scene if she didn't tell him where she got it. Jennifer played tough, but when her dad started dragging her out to the car, she told him—"

Lydia stopped talking and stared at the pipe.

I gave her a few moments. "Told him what?" I asked.

"Jennifer said she got it from Katie's boyfriend, Brad."

I smelled the pipe again. "This is marijuana?"

Lydia started crying. "No, it gets even worse. It's called hashish. Karen said it's worse than marijuana."

Lydia looked again at the dresser, then continued.

"When Karen told me Brad was selling drugs at the school, I told her she must be mistaken. When she accused me of hiding my head in the sand and told me Katie was probably doing drugs, I said she was flat-out wrong. And I hoped I was right. But then Karen said, 'Take me to Katie's room.' And when I did she walked straight to the dresser, opened the top drawer, and pulled out the pipe from underneath a pile of underwear."

I didn't know what to say. Lydia walked back to the bed and sat down. "What did we do wrong?" she said.

I took her hand. "I don't know if we did anything wrong," I said.

"So what do we do now?" Lydia asked in desperation.

"I don't know that either. But I know someone at work who might."

65

The next day, I called Tony Stiller as soon as I got to the office. Remember Tony? From the office Christmas party?

Well, Tony went on to become the head of travel and logistics for the entire company. He had a corner office and a secretary who might have filed a sexual harassment suit against her boss, had it been ten years later. Tony was the last of the *Flying Conquistadors*, the others having long succumbed to *The Commitment*.

"Hello, Angela," I said to the eighteen-year-old who picked up my call. "Is Tony in?"

"Of course, Mr. Richards. I'll put you right through."

"John!" Tony said in a deep, resonate voice, hand-crafted through years of chain smoking. "What's up? You increasing the travel budget?"

"Keep dreaming!" I said with a laugh.

"Well, I had to try," Tony said.

"And that's why they pay you the big bucks. But I'm not calling about business; I need some personal advice."

"Sure, where are you thinking of taking the little lady? Paris? London? Hey John, last month I was on this island off the coast of Greece. Incomparably beautiful!"

"I'm sure it was," I said. "But I need your help on a family matter. Can I drop by your office for a few minutes?"

"Sure, come on over! It's been too long, my friend. It'll be good to see you again."

I knocked on Tony's open door as he was handing a folder to Angela. The expression on her face said she was not comfortable having Tony's arm around her shoulder. I made a mental note to talk with him about it later, but first I needed *his* advice.

"John, come on in and have a seat!" Tony said as he lifted his arm but not his eyes off his relieved secretary, who hurried out the door.

He turned to me and winked. "Built in America!" he said.

We sat down at the coffee table, next to the window overlooking the lake.

Tony had added at least fifty pounds to the already heavy frame he had when I first met him at the company twenty years earlier. Although he lost the battle of the bulge and his understanding of women was absolutely pathetic, Tony was brilliant at solving problems others found hopeless, problems more pronounced than his Brooklyn accent. That's why he was in charge of travel and logistics. And that's why I was glad when he said,

"So John, what's the problem?"

I took a deep breath.

"Remember that situation a few years back? The one involving your nephews?"

Tony tapped his chin like he always did when he was thinking. "A few years back? Which nephews? Oh, you mean Robert and George? The booze and drug thing?"

"Yeah, that sounds right," I said. "How'd that turn out?"

"Oh, just fine. It was one of those teen things. Me and their dad—you remember my brother, Tommy—we took the boys aside and scared the livin'… uh, we had a little *talk* with them."

"And that's it? They're fine now?"

"Oh, yeah! Model students. Bobby's in his third year of pre-law at Northwestern and George is entering medical school this fall. Can you imagine that, John? A doctor!"

I was encouraged. I envisioned Katie a few years from now, smiling and laughing with her mother as they shopped at Marshall Field's.

"So John, what's the matter?" Tony asked, leaning back in his chair. "Having trouble with your girls?"

I told him about the pipe we found in Katie's dresser, and about her drug-pushing boyfriend. I told him how Lydia was at her wits' end.

He listened pensively as I spoke, and sat a full minute saying nothing after I stopped. He must have tapped his chin a couple hundred times.

"What's her boyfriend's name?" Tony finally asked.

"Brad Omer."

"What's he look like?"

"Well, he's tall and thin. He has brown, greasy hair, and a shabby, uneven beard."

"And he's in *high school?*" Tony said.

"No, he dropped out two years ago in his junior year—when he was *nineteen*!

"Oh. No relation to Einstein, huh?"

"We were told he sets up shop on Friday afternoons with two of his friends, a block down from the school."

Tony stood up and looked out at the lake. I could tell by his face he was so deep in thought he probably didn't even see the sailboats creeping along the waterfront.

A few minutes later, he grinned and started chuckling to himself, and continued to do so on and off for the next minute or so.

Finally he sat back down and extended his hand across the table.

"John, I have an idea, but I need a couple days to make a few arrangements. Meanwhile, you go home and hug that pretty wife of yours and tell her this thing will surely pass."

"Should we confront Katie about the pipe?"

This time, Tony replied right away. "No. Not yet. Give me a week."

"But—"

"No, seriously, John. This will all work out. Trust me."

66

Somehow, I did trust him. Or maybe I just didn't want to confront Katie—and I knew Lydia couldn't. At any rate, I felt better when I left Tony's office.

Lydia was not as comforted by Tony's unspoken plan as I had hoped, but then an amazing thing happened that Saturday afternoon.

Lydia and I were in the living room. I was skimming through the paper and Lydia was resting on the couch with her head on my lap reading a magazine when the doorbell rang.

Lydia sat up, her eyes nailed to an article on teenage drug use. "John, could you get that, Sweetheart?"

Before I could even put down the paper, Katie dashed downstairs from her room and flew to the door. Our first shock: she was wearing a dress! We hadn't seen her in a dress in over two years!

A minute later, Katie dragged her boyfriend into the room and the two of them stood before us. Our second shock: Brad had a haircut, he was clean-shaven, and he was wearing a suit and tie!

Lydia's mouth dropped, and I was filled with the hope that Katie and Brad had eloped and were planning to move away.

Brad cleared his throat after Katie poked his side with her elbow. "Mr. and Mrs. Richards," he said in a nervous voice, "Katie and I would like to take you to dinner to celebrate your anniversary."

Lydia could not speak. And the only thing I could come up with was, "Our anniversary isn't until next weekend—"

"We know that," Katie snarled.

Brad cleared his throat, loudly, and Katie fell into a more pleasant tone. "Uh, Brad and I just thought you'd have plans next week, so we wanted to take you out *tonight*."

"Uh, yeah," Brad said. "We would like to take you out to Al's Joynt.

Al's Joynt?

I had heard of it, but had never eaten there. I had a vague idea where it was, but other than that, I knew only what I had read in a review a few years earlier: *It is a clean but outdated steakhouse, a leftover from a bygone era, named after a former businessman from Cicero.* Still, I thought it was an offer we couldn't refuse.

"Princess, let me help you get ready."

"Al's Joynt?" Lydia said, in a daze.

"Yes. Isn't that wonderful?"

Brad insisted we take two cars, which I thought was strange, but what wasn't strange about that night? When we arrived at Al's, the place was packed and the man at the door said there was a two-hour wait. But when Brad mentioned we were the Richards Party, the man snapped his fingers and said to the waiter who appeared seconds later,

"Take Mr. Richards and his guests to see the boss."

The waiter led us through the noisy crowd toward the back of the restaurant, past table after table of people laughing and drinking and eating some of the best prime rib I had ever seen or smelled. Then we went down a long, dim-lit hallway to a private, corded-off room containing a single round table surrounded by five leather chairs.

A large plaque next to the entryway said:

The Boss's Room

The waiter removed the cord from the entryway and gestured us into the room where a second waiter held out a bottle of Champagne and said,

"A gift from Mr. Stillano."

Brad swallowed hard.

Stillano? I thought. *Oh brother, what's Tony up to now?*

After seating us, the waiter offered the bubbly. Lydia and I held our hands over our glasses. "We'll hold for now," I said.

The waiter moved over to Katie.

"She's under age," Lydia said.

The waiter slid over and filled Brad's glass. Brad downed it in a few quick gulps. "Can I have another?" he asked, appearing even more nervous.

Lydia lowered her head and pretended to adjust her napkin.

"He's acting a bit strange tonight," she whispered.

"When did he ever act normal?" I whispered back.

Lydia ordered a Teriyaki steak. I asked for the prime rib. Katie ordered only a salad. Brad said he didn't want anything, but poured himself another glass of Champagne from the bottle the waiter left at the table.

The thought came to me that maybe Brad was nervous because the restaurant was more expensive than he expected.

A glance at the menu told me the bill would run easily over a hundred dollars.

The waiter returned with our salads and a basket of bread just a few minutes after we ordered. Lydia bowed her head and slid her hand under the table, took my hand, and gave it the secret prayer squeeze we developed years ago in response to Katie's drama scenes whenever we gave thanks in public.

I bowed my head and returned the squeeze, in agreement of our joint gratefulness.

"Amen," we whispered together.

To our ongoing surprise, Katie went about her salad without saying a word.

Throughout all this, Brad's hands lay flat on the table, his eyes glued to the hallway.

I was half-finished with my salad when I heard Brad gasp. When I glanced over, there was a look of horror on his face. And when I turned toward the entryway, I saw the silhouette of a heavyset man standing behind two younger, well-built men. All three wore wide-brimmed hats and were impeccably dressed.

I stood up, and extended my hand.

"Tony?" I said.

67

One of the younger men rushed forward, slapped my hands out to the side, and patted me under the arms.

"Mr. Stillano don't like no one standing up too quick," he said in a thick Brooklyn accent.

"It's OK, Bobby," the heavy man said in the unmistakable brogue of Tony Stiller. "He's an old friend."

"Of course, Mr. Stillano." the young man said, smoothing out my jacket.

Tony walked up to me and smiled. "It's good to see you again, John." Then he gave me a hug and three strong pats on the back.

"Just play along," he whispered in my ear. "I'll explain later." And in a louder voice he said, "Are they treating you right in this joint?"

I had no clue what was going on, but figured Tony knew what he was doing. "Yeah! Great place!" I said.

Tony looked around the table. "Why don't you introduce me to your family again."

"Sure, uh, Mr. Stillano." I turned around and gestured to Lydia. "You remember my wife, Lydia?"

Tony grinned and nodded. "Ohhhhhh yes... *Lady* Lydia. I could never forget such a beautiful woman. You're a lucky man, John."

Lydia added a weak smile to the confused look already on her face.

"Indeed," I said before motioning to Katie. "It's been a while, so you might not recognize Katie—"

"What?!!" Tony howled in surprise. "Are you telling me this beautiful young thing is Little Katie?"

"Well, as you can see, she grew up a bit."

"She sure has!" Tony roared with a laugh. "I bet you turn a lot of heads, hey Cutie?"

"Most definitely," I answered for her before moving along to Brad, whose hands were trembling on the table. "And this is—"

"I know who this is," Tony said, sneering with disgust. "I know *who he is* and *where he lives*," Tony added, as if to remind Brad of something.

The room fell into silence as Tony and the two younger men walked over to Brad's chair. Brad was staring down at his plate when Tony slapped his hand on Brad's shoulder.

"You saved yourself a lot of trouble, Punk. Now beat it!"

Brad started to rise, only to be pushed down into the chair again. "You won't forget our little chat now, will you Punk?"

"N-n-no sir." Brad said.

"Good, then GO!"

Brad sprung up like a Jack-In-The-Box, grabbed Katie's hand, and rushed for the door.

"And take good care of Katie!" Tony shouted. "I'm her Godfather. I'd hate to see any harm come to her. *Capisce?*"

"Yes, Sir," Brad said before they ran out of the room.

"Katie, you drive," Lydia yelled as they disappeared around the corner. "He drank a lot of Champagne."

Brad's voice trailed off in the hallway. "I'll let her drive, Mrs. Richards."

I lifted my arms off the table in bewilderment and said, "Tony, what's going on?"

He put his finger to his mouth. "Shhhh!" he said. Then he turned to one of the younger men, the one who frisked me, and motioned for him to check the hallway. He did so, then turned around and announced, "It's clear."

Tony broke into the deepest laugh I had ever heard. The two younger men joined in. And soon Lydia and I, though still confused, couldn't stop grinning.

68

Tony sat down, emptied Brad's water glass into the ice bucket, and poured himself a large glass of Champagne. "To a problem solved," he said before downing the whole glass in a few gulps.

Then Tony introduced his nephews, Robert and George, just as Lydia's steak, my prime rib, and three other steaks were carted into the room.

"I hope I didn't wrinkle your suit," Robert said, without any trace of an accent.

Over dinner, Tony explained the plan I saw him concoct in his office. He had figured, correctly, that Brad had no gang or crime affiliations, and that he was just a dumb kid trying to make a quick buck on the street. So Tony and company waited in a limousine a block away from the high school until Brad and his two buddies approached their usual corner.

"My nephews and I were in the back," Tony explained, "and I asked PK to pull up the car."

"PK?" I said in surprise. "PK Chen, from accounting?"

"Yeah," Tony said. "His brother runs a limo service."

Tony continued. "We pulled up to the curb and stopped. Then Robert and George got out dressed in their suits and approached the three so-called dealers." Tony motioned to his nephews. "Why don't you guys tell 'em what happened next."

Robert spoke first: "I put on my fake accent and said, 'Which one of you is Brad Omer?' One of Brad's friends started pounding his fist. George calmly stuck his hand in his jacket and left it there."

George stood up. "Here, let me show you." He cocked his head slightly forward and to the side, stuck his hand in his jacket, creating a bulge, and looked at me with an expression so cold, I shivered. Then he turned to Lydia and presented the same look.

"I think you missed your calling," Lydia said. "You could be in the movies."

"Thanks," George said as he sat down. "I minored in theater."

"Yeah, yeah," Tony said. "So quit upstaging me."

We all laughed, then Tony went on with his story.

"So there's George reaching into his jacket and Brad's friends are backing off. Bobby walks up and puts his face six inches from Brad's. That kid starts shaking like a bag of... uh, leaves. Tell 'em what you said, Bobby—with that voice."

"Mr. Stillano wants to talk to you," Bobby said in a voice that had *gangster* written all over it.

Tony laughed and said, "By this time, PK steps out of the driver's seat and walks around the car. He opens the side door of the stretch with one hand and puts the other on the rim of his hat."

"Tell him about the hat, Uncle Tony," George said.

"Oh, yeah, that's right! PK wore one of those derbies. You mentioned movies earlier, Lydia? Well, PK looked like Odd Job from *Goldfinger*."

Everyone at the table must have gotten the same mental image, because we all broke out laughing hysterically.

Tony went on. "So Bobby and George hustle the kid into the car and sit down, Bobby on one side, George on the other, their linebacker frames squeezing the poor kid like a hot dog in a vise. Then Bobby says, 'This is the guy, Mr. Stillano.'"

Tony leaned back in his chair.

"So I'm sitting back in the seat and I say, 'Word has it on the street, you're working your own sales.' Then I leaned forward and poked my finger in his shoulder, hard, and said, 'You will cease and desist immediately. That means, in case you're as dumb as you look, you will stop all sales right away. *Capisce?*' Talk about a bag of leaves—that guy couldn't stop shaking if he was encased in cement, which he probably thought was coming next."

Tony broke out in a deep laugh again before going on.

"Then I say to him, 'Look, I know who you are. I know where you live. I know who your girlfriend is. Now here's what you're going to do: You're going to show up at Al's Joynt tomorrow. You're going to have a haircut. You're going to be clean-shaved. You're going be wearing a suit. And you're going to bring your girlfriend—and her parents, driving their own car. And make sure your girlfriend is wearing a dress.' I handed him a piece of paper with the address of the restaurant and said, 'I'll make a reservation for 6 PM under your girlfriend's last name. If you're not there when I show up at 6:15, I'll have you tracked down by 7:05. That's a promise. *Capisce?*'"

Tony slapped the table with both hands and roared. "Think bag of leaves again," he said. "Then I told him, 'Now get out of my car, you're stinkin' it up.'"

Tony laughed so hard I thought he was going to pass out.

"You know the rest of the story," he said.

We had the best laugh and the best steak we had had in a long time. Lydia even took a sip of Champagne after Tony filled her glass and insisted she try "the best of the house." We all laughed at the horrible face she made just before she coughed and said, "How can anyone drink this stuff?"

When we stood up to leave after dinner, I said "I'm picking up the tab."

Tony shook his head. "The tab's already been covered. My brother Tommy owns this place, and he owes me."

"You're kidding!" I said.

"No, I'm serious," Tony said with a big grin. "I got him this place cheap after the paper published a review about an outdated steakhouse—some of my best writing."

I remembered the review, and laughed again.

"Tony, I don't know how to thank you."

"You're a good man," Tony said. "I'm glad I could help." Then he turned to Lydia and gingerly picked up her hand, reminding me of the Christmas party years earlier. "And I hope I've been of help to you, *Lady* Lydia," he said as he bowed and kissed the tips of her fingers.

I could tell that Lydia was genuinely touched. And for a moment, I thought maybe Tony had at least a slim chance with the ladies.

Before Tony left with his nephews, he turned and said, "You two have one more surprise waiting for you at home. Heidi will tell you about it." Then he tipped his hat and left.

As Lydia checked Katie's chair to make sure she hadn't left anything behind, we wondered aloud about what was in store for us back home. Then we worked our way back through the crowded restaurant toward the front door. The Christmas party came to mind again as we passed the ladies room. "Do you want to wash your hand?" I said.

A puzzled look came to Lydia's face. "What for?"

69

When we walked into the house, Heidi was standing in the front hallway with one hand behind her back and a big smirk on her face.

"I think we're about to get our surprise," Lydia said under her breath.

"Mom, Dad." Heidi said, beaming. "The Lord answered another prayer." She twisted from side to side until we asked,

"Well, are you going to tell us about it?"

She brought Katie's pipe out from behind her back and showed us.

Lydia went limp. "Where did you get that?"

"Katie gave it to me."

"What?" I said.

"When?" Lydia asked.

Heidi explained: "An hour after you left, Katie and Brad came back to the house. Brad looked really scared, as if the FBI was after him or something. Katie didn't look much better. Brad told Katie to 'hurry up and get it,' so she ran to her room, came back with the pipe, and gave it to me. She said I could tell you guys everything. So did Brad. Then they left."

215

"Heidi," Lydia said in dismay, "you knew Katie, uh... smoked?"

"Mom, this is a *hash* pipe."

"You know about these things?" I asked, astonished.

Heidi laughed. "Oh, come on," she said. "I don't live in a cave."

"Heidi, this is not funny," Lydia said.

"I'm sorry, Mom. You're right, it isn't funny. The only reason I'm laughing is because after knowing all this for so long, and after praying so hard, I'm overjoyed at God's answer to prayer!"

With a little help from Big Tony, I thought to myself.

Lydia's eyes watered as she stepped in and hugged Heidi. "Oh Sweetheart, thanks for your prayers. I guess I had given up too soon."

Then Lydia stepped back with an afterthought. "Wait a minute; you knew about Katie's drug use and didn't say anything to me or your father?"

"Mom, you know my rule."

Heidi and Lydia recited it together: "*Never say anything about anyone that you wouldn't say if they were standing there with you.*"

Heidi went on to say, "As snotty as Katie can be at times, she knows I hold to the rule, and so she tells me *lots* of stuff— as do a lot of kids at school, from every caste."

"That's a good rule, Sweetheart," Lydia said. "But this was a serious matter. Katie could have been hurt, or maybe even die."

"If I had thought that, I would have told you and Daddy right away. But Mom, Katie doesn't do drugs. She *hates* not being in control. Remember that *one* time—that *only* time—she came home drunk?"

"How could we forget," I answered for the two of us.

"Katie told me afterward she would *never* do that again, and made me promise not to tell you. Until tonight, that is."

"Why would she make you promise such a thing?" Lydia asked.

"Mom, Dad: in her own way, Katie is frightened just like everyone else. The reason she's so demanding, so *controlling*, is because she feels so *out* of control. And she didn't want you or anyone else to know that."

Lydia thought for a moment, then asked, "What about Brad? Did you know he sells drugs?"

"He sells baked oregano and charcoal," Heidi answered.

"What?"

"I scraped residue from the bowl last month and asked Matthew to analyze it in Chem Lab after school. God made Matthew a genius, you know; it took him just a few minutes to determine the sample was little more than charcoal, flour, and oregano."

Heidi gave us a few moments to let it all sink in.

"Brad probably baked it at home," she continued. "And again, if I thought Katie was in danger, I would have come and told you. But I didn't want to scare you or violate Katie's trust without facts. That's why I asked Matthew for help."

Lydia sighed in relief, then asked Heidi, "Do you know why Brad and Katie came clean like this?"

"No," Heidi said. "But I've been thanking the Lord ever since! Like people say, 'God works in mysterious ways.'"

The restaurant scene played through my mind. It must have played through Lydia's too, because we turned to each other and started laughing.

"He certainly does," we said.

The Good...

70

In 1966, Clint Eastwood, Eli Wallach, and Lee Van Cleef starred in a western called *The Good, the Bad, and the Ugly*. It seems our family starred in a *Mid*western of the same name.

First, *The Good*:

I had been with Braxton-Becker for twenty-one years, head of the Chicago office for sixteen. I had turned down four promotions after taking the top job in Chicago. As far as I was concerned, heading the Chicago office was the best job in the company. It was big enough for a challenge, yet small enough to get my arms around.

I considered the people in the Chicago office my second family, and treated them accordingly. And they me. Through their dedication, I was able to deliver improvements to our business model, to our clients, and to the company's bottom line, year after year. And through the magic of delegation, I was able to deliver all this without shortchanging my family.

I still traveled once or twice a year, but only when I wanted to, and only where I wanted to go. And I'd always work out a way to take Lydia along, and sometimes the girls too.

Whenever an interesting travel opportunity came up, Tony gave me a call. From 1964 to early 1966, Lydia and I visited Rome, London, Hamburg, and Copenhagen. So when I picked up the phone in late 1966 after my secretary told me Tony was on the line, I wondered where we'd be off to next.

"Hey, John," Tony said. "How's Heidi doing?"

"Uh, fine," I said, surprised by his question. "She's growing. There have been a few setbacks, but I think we're managing her diabetes well."

"I'm not talking about her health," Tony said. "How's she doing with her religion thing? Does she still have it?"

I smiled and shook my head, glad Tony was not there to see it. "Well, she would put it another way: her religion has *her*—no, make that, *the Lord* has her."

"Then you might be interested in attending a conference," Tony said. "I'll send Michelle up with some brochures."

Five minutes later, Tony's new secretary showed up at my door and handed me a large manila envelope.

The aroma of curry chicken greeted me when I walked in the door that night. I put down the envelope from the office and picked up the mail, fingering through it quickly while thinking about mashed potatoes and gravy, string beans, hot buttered bread and, of course, the chicken.

I sambaed into the kitchen and wrapped my arms around the waist of the cook who stood at the stove, stirring a simmering pot of cut up potatoes. My lips found her neck and proceeded to make smooching sounds while my eyes jogged from burner to burner. "Mmmm, this is good," I said.

"What are you referring to?" Lydia asked.

"Mmmm, this is *very* good," I answered.

I turned my head and peeked into the dining room. There were only three place settings at the table.

"Katie's with Brad again tonight?" I asked.

"As usual," Lydia said, rolling her eyes.

At least we weren't as worried about Katie being with Brad after Tony and his nephews had their little talk with him. One week after the "training" at Al's Joynt, I took Brad out to lunch—alone, in spite of Katie's objections. We had what I thought was a good, friendly chat. Basically, I told him that when Katie was with him, he was responsible for her safety and *well-being.* "I don't know what I'd do if something bad happened to Katie," I told him. Brad didn't eat much of his lunch after that.

Being out of the house as much as she could was Katie's way of handling her relationship with her mother, a relationship that had deteriorated to the point where I wondered if they'd ever be friends.

My reminding Lydia that we should enjoy the girls for what little time we had them would not have helped matters any, so I just took my place at the table that night and smiled at Heidi, Lydia, and the feast set before us. We joined hands and bowed our heads. Why those spiritual giants always wanted me to say the prayer still amazes me.

"Be with us," I prayed, "and with Katie, tonight. Thank you for the food, for family, and for… surprises. Amen."

"Amen," Lydia and Heidi said.

Heidi slid the plate of chicken over to me. "Surprises?"

I speared two drumsticks. "Oh, did I say that? Hmmm, I wonder where that came from." I passed the chicken and reached across the table for the mashed potatoes. "Maybe it had to do with the brochures I got from Tony today."

Both girls turned to me. "Oh, are we going somewhere interesting?" Lydia asked.

"Give us a hint." Heidi begged.

"Well, we've never been there, but it's a place you—"

"ISRAEL!" Heidi squealed.

I laughed. "Tony called today and told me about a conference there. He also asked if you still had religion."

"You should have told him: *the Lord* has *me*!" Heidi said.

"Ha—I told him that very thing. And he figured you just might want to see Jerusalem."

"Oh, yes!" Heidi said, almost unable to contain herself. "Yes! Yes! Yes!"

"Is it safe to travel there?" Lydia asked.

"I think so," I said. "This is an international conference. They'll have security in place. I'm even thinking we can take a few extra days and visit the whole area."

I turned to Heidi. "Do you want to do anything in particular?"

"Oh yeah, for sure!" she cried. "I want to walk through Gethsemane where Jesus prayed, and climb the Mount of Olives! And Bethlehem—we gotta go see Bethlehem!"

She drummed on the table in her excitement.

"Can we go to Galilee?"

"Sure, why not."

"Oh, I'd love to wade in the Sea of Galilee—and walk on the hillside where Jesus fed the five thousand..."

Lydia and I leaned back in our chairs as Heidi lit up like the grand finale on the fourth of July.

After supper, we went to the living room and looked at the brochures from Tony. Heidi brought down her Bible—opened to the map section—along with a series of articles she had saved over the years. We spread everything out on the carpet, and the three of us got down on all fours and arranged and rearranged articles and maps and brochures.

Within an hour, we put together a four-day itinerary that I knew would be Heidi's trip of a lifetime.

The Bad…

71

I first became aware of the problem two weeks before Thanksgiving, 1966. I remember holding the phone to my ear and spinning the chair around to look out at Lake Michigan. The chair leaned back with me, lifting my feet to the ledge. There wasn't a cloud in the sky and the air was clear. I squinted and imagined I could see Michigan on the other side of the lake. I was wondering if that was even possible when a familiar voice answered at the other end.

"Accounting. This is Mary."

"Hi, Mary, is PK in?"

There was an uncomfortable pause, followed by a shaky voice. "Is this your idea of a joke, Mr. Richards? You were the last person I'd expect this from."

I dropped my legs to the floor and swung around to the desk. "Mary, I don't know what you're talking about. What's going on?"

There was another pause, then that unsteady voice again. "Did you fire Mr. Chen?"

"What? Of course not! Mary, why would you even think such a thing?"

"When I came in this morning, he was walking out, carrying a box of personal belongings. He told me to mail whatever else I found to his home in Evanston. He looked pretty upset. I assumed you fired him."

"Well, I didn't," I said.

I scanned down the agenda for the morning's conference call, stopping at the third item: Accounting Changes—Rob Martins.

"Did PK say anything else?" I asked.

"No, but he looked more worried than angry."

I glanced at my watch. "If he drove home, he should be there by now. Please call him and try to find out what's going on."

"Yes, Mr. Richards. I'll let you know what I learn."

"Thanks, Mary."

I hit the call button on the intercom. "Brenda, can you get Rob Martins on the line? He should be in New York."

Rob had joined Braxton-Becker a year earlier, two months after Milt Sievers was tapped for the CEO spot. Rob was Milt's right hand man, brought on board as part of Milt's plan to restructure the company. No one outside the Executive Committee knew Rob's credentials, but it was public knowledge—and the subject of numerous water cooler discussions—that the SEC had heavily fined Rob's former employer, and that arrests were made.

PK and I assumed Rob wouldn't have been hired had he been involved in the scandal, and we attributed the shroud of secrecy surrounding the executive office to Milt's style. But then an envelope, marked "Confidential", mysteriously appeared on PK's desk. It contained a copy of a memo that referred to the "Blue Books". PK called and asked if I had heard of them. I hadn't, and I told him so. He told me the memo added to his suspicion that the Executive Committee was keeping another set of books, and that he would know more before the conference call. That's why I tried to call him earlier.

The intercom chimed. I tapped the switch.

"Yes, Brenda?"

"Mr. Martins is in conference with Mr. Sievers. He will not be available before the conference call. Would you like to speak with his secretary?"

My watch said the call would start in fifteen minutes. "No, that's OK, thanks, Brenda. If PK or Mary calls, patch them through to the beige phone—even if we are in the middle of the conference."

"Yes, Mr. Richards."

The conference started at 10 o'clock sharp, Chicago time. All fifteen office heads were on the call, hosted by the three-man Executive Committee in New York. I put the call on speaker and hit the mute button, grabbed a pen and notepad, and settled back in the chair.

Milt opened the meeting with a warm and hearty summary of his accomplishments since he took the helm. Then he slid into the second agenda item: *Aiming High for the Seventies*. He was still sharing his "vision" when the beige phone rang.

It was PK.

"John, it's Peter," he said.

I was relieved to hear him say *Peter*, the name he used only with close friends.

"Sorry about this morning," he said. "I shouldn't have believed Rob when he told me you were going along with the change. I think—"

"Wait, Peter, slow down. What change?"

"They're moving all accounting functions to New York."

"No one mentioned anything about that to me."

"John, I think the Executive Committee is keeping another set of books."

"The Blue Books you mentioned last week?"

"Yes. I found some disturbing differences between our receivables and the company's published figures, so I called Rob at home over the weekend. He told me not to worry about it, that they were keeping separate records."

"What? He actually said that?"

"Yes, can you believe it? Whatever Rob's credentials are, they're certainly not in accounting or law."

I flipped to the next sheet of the notepad. "How long has this been going on?"

"For at least six months, based on our receivables and quarterly reports."

I scribbled a large "6" and circled it. "Six months! This is unbelievable—why weren't the office heads told?"

"John, the Executive Committee didn't even tell the corporate attorneys!"

"How do you know that?"

"Rob told me—he bragged about it!"

There was a long pause as I wrote more scribbles.

"OK, I got the picture," I said, and hesitated before asking one last question. "Peter, did Rob fire you?"

"No, but he said you were managing the accounting transition. Is that true?"

I tossed the notepad onto the desk. "If it is, you're the first to tell me about it. This is all new to me, Peter. How long have we known each other? How many barbeques have our families enjoyed together? Peter, I've never lied to you. I've never gone behind your back. And I have no plans to do so now or in the future. Let's meet over lunch. I'll call you when the conference ends."

I hung up the beige phone just in time to hear Milt say over the speaker: "The future belongs to companies that abandon back road strategies in favor of thoroughfare paradigms aligned with global economic realities. Rob Martins will come now and speak more to that. Rob?"

72

A fifteen-minute barrage of wind, smoke, and obfuscation followed — the only understandable part of which could be boiled down to one sentence: *All accounting activity will be transferred from Chicago to New York.*

Then I heard my name. "John," Rob said, "I'm counting on you to manage the transition."

I unmuted the phone and played dumb. "Rob, PK is director of accounting. Did you discuss this with him?"

"Chen and I talked last weekend," Rob said over the speaker as I jotted down another note. "John, as far as the Executive Committee is concerned, *you* hold all accounting responsibility. We are counting on *you, not Chen,* to ensure the transition goes smoothly. Do you have any questions about that?"

Oh, I did not like that guy — so arrogant, and stupid enough to believe I'd cower before him because he was on the Executive Committee.

"I need to talk with PK," I said.

Rob barked over the speaker: "Chen is out of the loop. This is *your* responsibility, John. Do you understand?"

"Yes, I understand. That's why I need to talk with PK."

"John, we can do this *with* you or *without* you."

"And just what does that mean, Rob?"

"You're either on the team or off," Rob said in a louder voice.

"And I repeat, *Rob*, what does *that mean?*"

Milt broke in. "Rob, John, we need to pull together on this. Now John, I believe we can count on you to do the right thing. Am I right?"

"Milt," I said, "You've known me long enough to *know* I will do the right thing. And that's why I need to talk with PK."

There was silence, and I knew they had muted their end and were arguing in New York.

"OK John," Milt finally said, "if you think that's best." I felt relieved when Milt tipped this one in my favor, even though it was becoming increasingly clear that Rob, not Milt, was running the show. "But let's work quickly," Milt added. "We'd like to complete the transition by end of fiscal year."

"I'll talk with PK today and get back to you by close of business."

I called Peter as soon as I hung up. We met for lunch and I filled him in on the conference call. He shook his head and said he couldn't believe what was happening. He handed me a summary of reported revenues versus actual revenues for the past three quarters. "I finished this just before you called," he said.

I studied the figures. "So the company's reporting false profits?"

"Yes, and I think they're doing it by booking revenues in advance."

"Which, of course, they haven't disclosed."

"That's right," Peter said. "They probably figure they'll cover the shortfall later since projections are up." He turned the summary over and pointed to a chart. "But look at these rates, John. If I'm right, then each quarter they'll have to reach farther into the future to make up for an ever-increasing shortfall. Sooner or later the whole thing will collapse and we'll have the SEC all over us."

I sat back in the chair. "Why are they doing this?"

"To boost the stock price."

As I thought about that, Peter took out a piece of paper and wrote down four questions. "Here," he said, handing me the list. "Ask these questions *in this order* when you talk with Milt this afternoon." A lump formed in my throat as I read silently through the list.

I went back to my office and asked my secretary to clear the schedule for the rest of the day and to hold any non-essential calls. Then I took a folder from my desk and went through news clippings I had collected after Rob joined the company.

I reread the articles in light of what I had just learned that day. I also looked at accounting reports for the previous four quarters, and reviewed the summary Peter gave me at lunch.

It all came together. By the time I finished the folder, I knew I wouldn't need Peter's four questions, and I knew I wouldn't complete my 22nd year with the company.

I picked up the phone and called Lydia. When I heard her voice, a montage of memories splashed through my mind: our walks through Scoville Park, our first kiss, the day she first told me she loved me. I started to weep.

"John, are you OK?" Lydia said.

I remembered her saying that years ago when I showed up at her apartment, half frozen.

And I chuckled as I cried, thinking about warming up in her bed with that towel around my head while she made hot cocoa in the kitchen.

"Oh, Lydia," I said. "I love you so much."

After a pause, she asked, "Are you having a rough day?"

"Mm-hmm… Maybe I should have these more often, to remind me how wonderful *you* are."

"John…"

"Lydia, what would I do without you?"

"My Johnny…"

"Talk to me," I said, clearing my throat. "Say anything. Just let me hear your voice."

...And The Ugly

73

I called Milt's office at 3:35, Chicago time. His secretary put me through to his desk.

"John," he said in a disgruntled voice. "I can't tell you how disappointed I was in your conduct during today's conference call. Our company is at a pivotal juncture. We need *all* the leaders—especially you, John—singing from the same page. Your little tiff with Rob undermined the unity I had hoped to establish on the call—"

I didn't wait for him to finish. "Rob's there now, right?"

My question caught Milt off guard. "Uh, yes, that's right," he said in a way that hid the question from Rob. "Unity is—"

"Milt, just listen to me. You know my history with the company. And you know PK's. Certainly, you realize—"

"Change is good," Milt went on to say, and I wondered if he had read anything in business school other than success posters. He was a textbook example of Good ol' Boys networking: dropped in the top spot of a company he knew little about, operating in an industry of which he knew even less. That's why Milt hired Rob—someone had to run the company. But run it into the ground?

"Milt, what do you know about the Blue Books?" I said.

I heard him cup his hand over the phone and the sound of muffled voices. Then Rob's voice took over the line.

"What's your problem, John?" he barked.

I hit him head on:

"Are you keeping a separate set of books?"

"I don't have to answer to you," he said.

"You *will* have to answer to the SEC, and most likely to a federal prosecutor if you're reporting false profits to the public. So get used to the question: *Are you keeping a separate set of books?*"

"And what if we are?"

"Didn't you learn *anything* from your last job?"

"Yes, I did," Rob said smugly. "And that's why this will work."

The U.S. Attorney's office disagreed.

The day before Thanksgiving, two weeks after Rob's arrogant boast, we were notified that our company was under investigation for conducting securities fraud using the mail. A U.S. Postal Inspector questioned me and Peter for over two hours.

Talk about a Turkey Day!

A week later, we were subpoenaed to appear as witnesses before a federal grand jury. We were never called to testify; fifteen minutes after the hearing convened, the grand jury had enough evidence to hand down indictments for Rob, Milt, and five of the fifteen office heads.

I called Peter into my office the next day and we talked about possibilities. We knew that many of our clients would have to distance themselves from us. We figured the company had about three months.

That proved too optimistic.

The board offered me a "damage control" position in New York. The new chairman called me personally and made it sound like a promotion. Arrogance and ignorance had already destroyed the company and the jobs of many hard-working employees—many of them my friends—and now the board wanted me to straighten out the mess, using my close relationships with clients to keep them from jumping ship. I declined the offer—which I would have done even if I had thought I could help.

I also refused the chairman's final order to fire everyone in the Chicago office to save the company unemployment insurance expense. I reminded him of my new friends in the U.S. Attorney's office, and strongly suggested the company lay us off instead.

We cleaned out our personal belongings and had a final party at the office. A lay-off party. Tony said it was the only office party that *everyone* attended. Families were invited. Lydia and Heidi came. There was lots of hugging, laughing, and stories. Only toward the end were the sounds of a few muffled sobs heard here and there.

And finally, against a background of lightly falling snow in the second week of February, 1967, we turned off the lights, and the Chicago office of Braxton-Becker International closed its doors for the very last time.

As office head, I was under a contract that had a separation clause. I flew to New York to review the settlement. With almost twenty-two years of service, I was handed a check that amounted to about three months salary. The meeting lasted less than five minutes. I flew back to Chicago that same day, and wondered what lay ahead.

Moving On

74

I remember arriving home that afternoon, tired and still in the fog of the past three months. Lydia and Heidi met me at the door. "Well, it's official," I said. They slipped their arms around me and escorted me to the recliner in the den.

"We'll do just fine, Daddy," Heidi assured me.

Lydia kissed my cheek. "You did the right thing. Let's have curry chicken tonight."

I woke in the recliner to one of my favorite smells, and the three of us had a surprisingly upbeat dinner, talking about things we would have done and places we would have seen had we been able to visit Israel.

Katie came home late that night, as usual, and was surprised to find me sitting in the kitchen, looking down into a cup of warm milk. After I told her what happened, she just matter-of-factly said, "Bummer, Dad. But at least you won't have me to worry about anymore; I'm moving out tomorrow."

We woke up the next morning and found a note on the table:

Off to the beat of a different drum...
                    —Katie

With all the flurry of activity, I had forgotten about Katie's 18th birthday. Had I not been so depressed by what happened at work, I probably would have grieved more when Katie left. The good relationship that I hoped would develop between Katie and her mother hadn't happened, and I was too numb to grieve for what probably ended up being for the better anyway, as terrible as that might sound. It certainly was more peaceful around the house. And it took on a more spiritual air.

I remember the first of many times I woke up in the middle of the night to find Lydia kneeling next to the bed, holding my hand as she prayed.

"What are you doing?" I asked.

"I'm loving you the best way I know how," she said.

One night, I woke and found her slumped on the floor, her hand still wrapped around mine. I got up and gently lifted her onto the bed and pulled the comforter over her shoulders.

"What's going on," she mumbled, half asleep.

I told her, "I'm loving the one who loves me the best way she knows how."

My full-time job was to find a job. Ongoing news coverage of the company's debacle made it an uphill battle. Affiliates distanced themselves from everything and anyone connected to Braxton-Becker. Even affiliates I had worked with, friends who trusted me and knew of my total innocence, could not or would not extend me an offer.

Weeks turned into months.

During all the years of our marriage, I never planned a budget. I figured our income was high enough that we didn't need one. Sometimes, when I was honest with myself, I realized the reason had more to do with the fact that budgets are not as free with money as I am. Maybe there was a little rebellion against my dad there, too. Who knows?

Lydia, on the other hand, believed in budgets—and assumed I kept one. So you can imagine the shocked look on her face when I explained how I had "handled" the finances, and that we had less than $2,000 in our savings account, not counting the severance check.

On the three-month anniversary of my unemployment, the alarm went off and I rolled over and hit the snooze button. Not that I was tired, I just wanted to take some time to count my blessings. There I was: out of work, no offers, and no prospects. And yet I was feeling grateful for all I had: a wonderful wife and daughter, good health, a nice home. And it wasn't as if we were flat broke; I figured we had enough money to keep us going for four or five months.

While I was thinking all this, Lydia rolled over in bed. And as I combed my hand through her hair, I remembered the embroidery that hung in her old apartment:

A Wife of Noble Character
Brings Her Husband Good
All The Days of Her Life

I leaned over and kissed her slightly-parted lips.
Her eyes eased open, and a smile woke up on her face.
"More," she said.
I kissed her again.
"Mmmm," she said. "And what can I do for you?"
"You can help me write a budget."
"Oh, I must still be dreaming."
My laugh convinced her otherwise.
Her eyes opened wide. "You want me to help you come up with a budget? Now? After all these years?"

I cuddled closer and kissed her cheek and neck. "Good point," I said. "It can wait another half-hour."

Later that morning, after sorting through five years of check registers and credit card receipts, Lydia knew where our money had gone. Our three biggest expenditures had been taxes; big-ticket items like the new car, furniture, and vacations; and what Lydia called nickel-and-dime spending. She set up budget categories and proposed reasonable allotments for each. The bottom line: with Lydia's budget, we had enough money to last over a year.

Lydia and I were in the kitchen standing by the table when Heidi walked in. I was holding the budget with one hand and Lydia with the other. Lydia's arms were wrapped around me.

"What's up?" Heidi asked.

"Your genius mother has devised a budget," I said, holding up the papers and waving them back and forth. "We are going to keep to this budget, and go on a one-month vacation."

Judging from their dropped jaws and furrowed foreheads, they must have been thinking Europe or South America—big budget items again. But all I was thinking was to take a month off from the job search, and to enjoy that time with Lydia and Heidi.

We made the most of the next thirty days. We visited the Shedd Aquarium, the Adler Planetarium, and the museums along the lake. We carried bag lunches up to the observation deck of the Prudential Building, and ate while watching boats sail around the breakwater.

We walked along the lakefront by the marinas, drove up and down Lake Shore Drive, and strolled Michigan Avenue.

We took photographs of the water tower that survived the Great Chicago Fire, and on a lark, we bought Heidi a pair of Bell Bottoms at one of those hippie shops in Old Towne.

We also reacquainted ourselves with Oak Park and River Forest. We saw where Hemingway lived, and toured the Frank Lloyd Wright Home and Studio. We took a sidewalk tour of Paul Harvey's house, and the house on Kenilworth where the Johnsons originated their radio show. We walked the paths of Thatcher Woods, chatted with the talking crow of Trailside Museum, and skipped stones on the pond out back.

When the month was over, I felt refreshed and encouraged when I sat down in front of the typewriter to spruce up my resume and type two cover letters—one to a company in Nashville and the other to a company in Atlanta. Neither company had what I wanted, but then I couldn't be as picky as I once was. Plus, I knew it would be a dream come true for Lydia to move to Atlanta so she could spend more time with her mom.

Hope is a powerful gift. I used to wish I could see into the future, but now I realize that doing so would undermine the power of hope and the joy of longings fulfilled. I mailed those letters with hopeful anticipation, a feeling I would have missed had I been able to look into the future and see that the effort would amount to nothing, and that I wouldn't see employment for another year.

Bittersweet Forgiveness

75

As turbulent as 1967 had been, it ended with a peaceful and memorable Christmas, which began with an unexpected wakeup call on December 24th.

Lydia rolled over and picked up the phone. I could hear the tinny murmur of Katie's voice over the line, but couldn't make out what she was saying. Lydia wiped tears from her cheeks after she hung up.

"What was all that about?" I asked.

Lydia rolled onto her back and stared at the ceiling. "Katie is coming for dinner."

"Well," I said in surprise. "Isn't that wonderful?"

Another tear rolled down Lydia's cheek. "Yes, it is."

The troubled look on her face told me she was keeping something back. "What's the matter?" I asked.

She was not ready to tell me.

"The important thing is that Katie is coming home for dinner," she said. "And we will spend Christmas Eve as a family again." She threw off the covers and rolled out of bed. "There's something I have to do."

She spent a half-hour in Katie's room. The door was closed but I could hear her going through the closet. She came out with a box and headed toward the attic where she spent another half-hour. Then she came downstairs, wrapped the mystery box and put it under the tree next to the other gifts.

Lake-effect snow visited the area that afternoon, bringing in a much-wished-for White Christmas. The wind picked up from the east, and by four o'clock three inches of the fluffy stuff was on the ground in Oak Park.

Heidi and Lydia, dressed in black slacks and matching holiday sweaters, were already waiting by the picture window when I came downstairs in the reindeer sweater Katie gave me a half-dozen Christmases earlier.

We stood in silence and watched the big flakes float in and out of the porch light. The table was set, the candles lit, the scent of pine hanging in the air. Carols played over the radio and the soft glow of the nativity set grew brighter as the room darkened.

A rusty Studebaker pulled up to the curb at 4:30. Katie got out and shuffled up to the front door. She wore no hat, and her chin was buried in a tattered coat held shut with bare hands.

We waved from the window, but Katie didn't see us. Heidi said, "Let's yell *Merry Christmas!!!* when she comes in."

But instead of barging in like she always did in the past, Katie knocked and waited on the porch. And even when we opened the door and shouted our greeting, Katie just stood there, shivering.

"Can I come in?" she finally asked.

"Of course you can," Lydia said. "This is your home, and you're welcome at any time."

I can barely believe what happened next.

Katie brought her hands to her face and began to weep. Then she reached out and threw herself into the open arms of her mother. "I'm sorry, Mom."

Lydia burst into tears. "I love you, Sweetheart."

It was as if the difficult, sometimes unbearable, 18-year struggle with Katie had never happened. As if Katie and Lydia had never fought. As if Katie had never sworn at her mother, or gave her the finger, or spoke disparagingly about her to friends while Lydia was there to hear.

Later at the table, we enjoyed the full complement of holiday fare as we revisited memories of our years in The Pink House. It was good to see the three girls laughing together again and enjoying each other's company. And somewhere in the middle of it all, I realized Katie didn't smell of smoke.

"Did you stop smoking?" I asked.

Katie looked embarrassed. "Yes," she said. "About a month ago." Then she turned and smiled at her mother, as if they shared a secret.

After dinner, we went to the den and sat around the tree. Lydia turned to Katie. "Are you sure you can't stay with us?"

Katie's eyes welled. "Mom, you know it's best this way."

Lydia stood up and walked to the tree, pulled out two gifts, and handed them to Katie.

"Merry Christmas, Sweetheart."

"Which is the one we talked about?" Katie asked.

Lydia pointed with her eyes to the larger box, which Katie set off to the side. "Thanks, Mom."

"Go ahead and open the other one now," Lydia said. "We got it for you in case you came home for Christmas."

Katie carefully removed the wrapping paper and opened the box from Marshall Field's. Inside was a wool sweater. Red, Katie's favorite color.

The remaining gifts would wait under the tree until Christmas morning. We spent another hour talking in the den before Katie stood up and said it was time to leave. Lydia asked her to wait a few minutes while she got something from upstairs. That gave me time to slip out and open a path in the snow.

Lydia returned a few minutes later with a winter coat, hat, and a warm pair of gloves. Katie put them on, then wiped her cheeks. "You might as well keep the coat I wore here," she said with a tearful chuckle.

We walked Katie out to the car and loaded her presents into the back seat. I gave her a hug, as did Heidi. Lydia hugged her last, and handed her an envelope with rainy-day money in it. "You take this," Lydia said.

Five months later, we received a package from a home for unwed mothers in Iowa. In it was a letter from Katie and pictures of our granddaughter, Sarah, wearing clothes from the mystery box.

A Budding Romance

76

Midway through her junior year in high school, Heidi caught a bad case of the flu, which landed her in the hospital for a week. She spent another two weeks at home, mostly in bed.

Every afternoon, Matthew faithfully brought over her school assignments, on which she'd spend an hour or two every day when she could find the strength.

When Matthew came over, Lydia would invite him in for hot cider and call upstairs for Heidi to join them. But as weak as she was, Heidi could barely open her door and say in a hoarse voice, "I better stay in my room. Thanks for bringing my assignments, Matthew."

Near the end of the two weeks, when Heidi was feeling better, she came downstairs in her bathrobe and sat with Matthew and Lydia at the kitchen table.

She had lost ten pounds, tipping the scales at ninety-two. Her face was pale, her eyes slightly darkened. Even so, Lydia told me, Matthew was moonstruck as he looked at Heidi from across the table.

The twins walked Matthew to the door, and Heidi thanked Matthew again. He hesitated, then lifted his hand and cupped Heidi's arm.

"I hope you get well soon," he said. "We all miss you at school… I miss you." His face grew flush, then he turned and thanked Heidi's mother for the cider.

Heidi and Lydia watched Matthew walk down the porch steps, and waved when he looked back from the sidewalk.

"Mom," Heidi said, "what do you think of Matthew?"

Lydia put her arm around Heidi and kissed her hair. "He's a fine young man. I've thought so ever since your 13th birthday party. Remember how frail he looked backed then?"

Heidi sighed. "Not anymore."

Lydia let out a chuckle. "No, not anymore."

"He's captain of the varsity football team," Heidi said. "And he's only a junior."

"And you and your dad keep reminding me how smart he is."

The twins stayed at the window long after Matthew had disappeared up the street, leaving a trail of large footprints in the snow.

"Mom," Heidi said softly, "do you think I'm pretty?"

Lydia smiled. "Look at me," she said. "Do you think *I'm* pretty?"

Heidi's face brightened. "Mom, you're gorgeous!"

Lydia brought her hands to Heidi's cheeks.

"Then remember what people say: you're my twin!"

77

Within another week, Heidi's strength had returned and she was itching to get back to work at the homeless shelter. Matthew's face lit up when Heidi asked at school if he would help her carry items to the church that Sunday night.

"And could you ask Martha to join us?" Heidi said.

The doorbell rang the following Sunday at 4:30, and Matthew had shaken the snow off his coat and shoes by the time I opened the door. Heidi was in her bedroom with her mother, packing loose clothes and a few toys into two medium-sized duffle bags.

"Are they here?" Heidi yelled down to the foyer.

"Matthew's here," I shouted.

"OK, I'll be down in a minute," Heidi said.

I raised my eyebrows and said to Matthew with a chuckle, "Yeah, we'll see about that."

I motioned for him to come into the living room and sit down. He chose the chair opposite mine, on the other side of the coffee table—which surprised me, since he appeared to be strangely nervous and uncomfortable.

"Would you like something to read," I asked, pointing to a pile of magazines stacked neatly in the corner.

"No thank you, Mr. Richards."

I went back to reading my newspaper, over the top of which I could see Matthew sitting at attention, his body squared off to mine, his hands frozen around his knees. Every minute or so, he looked toward the foyer and drew a deep breath which he let out slowly through pursed lips.

I didn't know what was going on, nor did I think it best to ask. So I turned the page of the paper and tried to act nonchalant. This seemed to relax Matthew; he loosened a bit, and his hands started sliding back and forth on his thighs as he rocked in the chair.

By this time, I had forgotten which article I was reading, so I dropped my pretense and said, "Matthew, is everything OK?"

"Mr. Richards," he blurted. "Martha's not here because I didn't tell her about the homeless shelter tonight."

I had no idea what he was talking about, but was curious enough to ask, "Why?"

Matthew stopped rocking and locked onto his knees again. "I—I just wanted to be with Heidi… myself."

I leaned back in the chair. "Oh, I see."

He drew another deep breath and said, "Mr. Richards, I like your daughter… a lot." And after taking a few minutes to explain his feelings for her, he asked me something I had never been asked before.

Meanwhile, up in Heidi's bedroom, the duffle bags had been packed and lying on the bed for over five minutes. Heidi sat at her desk and looked into a small mirror that Lydia had brought into the room.

"Are you sure it's OK, Mom?"

Lydia looked at Heidi in the mirror and smiled.

"It's fine, Sweetheart," Lydia assured her. "It's only a little makeup."

"It doesn't look like I'm trying to… you know…"

"Don't be silly," Lydia said. "It looks fine."

Matthew and I heard two sets of footsteps coming down the stairs. Heidi and Lydia appeared at the entrance to the living room a few moments later.

Lydia slid the duffle bags off her shoulder, onto the floor.

Matthew and I stood up and faced the twins.

I think Matthew picked up the extra color on Heidi's face right away; I noticed he was breathing a little deeper and faster. The makeup was subtle, certainly not overdone by any means, just enough to give Heidi's skin the natural tone that Matthew hadn't seen in a while. After our little talk, I knew Matthew already thought Heidi was the most beautiful girl in the world. I think the makeup stirred him only because he hoped she had put it on for him.

"Wow, Heidi, you look great!" Matthew said. "How are you feeling?"

More color came to Heidi's face, along with a soft smile.

"Thank you," she said. "I feel pretty good."

Lydia and I watched Heidi and Matthew look at each other as their minds drifted to that place where thoughts speed up and slow down at the same time.

Matthew's face softened.

Heidi's smile widened.

And we all stood in the quiet of the room until the silence grew too loud.

"Uh, where's Martha?" Heidi finally said.

I spoke before Matthew could answer. "It looks like it's just going to be the two of you tonight."

"Oh," Heidi said. "Well, I... I guess that's OK." Ridges appeared on her forehead as her eyes volleyed back and forth between Lydia's and mine. "Isn't it?"

By the questioning look on her face, we knew she was asking permission to go with Matthew alone. In her mind, that would constitute a date. While Heidi knew many boys from Dorks Club and church youth group, she never had a boyfriend. She had gone on group dates to the movies and on youth group outings, but she had never been alone with a boy. We never set dating rules for Heidi, as we had with Katie, which Katie ignored anyway.

"I'm sure the two of you can manage by yourselves," Lydia said, nodding at Heidi, trying to assure her. Then she turned to Matthew and motioned to the duffle bags.

"Do you think you can handle both of those?"

"Yes, Mrs. Richards," Matthew said, slinging the bags over his shoulder as if they were filled with feathers.

78

Lydia and I watched through the picture window as Heidi and Matthew walked down the sidewalk toward the church.

"I think Heidi is in love," Lydia said with a sigh.

I squeezed Lydia's hand. "I *know* Matthew is."

"Did you figure that out by yourself or did he have to tell you?"

I lifted her hand to my mouth and kissed it. "I refuse to answer on the grounds that it might make me look stupid."

Lydia let out a chuckle, then turned and slid her arms around my waist and brought her face close to mine. "Remember when we first fell in love?"

"The shiver running down my back tells me I do."

"Remember our first kiss?"

"You mean the one in front of your apartment? In the soft light of the hallway? When I eased toward you, like this? And you eased toward me? ...Yeah, like that... And our lips touched, like this... and I couldn't imagine life getting any better."

"We had a wonderful courtship," Lydia said.

"Had?"

She smiled and kissed me. "You know what I mean."

"Mmmm."

"I hope Heidi has as wonderful an experience falling in love as we've had."

"She has time…" I said.

Lydia leaned forward and rested her head on my shoulder. We both knew Heidi's health was deteriorating. Her sugar levels were harder to control, she was tired most of the time, blood work from her previous stay in the hospital left doctors concerned about her liver function.

"I think falling in love will do Heidi good," Lydia strained to say.

"You're right," I said. "And what's to stop her?"

We swayed in each other's arms as the sun slipped down and away. Lydia lifted her head, revealing tears on her cheeks. "Heidi thinks no one will want her, because of her health."

I forced a smile to hide the groaning inside. "Others don't think that way. Matthew certainly doesn't."

"I know," Lydia said, with hope in her voice. "You should have seen the moonstruck look on his face last week when he and Heidi talked in the kitchen."

"He asked me tonight if he could take her out to see a movie."

Lydia brightened up and ran her finger slowly across my lips. "And I thought *you* were shy, taking five weeks before you'd even kiss me," she said. "What did he do when you said yes?"

"I didn't say yes."

"What?"

"I told him he should ask *her*, and that it was OK with me."

"Oh… Well, I wonder if he'll ask her tonight."

"I don't think so," I said. "He asked me to ask her for him."

"You're kidding," Lydia said in surprise. "Matthew could get a date with any girl at school. With all he has going for him—looks, brains, talent—are you telling me he doesn't have the confidence to ask Heidi out?"

I laughed and rested my forehead against Lydia's. "Take it from someone who knows: it takes a lot of courage to ask a beautiful woman for a date."

Lydia and I were snuggled on the couch in front of the TV watching *Bonanza* when Heidi and Matthew returned to the house a half-hour early.

"Back so soon?" I said.

"I was feeling tired so I asked Matthew to walk me home."

"Do you want to watch TV with us?" Lydia asked. "Your father could make some popcorn."

"I have a better idea," I said, looking up at Matthew and Heidi. "Why don't *you two* make the popcorn?"

Heidi turned to Matthew. "Can you help me, and stay for some TV?"

His widened eyes said *yes* before his mouth could open, and the two made their way to the kitchen. We turned down the TV and listened to them clanging pans in search of a suitable one. We could hear their voices, but couldn't make out what they were saying. But as the popping grew louder, we heard Heidi laughing hysterically, and how great it was to hear *that* again.

They returned from the kitchen and put a big bowl of popcorn and four smaller bowls on the coffee table.

Lydia and I sat up on the couch as Heidi scooped popcorn into the small bowls and handed them out.

Heidi and Matthew sat in separate chairs across the coffee table from us, and Lydia briefly explained what had happened so far on the show: "A beautiful, young lady was blinded in a riding accident. She's staying at the Cartwright's ranch."

We all munched popcorn and watched Little Joe fall in love with the woman.

Later that evening while I sat in the living room reading the newspaper, I heard Heidi cough upstairs and close the bathroom door. A few minutes later, I heard her walk back to her room, and I went upstairs to make sure everything was all right. I tapped lightly on her door, cracked it open a bit, and peeked in. Heidi was rolled up in a ball under the covers, facing the wall, her back toward me.

"Are you OK, Little Princess?"

She rolled around under the covers, reformed into a ball, and hugged the blankets under her chin. "I love you, Daddy."

By the way she said it, I knew something was weighing on her. "I love you too," I said. "Are you OK?"

"Yes, I was just thinking."

"About what?"

"Oh, just things."

"Did *things* go well at the shelter?"

"Yeah—oh, and Mrs. Madison is back from the hospital. She wanted me to thank you and Mom for the card."

"Did you get everything to the church OK?"

"Yes. Matthew was a great help."

"Matthew is a fine young man," I said.

Heidi sighed. "He is, Daddy… he really is…"

My heart took on a warm smile.

"Matthew and I had a little talk downstairs while you and mom were up here getting ready," I said. "He asked me something I've never been asked before."

Heidi hugged the blankets closer. "What did he say?"

"He said he'd like to take you to a movie. And he asked me to ask you if that would be OK."

A slight smile played across Heidi's face. "Yes, Daddy, that would be OK." And as I was about to back out the door, I heard her add softly: "That would be *wonderful*."

After that movie at the Lake Theatre, Matthew became a frequent dinner guest at our house, and he and Heidi started spending a lot more time together.

And as Lydia had predicted, Heidi's health took a turn for the better; the three of us caught colds in February of that year, and to our surprise, Heidi was the first to recover. The shading under in her eyes disappeared, and she took on the energy of her junior-high days.

Never underestimate the power of love. If someone could put that power in pill form, they'd have the best selling medicine of all time.

Heidi's Hope

79

Two weeks before her 17th birthday, the weather turned mild and Heidi rode her bike over to Thatcher Woods to walk along the paths and pray. On the way home, she was cut off by a pickup truck that suddenly switched lanes. The driver hadn't seen her. Heidi slammed the brakes just before the collision that threw her over the handlebars and into the bed of the pickup.

The driver—ironically, an Emergency Room doctor— jumped out to help. Heidi was conscious but groggy, and said her neck and right side hurt. The doctor offered to take her to the ER. Heidi told him she was fine and that she lived just a block away, but when she seemed unable to get her bearings, the doctor insisted she get medical treatment.

We arrived at West Suburban Hospital within fifteen minutes of receiving the call. Heidi was alert, but still confused. We registered, and they sent her to x-ray for films of her head, neck, and chest. The head and neck were fine. The chest film and examination suggested only a bruised rib. The neurological exam was negative, but based on her confusion, the doctor suspected she suffered a mild concussion.

When the doctor found out Heidi was diabetic, he wanted to admit her to the hospital. "At least overnight," he told us, "just as an extra precaution."

Lydia stayed with Heidi while I drove back to the house to pick up some things for her stay. By the time I got back to the hospital, Heidi was already in her room, in bed, praying with her mother.

I panicked, thinking they had been given bad news. I rushed over to the bed and put my hand on Heidi's shoulder. She opened her eyes.

"Hi, Daddy," she said with a cheery smile. Lydia looked up too.

"Is everything OK?" I asked.

"Yes," Heidi said. "We were just thanking the Lord that nothing more serious happened."

Shortly afterward, a nurse and an orderly showed up with a wheelchair to take Heidi to x-ray again. Heidi told us she would be fine and that we should go home. We asked if we could bring anything back for her.

Yes," she said, "Bring Zaccheus."

It was only 8:15 PM, but Lydia and I were exhausted by the time we got home and plopped on the bed. I pried my shoes off with my feet and felt prepared enough to retire for the night, lying on my stomach, fully clothed. But then Lydia sighed and said in a low voice: "Zaccheus."

My eyes barely opened before they closed again.

"Tomorrow," I moaned.

A minute passed and Lydia sighed a second time. "Can you get him now?" she mumbled. "So we won't forget?"

"OK," I said, but apparently my body wasn't listening. Another minute passed.

"Please, John?"

I rolled over and sat up on the edge of the bed just as a passing bus squealed its brakes in front of the house, sending enough of a shiver through me to get me on my feet.

"Just grab him and set him by the back door," Lydia muttered. "We can't forget him then."

I shuffled toward the doorway and almost tripped over the basket of laundry that had been abandoned earlier when the hospital called. I dragged myself through the hall and opened Heidi's door that greeted me with its usual squeak. Her room was clean and organized. The sweet smell of potpourri hung in the air.

A herd of stuffed animals had gathered on Heidi's bed, waiting for their best friend. Zaccheus was among them, begging with opened arms for me to pick him up.

Zaccheus was the most cherished of Heidi's three bears. The little blue one that Grandma made, the one who survived two surgeries to repair his seams, the frailest of the three—which alone would have been reason enough for Heidi to favor him.

I picked him up and whispered so the other animals wouldn't hear and feel left out. That's what Heidi would've done, and the type of thing I do when I'm half-asleep.

"Zaccheus?" I said. "Heidi wants to see you."

As we turned to go out the door, my eye caught the bright letters of a new addition to Heidi's board. At the top it said:

HEIDI'S HOPE: To hear Jesus say,
"Well done, thou good and faithful servant."

I stood there, reading it over and over again, out loud. Just eleven words, only fourteen syllables, yet the more I thought about Heidi's hope, the more I wondered how I ever got to be her dad.

As I was wondering, my eyes drifted down to another addition, at the bottom of her board.

In small blue letters, it said:

heidi's wish: a baby blue volkswagen.

Suddenly, I had the closest thing I'll probably ever get to an inspired idea. "Zaccheus," I said with a grin, "let me show you how to use a phone book."

Heidi's Wish

80

I carried Zaccheus into the kitchen and set him on the table, then reached over and grabbed the phone book from the shelf. Zaccheus leaned against the fruit bowl and watched attentively as I turned to the business listings.

"It's easy," I said. "We're looking for a *Volkswagen,* which is an *automobile."*

I flipped through the pages starting from the back, passing *pizza, homebuilders,* and *dog groomers* along the way.

"Ah-hah! *Automobiles!* See how simple this is, Zaccheus? OK, now what do we want? *Service?* No-o-o-o. *Parts?* Sorry, not today. Ah, here we go, *Dealers! Volkswagen Dealers!"*

"OK, now the fun part. Can you grab a pen for me from the drawer?"

Zaccheus just stared, dumbfounded, probably wondering how I found the section so fast; it would have taken him forever.

"Never mind," I said. "I'll get the pen. Help yourself to a piece of fruit."

I grabbed a pencil and returned to the chair. None of the fruit was missing.

"OK, let's find some local dealers." I circled three names and numbers, then picked up the phone.

None of those dealers had anything in baby blue.

I glanced at my watch. 8:30. The library was open until nine. Zaccheus watched me put on a light jacket. "I'll be right back," I told him.

Forty minutes later, I showed Zaccheus a piece of paper with the names and numbers of a dozen metropolitan-area Volkswagen dealers scribbled on it. Strangely enough, a piece of fruit *was* missing from the bowl, but I didn't have time to think about it then.

I dialed the first number and talked to Dan, who told me they were already closed, but that he'd stick around if I came down right away. I asked him about baby blue. "We got every color you can imagine," he told me. "Hurry down. Let's pick something out."

It sounded like a tune I'd heard many times before. "Dan, it has to be baby blue."

"We got blue," he assured me.

"*Baby* blue?"

There was a long pause before Dan said, "They stopped making baby blue. It's not a popular color. But hurry down now and I'll fix you up with a good deal."

I thanked him anyway and said goodbye, just as Lydia walked into the kitchen, nibbling on a pear. She leaned over, kissed my cheek, and licked off the juice.

"I heard you leave. Where'd you go?"

"To the library."

"Why?"

"To look up Volkswagen dealers."

Lydia looked down at the bear. "Was this your idea, Zaccheus?"

I told Lydia what Heidi wrote on her board. Lydia gasped and cupped her hands over her mouth. "Wouldn't it be wonderful if we could get her one," she said.

"We *are* going to get her one."

"What about watching expenses?"

In a brief swap of roles, I grinned at her and said, "Sometimes, you just gotta have faith."

81

Two days before Heidi's birthday, I found a used '67 baby blue Volkswagen in the classifieds. And for just $850, I saved it from being repossessed from a spoiled teenager whose father decided the kid should learn how things work in the real world.

While Heidi was at school, I drove the car home and picked up Lydia, who wanted to take it for a spin herself until she saw the stick shift.

"Does Heidi drive stick?" Lydia asked.

"Sure, Matthew taught her."

We drove around Oak Park, careful to avoid the high school area. Lydia thought the engine was going to explode whenever I downshifted. Maybe that's why she declined my offer of driving lessons.

We parked the car two blocks away from Matthew's house and put the key under the floor mat, as I had arranged with Matthew. He was to pick up the car and park it in his garage until Heidi's birthday.

We walked the eight blocks home under a mild and sunny sky, talking all the way about Heidi's surprise.

When we reached our porch, I pulled an unexpected letter from the mailbox and looked at the return address.

"Sedgwick, Baker & Hunt?" I muttered under my breath. "They're still around? I wonder if Rich Staler is still there…"

I opened the envelope and unfolded the letter. "Oh, I guess he is… Hmmm… President! Why am I surprised? He's a good man."

I had just finished the first sentence—*It has been too long, my friend*—when Lydia let out a scream and pointed to the third paragraph.

"John! They're offering you a job!"

My eyes leaped down the page to where it said, *"I can think of no one better to open the Chicago office than you…"*

Lydia squealed and kissed my cheek.

"This is wonderful," she said.

I read the entire letter. The salary was $5,000 lower than what I had been making at Braxton-Becker, but because it was a new office, I'd be able to bring in my own people. Peter and Tony immediately came to mind. "Yes, this *is* wonderful!"

"An answer to prayer," Lydia said with tears in her eyes. "Heidi will be so excited."

I drew a deep breath and thought about the job and about the Volkswagen parked eight blocks away.

"Wait," I said. "Let's not tell Heidi about the job yet. Let's wait until after she gets her birthday present. I don't want anything competing with *that* surprise."

82

We could not have asked for a better March 21, 1968. The sun rose over the cloudless equinox sky on its way to warm the day to sixty-seven degrees. Heidi had already been up for over an hour when I woke at 6 AM. The open door to the attic told me where she was and what she was doing.

I tiptoed up the grouchy steps and found her slumped in front of the window, facing the rising sun. Her marked-up Bible lay in her lap, opened to Psalm 19, and her fingers rested beneath words she had underlined in gold long ago:

> *The heavens declare the glory of God;*
> *and the firmament sheweth his handywork.*

Not a sound came from her slightly opened mouth as she sipped orange sunlight through the window. Her olive skin glowed. Her ebony hair took on a morning shine. Her face radiated all the beauty of her mother and grandmother.

I eased beside her and wondered what she was dreaming.

Was she soft on the trails of Thatcher Woods? Or off on a prayer walk at school?

Was she comforting children on the wards? Or serving the homeless at church?

Was she on the porch with Matthew? In the midst of a goodnight kiss, under a moon-lit sky?

Was she even on the earth? In the midst of her reading and praying, had she ascended into the heavens, leaving her hand frozen to the page while her spirit soared high above the clouds, declaring with all God's creation:

GLORY, GLORY, GLORY TO GOD !

I wrapped my arm around her shoulders, and sang in a soft voice:

> ♫ *Praise God from whom all blessings flow;*
> *Praise him all creatures here below…*

Her eyes eased opened, and she whispered along:

> ♫ *Praise him above ye heavenly host;*
> *Praise Father, Son, and Holy Ghost.*

"Amen," she said, caressing my hand. "I must have dozed off. I came up to read and pray, and I… just dozed off."

"What were you reading?" I asked *"Genealogies?"*

She chuckled and pointed to the underlined passage. "No, Daddy… here, Psalm 19: *'The Heavens declare the glory of God.'* I was dreaming about all the wonderful things God has made. I saw his creation, gathered in worship. Things in heaven and things on earth. Valleys and mountains; plains and forests; rivers, lakes and oceans; the sun, moon and stars; the farthest galaxies—all declaring God's Glory to the world, in every language and tongue, leading all creatures on earth to sing in praise, and all the trees and flowers to dance for joy."

She was talking like her old self again, like she did before her growing frailty started wearing her down and filling her with doubt. I drew her nearer and combed my fingers through her long, beautiful hair.

"Maybe I don't understand your faith," I said. "but I think I understand your hope. And for what it's worth, I've never met anyone so *full* of hope, and committed to it, as you."

Heidi lifted her head and kissed my cheek.

"Thank you, Daddy," she said in a whisper.

When we stepped downstairs to the kitchen, Lydia was putting breakfast on the table.

"I was just about to call you down," she said.

She handed me a platter of bacon and eggs, then gave Heidi a big hug. "Happy birthday, Sweetheart!"

Halfway through breakfast the phone rang. Lydia looked at Heidi and smiled. "I'll bet that's Matthew."

Heidi ran and picked up the handset, and we heard Matthew and his parents singing happy birthday over the phone, bringing a big grin and blushed cheeks to Heidi's face.

For the next few minutes, Heidi twisted the phone cord around her fingers as she talked with Matthew, sometimes in a whisper.

Before she hung up, she turned to the side and blew a kiss into the mouthpiece. "And I, you," she said in a soft voice, not that we were listening.

She was still blushing when she got back to the table.

"So what's going on?" Lydia asked.

"The Karlssons have invited us over for ice cream."

"Ice cream?" I said, acting surprised, even though Lydia and I had set the whole thing up with Matthew and his parents.

"Yes, for my birthday. Two o'clock."

"Speaking of birthdays," Lydia said, handing a jewelry box to Heidi, "you better open your present before you go running off."

"Is it—"

"Yes," Lydia answered.

Heidi opened the box and held up the dove necklace. And she choked back tears when she opened the card and saw the words: *Well Done...*

"Someday," Lydia said softly, "He will tell you himself."

83

Heidi returned at noon after visiting kids in the pediatrics ward at the hospital. And after a quick nap, she joined us in the kitchen for a light lunch.

"It's so beautiful outside," she said, grabbing a sandwich.

"Maybe we should *walk* to the Karlssons'," I suggested.

We left the house at one-thirty and walked west on Chicago Avenue, past Kenilworth and Woodbine to Forest, where we turned south and then west onto Erie.

When I looked down the block, I saw the Volkswagen parked across the street from Matthew's house. I saw Heidi eyeing it too, but she didn't say a word, not even when we passed it just before turning up the sidewalk leading to the Karlssons' porch.

Matthew waved from the window before he and his parents, Peder and Edna, came outside as we walked up the steps.

"Welcome, welcome, and happy birthday, Heidi!" Edna said, beaming.

Peder extended his hand. "Good to see you again, John."

Edna took in a deep breath and looked to the sky. "Seeing that the weather is so nice, would it be OK to have our birthday treat here on the porch?"

The vote was unanimous.

"Good," Edna said. "Matthew, why don't you and Heidi bring out the tray from the kitchen."

When the kids had gone inside, the four of us huddled on the porch. Peder passed me the keys and said: "She's cleaned and waxed, all gassed up, and ready to roll."

"You did a beautiful job," Lydia said, looking across the street. "It looks brand new."

Edna nodded. "Matthew spent hours on it."

"A labor of love," Peder added.

We sat down at a table set up for the occasion, leaving the two seats facing the street for Heidi and Matthew. The kids brought out the tray and Edna passed around bowls of ice cream and vanilla wafers.

Matthew held up a heaping spoonful and announced: "To the Birthday Girl!"

"Hear! Hear!"

As we ate and talked, I noticed Heidi's eyes jogging back and forth between her bowl and the light blue bug parked less than 100 feet away. When we finished eating, I twisted in my chair and looked over my shoulder.

"What do you keep peeking at?" I asked.

"Oh, nothing," Heidi said.

By this time, everyone had turned and was looking across the street.

"I think that little Volkswagen caught her attention," Matthew said. "She's been telling me for months how she's wanted one."

"You have?" I said.

Heidi blushed. "Well, yeah… it's even the color I want."

"It was there when I woke up this morning," Peder said.

I set my bowl down and stood up. "Let's get a closer look at it. Maybe Heidi can explain the big attraction."

We all got up—all except Heidi, who put her hands over her face to hide her embarrassment. Matthew reached over and tickled her. "Come on," he said. "Let's check it out."

We all paraded across the street and gathered around the car, leaving a wide-open space by the driver's door for Heidi.

"Look in and give us the tour," Lydia suggested. Heidi looked cautiously up and down the street and at the nearby house, then she grinned and leaned into the window, cupping her hands around her eyes as she surveyed the interior:

"Four-speed on the floor…AM/FM radio…bucket seats— Oh yeah, this is one fine automobile."

I leaned over and pulled on the handle. Heidi gasped when the door opened. "Daddy!"

"Why don't you get in and see how she feels," I said.

Heidi jolted back and looked up and down the street again. "You can't just open someone's car and get in!"

"It's not like we're stealing it." I said.

"Go ahead and try it, Sweetheart," Lydia pleaded.

Heidi's mouth dropped. "Mom, I can't believe you'd even suggest such a thing!"

"Look at how well kept it is," Edna said. "Obviously it's owned by someone who takes pride in the vehicle. Why would they mind if someone else admired their car enough to step inside?"

"I'm sure they wouldn't mind at all." Peder said.

Heidi looked at us as if we had all lost our minds. Lydia leaned in close and whispered in Heidi's ear, "Just get in, Honey. You don't want to embarrass the Karlssons."

I opened the door wider and nudged Heidi. And the five of us crowded around after she sat down in the driver's seat.

"Well, how does it feel?"

"I'm too frightened to feel anything," Heidi said, keeping her hands to herself, afraid to touch anything.

"Come on, just take a deep breath and relax."

She closed her eyes and tried to do so.

"That's good," I said. "Now let it out slowly."

Her face relaxed a bit.

"That's it… Now breathe in again… That's my girl…"

I quietly pulled the keys out of my pocket. "Now keep your eyes closed and pretend you're driving."

At first she hesitated, but then a smile came to her face as she lifted her hands and grabbed the steering wheel.

"If we could start this thing," I said, "would you take it around the block?"

Heidi popped open her eyes and looked at us. "Now *that* *would* get us arrested."

I held up the keys and passed them through the window. "Only if you press charges against yourself."

And with that, everyone outside yelled:

Happy Birthday, Heidi!

It took a few seconds for reality to sink in, then Heidi let out the loudest scream I ever heard.

"Ahhhhhhhh! Someone, hop in back!" she said. "I'll take you around the block!" Then she motioned to Matthew and patted the front passenger seat. "Get in!" she squealed. "I'll drive *you* for a change!"

Lydia and Edna jumped in the back seat. Heidi started the engine, dropped into first gear, and slowly let out the clutch. The car jerked a couple of times, then peeled away from the curb.

Five minutes later, Peder and I traded places with our wives. Matthew patted Heidi's hand as it rested on the stick shift. "Well done!" he hollered. "Let's go again!"

Heidi pulled away, flawlessly this time, screaming with joy like a child on Christmas morning.

"This is so cool," she said. "Thank you, Daddy!"

That moment—the wind in her hair, the surprise in her voice, her strength and confidence behind the wheel—is indelibly etched in my mind. It replays like a favorite movie every time I sit in the back seat of her car. Sometimes it comes to me when I'm in bed, about to drift off into sleep. It kisses me goodnight, and sends me off to dream about her journey through life, her adventure in faith, her struggle to live...

84

Heidi and her VW were inseparable. We half expected her to sleep in the back seat. After church on the Sunday after her birthday, Heidi picked up Matthew and drove west on Roosevelt Road, through the western suburbs, past Wheaton and Geneva, through the rural stretch leading to Cortland and DeKalb, past quaint country cemeteries and awakening fields that would host armies of soybeans and corn later that year.

And when autumn came, she drove Matthew to the Halsted Outdoor Theatre in Riverdale to see *Romeo and Juliet*, starring Leonard Whiting and the lovely Olivia Hussey—who was almost as pretty as Heidi, by Matthew's account.

On a more utilitarian note, Heidi used the car so that she, Matthew, and Martha could make weekly rounds at Loyola and Children's Memorial, to encourage *the little lambs*, as Heidi called them.

With the car, she also was able to increase the ranks of her volunteer force by offering rides to kids who otherwise had no way to get to assignments. At one time, she had forty kids from school—mostly Dorks, but over a dozen Doopers, and even a handful of Zombies—all organized and working at the homeless shelter, visiting hospitals and nursing homes, and picking up items for food and clothing drives.

Speaking of kids from school: in accordance with her seventh directive—*Share God's Love With Others*—Heidi started mingling with the Zombies who hung out at Scoville Park.

She listened to them rant and rave about the government, the Vietnam War, and the need to legalize marijuana. Then she told them about the Sermon on the Mount, the love of God, and their need of Jesus. At first, they thought she was joking. When they realized she wasn't, a few walked away, but many stayed and listened, especially after Heidi told them how Jesus stood up to the authorities in Jerusalem.

As word got around, more and more Zombies showed up week after week to hear her. After the police came twice, thinking the kids were up to no good, Heidi knew they wouldn't be able to meet in the park much longer, so she handed out paperback Bibles one night and said,

"I thank God that so many of you come back every week—even those of you who are honest critics. But our growing numbers have attracted complaints."

"Let the pigs complain!" someone shouted.

"The police are only doing their job," Heidi said. "And when they see us orderly, they leave us alone. Still, it's time to move on. Gonner Church has offered us a room where we can meet, but I know many of you will not set foot in a church. That's why I'm handing out these Bibles. They are my gifts to you, in case I don't see you again.

"I hope you'll read your copy," Heidi went on to say, waving her own Bible high over head. "In it, you'll find everything of importance we've talked about, and much more. It's the most important book you'll ever own."

Heidi was right: most of the kids didn't show up at the church the following week. But those who *did,* shared in Heidi's zeal, and their numbers grew over the next four years as they sang, studied the Bible, and prayed together every Friday night.

From the Mountains, to the Valleys

85

Regardless of all she had done, Heidi felt it was never enough, and this weighed heavily on her. It was a recurring theme in her diary which she kept open on her nightstand for anyone to read—even those parts I would have hidden, had I written them.

Heidi told me she didn't care who read her diary because she knew she couldn't hide her feelings from the Lord. "And if the Lord knows," she said, "what difference does it make if others know I struggle with feelings of inadequacy?"

Interestingly enough, as the weight of her struggle grew, so did the number of people who became aware of her efforts to help others.

At Heidi's high school graduation, officials made their annual plea to parents and friends to hold their applause until all the graduates received their diplomas.

Yeah, right.

One by one, as the names of the class of '69 were called, graduates took their diplomas and shook the principal's hand. There were the usual short, spontaneous outbreaks for the popular kids, and for the kids with boisterous relatives.

I wasn't surprised when applause broke out for Matthew, he being captain of the football team and having just delivered the funniest valedictorian speech I had ever heard.

What *did* surprise me was the sustained applause and cheers that broke out when Heidi's name was called. People stood up—graduates, undergraduates, and parents alike. Even the principal broke his own protocol and said over the P.A., "It sounds like you have quite a following, Heidi," which brought a second round of cheers and applause.

After the ceremony, we popped out the cameras and shot photos of Heidi and Matthew in their caps and gowns. Heidi wanted a photo with as many Dorks as possible. We got over a hundred kids in the shot, and had it blown up into a poster that Heidi hung on her wall, a timeless reminder of a happy passage in life.

She had graduated, she had a boyfriend, she had a car, she was appreciated by people she didn't even know.

She looked to be on the mountaintop.

But after her graduation, she started coming down. She tired more easily, and found it harder to control her sugar levels.

It didn't help that Matthew was registered to attend the University of Illinois in downstate Urbana while Heidi was set to attend the UICC campus in Chicago. Matthew had over a half-dozen, full-scholarship offers from big-name schools across the country. One reason he picked Urbana was because it was close enough for him to drive up to be with Heidi, if only for the weekends.

Then in July, Matthew surprised us all when he announced he had changed plans and decided to attend UICC. He made the announcement in Heidi's hospital room during one of her week-long stays that year.

It was an emotional time for us all. Heidi protested in tears, knowing how much Matthew wanted to attend Urbana.

They carpooled to school together, with Matthew doing most of the driving. Though Heidi was out sick at least two weeks every quarter, she managed to finish her freshman year with a B average. And after resting over the summer, she got an A in every class during her first quarter as a sophomore, and continued to do well in the winter quarter until she caught pneumonia and landed in the hospital again.

Had you met Heidi on the street, you would not have known how sick she was. Yes, she was thin, but not like some her age who based their standards on half-starved models and cover girls. Yes, she tired easily, but she hid it well; a smile was usually on her face, and she wore the inherited beauty of her mother and grandmother with natural elegance.

However, those closest to her knew her drive was waning. With the help of Matthew and Martha, she was able to keep her army of volunteers active throughout the community, but she had little choice than to curtail her personal involvement with the down-and-out people she had grown to love.

Despite her failing health, Heidi refused to give up her visits with the kids at Children's Memorial. Every Saturday, Matthew drove her downtown so she could make her rounds, encouraging those who fought against hope, even as her own world grew darker.

Fender Bender

86

Over the summer of '72, Heidi drove her car only if no one else was available to drive. Lydia and I figured something was going on, and that Heidi would tell us in her own good time.

One mild day in August, she asked if I wanted to drive her to Wieboldt's in the Volkswagen so she could buy a sweatshirt. I told her I'd tag along, but only if she'd drive. She laughed and said, "Come on, how long has it been since you've driven a *real* car?"

When I told her I just wanted to be a passenger for a change, her face went blank, as if she was weighing something in her mind.

"OK," she finally said. "I'll drive."

We walked out of the house and into the dim garage. Heidi knocked over the garbage can on her way to the car. After buckling up, she reached back and over her head to turn on the interior light. Even with it on, she had to grope the controls to find the ignition switch.

"Your eyes must be thinking they're still out in the sun," I said.

She turned the key and brought the engine to life. And after squinting at the rear view mirror she said,

"How does it look back there?"

I looked back into the bright patch of sunlight.

"All clear."

She stepped on the clutch and slid the stick into reverse. As she inched out of the garage, her eyes volleyed between the mirrors until the sun hit the back window, filling the car with light. She slammed on the brake and checked the mirrors again, then continued to creep back until we were halfway out of the garage, giving me a clear view up both sides of the alley.

"How does it look now?" she said.

"It looks fine. My, you are one cautious driver today."

A nervous smile briefly lit her face. She turned the wheel and backed into the alley until the car faced south. Her eyes grew wide as she stared out the windshield, wiggled the stick into first gear, and let out the clutch.

She stayed in first all the way to the end of the alley, letting the engine roar before she finally stepped off the gas and onto the clutch. This was not the same driver who raced around the block on her 17th birthday.

"Are you OK?" I asked, careful not to sound concerned.

"I guess I'm tired and not adjusted to the light," she said.

I took off my sunglasses and handed them to her. "Would these help?"

She turned toward me and squinted, trying to refocus her eyes.

"Oh, no thanks. I'm fine. I'll just take it slow for a while."

Even when we were on the main streets, she stayed in second gear until the engine's whine was too loud to ignore. I rolled down the window and stuck my elbow out, trying to look more relaxed than I was.

And even when she was less than a half-block from her turn and traveling faster than I would have been, I didn't say anything—until she entered the intersection.

"Uh, wasn't that your turn?"

She gasped, stomped on the clutch, and readied her other foot above the brake.

"It's OK," I said. "Just go down another block and we'll circle around."

She froze down on the clutch and coasted, her quick and shallow breaths revealing her near state of panic. At the next corner she downshifted into second, and even though she fought the steering wheel with all her strength, she still made too wide a turn onto the narrow street.

I don't think she even saw the parked car.

"Hit your brake!" I shouted.

87

Heidi pounced on the clutch and brake pedals. The tires screamed. I heard the rush of air gushing in and out of her mouth, and saw the frightened look on her face as she strained to see out the front window.

Just before the car came to a stop, it lightly bumped into a red, '69 Mustang convertible. We jerked forward, then back into our seats. Heidi gasped for air, her hands frozen around the steering wheel, her eyes filled with uncertainty.

"It's OK," I assured her, putting my arm around her shoulder. "It's OK."

I stayed with her in the car as a young man rushed out of the nearby house, down the porch steps, toward the Mustang.

"It's OK," I assured her again. "I'll go talk with him."

By the time I got out, the young man was already assessing the damage. As he did, the scowl on his face dissolved and his tense arms relaxed. Heidi's left fender sported a slight dent. All the Mustang sported was a light blue smudge on the bumper, which the young man was able to rub out with some spit and his T-shirt.

"It could have been worse, huh?" I said.

The young man sighed in relief.

"I guess so, Mr. Richards."

Before I could ask how he knew my name, he motioned to the Volkswagen. "Is Heidi OK?"

"Oh, you know Heidi?"

The young man laughed. "Everyone knows Heidi."

He extended his right hand to me. "I'm Randy Bollner."

"Ahhhh, you were co-captain of the football team. I've heard Heidi and Matthew talking about you."

"Good things, I hope."

"Of course," I said. We both laughed. And I glanced over and saw Heidi break into a nervous smile when she heard our laughter.

Randy looked her way again. "Is she OK?"

"She's a bit shaken up, but I think she'll feel better once she finds out she didn't damage your car."

Randy walked over to Heidi's door, tapped on the glass, and motioned for her to roll down the window. Then he bent over and said, "How are you doing?"

"Randy, is that you?" she asked. "Sorry about your car. I'll pay for any damage."

"No damage done, just a paint smudge that I've already wiped off."

Heidi broke into tears.

"Don't cry, Heidi," Randy said. "It was nothing."

When she didn't stop crying, he asked, "Are you hurt?"

Heidi caught her breath and sighed. "No," she said. "I'm just tired." Then she started weeping again.

I walked over and opened the door, took her hand and helped her out of the car. She buried her head into my shoulder and cried as I rocked her gently back and forth.

"No harm done, Heidi," Randy assured her again as he slowly backed away and headed up to his house.

"It's OK, it's OK," I said in a soft voice. "No one was hurt, no damage done to Randy's car. Only a slight dent on yours. We'll get it fixed."

"Will you drive home, Daddy?" she asked. "I don't want to drive anymore."

I could feel her trembling.

"Honey, I think you should drive; it will restore your confidence. Don't think about it. Just get behind the wheel and drive home."

"I can't."

"Of course you can," I said.

"Please…"

I kissed the top of her head and stroked her hair.

"It's less than a mile," I said. "You can take the side streets if you want."

She eventually settled down and nodded her head in my shoulder. I helped her into the car and kissed her cheek, then walked around and got in. As I buckled up, she rolled up her window and turned on the heater, even though it was a comfortable seventy-four degrees outside.

She shivered all the way home, driving slowly and unsteadily down deserted side streets and alleys.

Less than a block away from the house, she wept and whimpered, "But *why*, Father?"

I knew she wasn't talking to me.

She pulled up to the garage and stopped.

"Only a few more feet," I said.

She slipped into first and let the clutch out until the car lunged into the dark space. Seconds later she slammed the brake hard, stopping the engine and bending our bodies forward as the car jerked to a halt.

We sat a few moments in silence. Then she leaned into the steering wheel and started weeping again.

I softly rubbed her shoulder, "You did well. It's all behind you now. Everything's OK."

"I'm not OK," she said softly. "I'm tired and cold and I—"

"You're just a bit shaken, that's all."

"No," she said. "I'm getting worse. I'm tired and cold most of the time. And I… I…" She lifted her hand and wiped tears from her cheeks.

"What, little Princess?" I said. "Just tell me. What's been bothering you so much lately?"

Her mouth was trembling when she turned to me.

"Daddy…" she whimpered, "I'm losing my sight."

And with that, Heidi sighed in relief, as if a huge burden had been lifted from her shoulders. She wiped her face with her hands, then leaned back in her seat and took several deep breaths.

I couldn't speak. Her words hit me like a truck. I didn't know what to say, what to do. I just sat there and stroked her hair until I worked up enough composure to ask if she wanted me to help her into the house.

"Just hold me for a few minutes," she said, leaning into my side.

I held my tears until late that night, when I walked to the garage and climbed into the back seat of the slightly dented baby-blue Volkswagen that Heidi would never drive again. I wailed, as I had never done before, or since. It was the second worst day of my life.

88

Heidi had known for six months that her eyes were failing. She had talked with Dr. Nichols at church and had seen a specialist on her own. She asked Dr. Nichols to keep her condition confidential, which he was legally obligated to do since Heidi was over eighteen.

She didn't want us to worry, especially since there was little that could be done back then.

Now that her secret was out, Heidi made the most of every moment. She and Matthew went for unhurried walks in Thatcher Woods and along the Chicago lakefront. They drove to Indiana Dunes State Park and walked barefoot along the water's edge, when reflections off the lake could still send sparkles into Heidi's darkening world.

Leah flew up from Atlanta the week before Christmas, 1972. We picked her up at O'Hare mid-morning in a heavy, steady snow. I played chauffer while the triplets born decades apart rode in the back seat, Heidi in the middle. The rearview mirror revealed a wide grin under Heidi's blank eyes as she leaned against her grandmother.

Leah was not dressed for the weather, wearing only a light coat and no boots. As the girls chattered in the back seat, I wondered how we'd get Leah into the house through all the snow. In the rush to get to the airport, we left the sidewalks to fend for themselves, and I was sure there would be two-foot drifts standing by to welcome Leah to The Pink House.

I had played with the idea of *carrying* Leah into the house, but when I pulled over and announced our arrival, the walks were clear. And Matthew, wearing a parka and shouldering a shovel, stepped down from the porch and headed toward the car.

Leah gasped when she saw him. "Who is this tall, handsome, strapping young man walking our way?" she said.

Heidi giggled like a school girl. "Is it Matthew?"

"It is," Lydia said. "Bless his heart—he cleaned the walks!"

"Land sakes, Heidi," Leah said in grand, southern-belle fashion. "That's some man you've got there, Honey!"

Unaware of his favorable review, Matthew opened the door, leaned down, and offered Leah his hand. "Welcome to snow town, Mrs. Bowman."

Leah reached up. "Thank you, young man."

The wisps of snow that flew into the car could not blow the smile off Heidi's face as she turned in Matthew's direction. "Take good care of my Grandma," she said.

Lydia dipped into her purse, pulled out her keys, and handed them to Matthew. "Let yourselves in. We'll pull around to the back."

By the time we spun and swaggered around the corners and plowed our way through the alley, Matthew had already gotten Leah into the house and was clearing the sidewalk to the garage. He finished the path and harpooned the snow with the shovel just as we pulled in.

When the car stopped, he was there to open Heidi's door. "Hey, Gorgeous," he said, slightly out of breath. "Need an escort?"

He leaned in and took Heidi's outstretched hand. She got out and stood up, her lips quivering from the cold. When Matthew took off his parka and wrapped it around her tiny frame, I was reminded of Lydia in her oversized stadium jacket years earlier.

Heidi reached toward Matthew. "Warm me up," she said, her teeth chattering. Matthew reached into the parka and drew her forward. She sunk her face into his chest and thrashed her arms playfully around him while Lydia and I stood to the side.

Matthew looked at us over his shoulder, wearing a sheepish grin. "Just warming her up," he said.

Lydia smiled. "We'll go heat up some milk. Can you join us for hot cocoa, Matthew?"

"Sounds great, Mrs. Richards."

Lydia and I walked out of the garage, and when I turned around to close the service door, I saw Heidi lift her chin, her lips slightly parted, searching for Matthew's.

"Let's go," Lydia whispered, tugging my arm. "It's too crowded out here..."

89

Leah's visit led to a spiritual summit for the triplets. Leah, her body set one hour ahead of ours, got up early each morning and had breakfast on the table by the time the rest of us joined her in the kitchen. I'd have a quick bite before shuffling off to work while the triplets, dressed in robes and slippers, read their Bibles out loud and prayed at the table.

Heidi called the Christmas of '72 a time of still waters, a restoring of the soul. She glowed in it—even more so when Matthew joined the summit during the second week of Leah's stay.

Seasonal energies were redirected that year. The tree was not as extravagantly adorned as it had been in years past, but much attention went into the arrangement of the nativity set on the mantle.

There were more shepherds and animals, and a bigger stable to accommodate them all. It was the year we installed a spotlight in the ceiling to shine down on the manger, as if it were that ancient star the wise men followed long ago.

They held three services at church that Christmas Eve. We attended the first, arriving twenty minutes early and taking a seat near the front, beneath a giant balsawood angel suspended from the ceiling.

Out of the corner of my eye, I saw Heidi, beaming and holding tightly onto Matthew's hand. It was the first time Matthew had been to a service in almost fifteen years.

Musicians filled the sanctuary with songs of the season, and voices echoed the angelic choir that brought Good News to the shepherds living outside Bethlehem 2,000 years ago.

"Christmas should be pronounced CHRISTmas," the pastor said a half-hour later, his voice resonating throughout the crowded but silent church. *"For Christmas is about the Christ, who came to earth to die, to rise again, and to take away the sins of the world.*

"The word 'Christ' means 'anointed one.' He is known by other names as well—like Immanuel, which means: 'God with us.'

"Today, we wait for Christ to return to earth. And every year as we wait, we celebrate Christmas in remembrance of that earlier visit two millennia ago, when He came in humble surroundings, in the form of a baby, and was given the name Jesus..."

After the sermon, the choir and orchestra performed in the background as families were invited to the platform to receive a blessing.

Heidi leaned against Matthew and asked him to join us.

We went forward and knelt in front of the Communion table. Leah was at one end, then Lydia, me, Heidi, and Matthew. The pastor worked his way around the table, finally coming to the five of us. He leaned over and spread out his arms, cupping Leah's shoulder with one hand and Matthew's with the other. Before the pastor prayed, he asked if we had any specific requests or concerns.

I thought of my two girls, and whispered their names:
"Heidi... Katie..."

Heidi squeezed my hand. I turned and saw a gentle smile on her face, her blank eyes staring off in the distance as if she were looking out over still waters—still waters I *longed* to see as I thought about my girls again, and hoped beyond hope.

Last Man Out

90

We returned home to the smell of apple pie and a small mountain of gifts waiting under the tree. Lydia walked to the front door and pulled off the envelope she had taped there earlier, in case Katie dropped by to surprise us.

She hadn't.

We were opening presents when the phone rang.

Lydia picked up. A smile came to her face seconds later, and after listening a few moments she started bouncing up and down on her toes. "Tony, that's wonderful!" she said. "Here, let me put John on the line."

At the age of 55, Tony Stiller—the one-time mobster impersonator and the last of the *Flying Conquistadors*—told me in his deep, raspy voice: "John, you won't believe it, but I just dove off bachelor's bluff and am about to plop into the uncharted waters of marriage."

"You're kidding!" I said. "You old son-of-a-gun."

I wasn't surprised when he told me his fiancée was in her mid-20s. But I *was* surprised when he told me he had proposed to her *in a church*!

"I never figured you for the church type," I said.

"I'm not," Tony replied. "But as I got to know this girl over the past two weeks and found out she was as religious as she was beautiful, I figured going to church was a small price to pay. Are you following me here, John?"

I laughed, and Tony playfully chided me over the phone. "Yeah, go ahead and laugh, Mr. Religion. But if my memory serves me right, my situation ain't much different from what you had going with Lydia when *you* got hitched."

He had me on that one.

"And look," he said, "in addition to Lydia, now you got Heidi, who'd probably be declared a saint if she was Catholic. Two Bible scholars live with you John, and you probably don't even know who was at the First Supper."

"You mean the *Last* Supper?"

"Whatever! Listen John, you guys gotta help me!"

I chuckled, *under* my breath this time as I thought of my own antics back when I courted Lydia: searching the Bible for her name, trying to come up with clever prayers, living in fear she'd discover our spiritual disparity and dump me.

"OK, Tony. What do you need us to do?"

"Well, not so much you, John," he said. "I was thinking more along the lines of Heidi and Lydia. You see, tonight at church, some high school kid sang a song. Uh, what was it... Oh yeah—'Ave Maria'—ever hear of it?"

"Yes."

"The kid wasn't bad. With the acoustics of that place— John, you should see it, it's beautiful... Uh, where was I?"

"Heidi... Lydia... kid singing... acoustics—"

"Yeah, *acoustics*! With the acoustics in that place, the kid sounded pretty good. Francine—that's her name, John—she got all choked up thinking about that song after the service. We stayed in our seats until everyone else left, then she told me she'd love to have that song at her wedding someday.

"And John," Tony went on to say, "I gotta tell ya... I was going to spring the ring on her later tonight, but I figured right then and there, *now* is the time to do it—in a religious setting. You know what I mean?"

"Yeah," I said, not so much in answer to *his* question as to the one I asked myself: "Were Lydia and I *this much* of a spiritual mismatch?"

Tony continued. "So I told her: 'My friend has a wife and daughter who sing like angels.' Then I showed her the ring and said, 'Maybe they could sing "Ave Maria" at *our* wedding.'"

Tony waited for me to respond, and when I didn't soon enough, he added: "She cried out and said YES! Isn't that great, John? We're getting married next spring!"

91

After a bumpy engagement (surprise!) Tony and Francine were married on April 7, 1973.

I remember so much about their wedding that it's strange I can't think of the name of the church. I know it was on the near-north side, within a mile of the lake. And when I pulled up to the front door to drop off Lydia, Heidi, and Matthew, the size of the building told us it wasn't an ordinary church. Built in the 1890s for who knows how much then, we could only guess how many millions it would cost to build today.

I parked the car in the side lot and entered two sets of heavy double-doors. The smell of freshly polished wood greeted me, as did a purple carpet pointing down a corridor adorned with religious art and a painting of the Pope.

Another set of doors opened to the cavernous sanctuary, to the sounds of voices and echoes. A vibrant host of colors splashed through stained glass, and the scent of fresh-cut flowers waltzed around my head when I reached the front and looked high into the dome above.

Lydia and Heidi were on the platform talking with the wedding planner who told them—in excruciating detail—

where they should sit, how they should walk up to the platform, and where they should stand for the duet.

I joined Matthew in the third row, and looked on as the planner consulted his watch every minute or so while he paced the platform making frantic comments about this, that, and the other thing.

Tony had warned us that the planner—Francine's mother's second cousin, once removed—was "totally anal" and nervous about bringing in unknown talent.

The planner turned back to Heidi and Lydia, who were still on the platform. "Can I hear you sing just a few measures?" he asked, chewing on a fingernail.

Lydia and Heidi cleared their throats, and even though they had not warmed up, a look of relief came over the planner's face as they sang *a cappella*. He applauded, then motioned for them to stop. "Wonderful!" he said with a big grin. "Francine will be so pleased."

Less than three hours later, after Tony and Francine faced each other and exchanged vows and rings, Lydia and Heidi stood up and approached the platform.

Probably fewer than a half-dozen of the two-hundred in attendance knew Heidi was blind. She and her mother walked close together, the back of their wrists slightly touching, communicating the ascent up the steps.

They turned and faced the rear stained-glass window and waited as the sound of an O'Hare-bound jet faded in the distance. Heidi, though a bit pale and not standing as straight as her mother, was nonetheless radiant.

Then at the end of the piano opening, after the witnesses settled in stillness there, Lydia sang with the voice of an angel sweet, as if the heavens were opened and listening.

♪ *Ah-veh-Mah-ree-ee-ah…*

295

Heidi joined with equally affecting voice, giving birth to a chorus of echoes that danced above our heads—reaching crescendo, then tapering off like a wave returning to sea, in harmonic retreat to the solemn last chord.

Matthew trembled and wept. And as Heidi and Lydia took their seats, before the priest made the announcement, hushed weeping could be heard throughout the church.

My tears were two-fold: I was proud of my wonderful wife and daughter, and I grieved with Matthew over Heidi's unwinding health.

I remember looking up into the dome and thinking:

If you're here, please help Heidi. Look at all she's done for you. Please...

To Every Thing, There Is A Season…

92

By the beginning of May, 1973, the flowers in Heidi's garden broke ground to watch the sun mosey across the sky. The birds, back from winter vacation, sang and built nests in the towering oaks and elms. Less than a mile away at the high school, students raged with spring fever and looked out the windows as their teachers droned on and on.

On the weekends, Trailside Museum swelled with visitors marching through exhibits and wandering out back by the pond. Scoville Park blossomed with flowers, and with couples like Heidi and Matthew, strolling hand-in-hand like countless couples had done before.

Life seemed to go on.

But by the middle of May, Heidi was back in the hospital for what would be the last time.

If you had seen her that first night in her hospital bed, you wouldn't have suspected her time was near. Yes, you would have noticed she looked thin and tired, and you might have noticed she was blind. But you wouldn't have thought things were as bad as they were; you wouldn't have thought her body was shutting down. Her gentle, persistent smile would have fooled you, as would the ever-striking features of her face and the shine of her long, ebony hair as she lay on the pillow.

She was beautiful...oh, so beautiful...

Lydia and I knew this stay was different when Heidi didn't ask for Zaccheus until after she had been in the hospital for almost a week. Even then, she asked for him only as an afterthought:

"Please find Katie and ask her to come see me," she said. "Oh, and bring my bear, if you remember."

We hadn't heard from Katie in over a year and had no idea where she was or how to contact her. When we got home, I went into Heidi's room to get Zaccheus so I could put him by the back door as a reminder. I didn't pay much attention when the phone rang, knowing Lydia would answer it.

I found the bear tucked under the covers, his head resting on the pillow. "Zaccheus," I whispered. "Heidi would like to see you."

As I turned toward the door, Heidi's board caught my eye. The line at the bottom—her wish for a Volkswagen—had been erased, replaced with a Bible verse. And at the top of the board, three underlined words stood out:

HEIDI'S HOPE: To hear <u>Jesus</u> say:
"Well done, thou <u>good</u> and <u>faithful</u> servant."

Below that were the seven directives Heidi had written years earlier, along with the dates and notes she had added next to all but one of those directives: *Go Unto the Prisoners.*

I was still reading her notes when I heard Lydia gasp down in the kitchen. I put Zaccheus into my shirt pocket and hurried downstairs.

Lydia was smiling and wiping tears from her face when we walked in on her. When she saw me, she said over the phone, "It's a miracle that you called. Here, talk with your father."

"Heidi?" I said.

No. It was Katie. She had taken a job in New York for a small cosmetics firm and was in Chicago on a two-day business trip. She wanted to know if she could meet us somewhere for dinner.

Lydia had told her about Heidi being in the hospital, and about Heidi wanting to see her. We offered to pick her up downtown, but Katie insisted we stay in Oak Park in case the hospital called.

"I'm at the train station now," Katie told me. "I can be in Oak Park within 30 minutes."

"OK, your mother can drop me off at the hospital then pick you up at the station—Oh, and Katie—this *is* a miracle!"

93

Matthew was leaning over the bed and had just given Heidi a kiss when I walked into the hospital room. His face was wet from crying.

Heidi groped the air until she found Matthew's hands. "Always remember what we talked about tonight," she said in a soft voice. "I'll be disappointed if you're not there."

Matthew's face contorted in a futile attempt to hold back a second wave of tears. He drew a deep breath and blew it out slowly, then lifted Heidi's hand to his mouth and kissed it.

"I love you, Heidi Richards," he said.

Heidi turned her head toward his voice. "And I love you, Matthew Karlsson."

Matthew lowered Heidi's hand, then turned to me and nodded. "Good night, Mr. Richards."

"Thanks for dropping by, Matthew."

I closed the door after he left, then walked over and stood by the chair next to the bed.

"Did you bring Zaccheus?" Heidi asked.

"I did."

Heidi smiled and lifted her arms. "Where is he?"

I placed the pudgy bear in her hands and she gave him a squeeze. "Hey, little guy," she said. "You and I go back a long way..."

I chuckled. "Do you remember when me and your mom played peek-a-boo with you and Zaccheus?"

"Yes, I remember," Heidi said. "You used to pull the blanket over me, and I thought Zaccheus had done it."

"And you would have gone on thinking that if Mom hadn't told you it was me."

We laughed, and some color flowed into Heidi's cheeks. I leaned down and kissed one, then scooted the chair over and sat down beside her.

She took my hand in hers.

"We've had some wonderful times," she said.

"Yes, we have."

The room grew quiet, save for an occasional beep from the monitors and the muffled sounds of people and carts bustling about in the hall. Heidi turned her head and stared through the ceiling, as if looking into heaven.

"I am so blessed," she said, "to be part of his surprise."

"What surprise?" I asked.

She squeezed my hand and turned her face back to me. "The surprise of being."

"Of being what?"

"Just *being*," she said. "Even the thought of it overwhelms me at times, in a good way..."

I leaned in closer and said in a quiet voice, "Sometimes I'm overwhelmed by how *rarely* I'm overwhelmed. There are times when I feel that I've squandered my life, that I've fallen short of something more important, something I can't seem to get my mind around... Then I think of you, and your mother, and about the blessings that come my way through you two...

I've wondered what I've done to deserve such blessings, and I've gotten this feeling—no, this *realization*—that it has nothing to do with me or what I did or deserve. I realize that it's a gift. It's *all,* a gift."

Heidi drew my hand to her mouth and kissed it.

"I love you, Daddy. *You* are a wonderful gift."

"I don't know," I said. "I've let so much go by."

"Me too," Heidi said.

I fought back tears. "Little Princess, your board is almost filled. What else could you have done?"

"Well, I had a lot of help," she said. "And even so, I didn't finish all I set out to do."

"If you're talking about visiting jails—can't you find someone else to go?"

Heidi lifted her head. "I've been thinking about that... and wondering if you'd go for me."

"Would you still get credit for it?"

Heidi chuckled. "Oh, Daddy," she said. "It's not about who gets the credit; it's about getting the work done."

"Well, I—"

"If you don't know what to say, just take some of the tracts from my top shelf and hand them out."

"Tracts?"

"Yeah—you know, those pamphlets."

I remembered how Heidi used to hand out pamphlets and talk with people out on the street, and how strange I thought that was at the time. But somehow, there at her bedside, her request seemed like something I should do, something I *wanted* to do, for her.

"OK, I'll go," I told her.

Heidi eased her head back down on the pillow. "Thank you," she said, "and if you think of it, go to my room tonight and write a note for yourself on my board."

I brushed the back of my hand softly against her cheek. "Consider it done," I said. "And who knows? Now that I'm one of your disciples, maybe *I'll* get into heaven."

"Oh Daddy," Heidi said with a chuckle, "you know better than that." Then she reminded me for the zillionth time:

"Heaven comes through faith… in Jesus."

"So you and your mother have been telling me all these years."

Heidi whispered, "Expect God to surprise you."

A moment later, we heard the door ease open, and the voice of a young woman saying,

"Is there a little sister in here?"

94

Heidi cried out, "Katie!"

I fetched two more chairs from the other side of the room and the three of us sat around Heidi's bed. It was the first time the whole family had been together in over five years.

We laughed as we recalled adventures of growing up in The Pink House. And Katie laughed the loudest when we relived the "Godfather Tony Incident".

Heidi told Katie about Matthew and her Volkswagen. Katie told us about her job and five-year-old daughter, Sarah.

"Sarah means *little princess*," Heidi said.

Katie nodded. "I was thinking of you when I named her."

"When did you get married?" Heidi asked.

Katie blushed. "That's a long story..."

"Well, tell me what Sarah looks like."

Katie chuckled as she dug in her purse. "You wouldn't believe me if I told you, so I'll hand a photo to mom and she can tell you."

I looked over Lydia's shoulder and our jaws dropped.

Lydia asked Katie, "Is this a joke? Did you get this from one of our baby books?"

"No mom, I swear. This is Sarah. I took this picture two weeks ago."

"Come on!" Heidi cried. "What does she look like?"

Lydia swallowed the lump out of her throat. "She looks like you did when you were five. And like me, and grandma."

"Quadruplets!" I shouted.

We talked and laughed for another hour. I think it was the closest time we ever spent as a family.

"I'm so glad we could be together," Heidi said afterward. Then she held out her hands. "Come here…"

We leaned over the bed and she said to each of us, in turn:

"I love you, Katie…

"I love you, Mom…

"I love you, Daddy…"

It was an oddly dreamlike moment, simple in so many ways, transcendent in so many others, one of my most treasured memories.

A few minutes later, an aide walked into the room. A towel was draped over her shoulder, and in her hands were a small plastic tub and a sponge.

"Well," the stocky, 30-ish woman said in a thick drawl, "like my daddy used to say back in Miss'ippi, anyone not taking a bath has gotta go!"

Katie looked at her watch and gasped. "Wow, time got away from us!"

We took turns leaning over the bed and kissing Heidi. "Dad and I will be back first thing tomorrow," Lydia told her.

On the way out of the building we offered Katie a ride downtown but she refused. "You guys stick around in case Heidi needs you," she said. "I'll take the train, just drop me off up the street."

No one said a word as we headed south on Austin Boulevard toward the train station; I guess we were all just thinking back on our visit with Heidi.

We got a red light before the expressway and Katie leaned forward from the back seat. "I can get out here; there's no need to stop on the bridge."

She opened the door and turned to us after putting one foot out on the pavement. "Why did all this happen to Heidi?" she said. "It's not like she was a bad person."

Lydia reached over and put her hand on Katie's. "And how did you happen to call today, when Heidi needed you? Some things we just can't understand now."

Katie fought back tears and got out as the light turned green.

It drizzled on the way home, filling the car with the sounds of windshield wipers and traffic whooshing through the streets. It wasn't until after I turned off the engine in the garage that I heard Lydia softly weeping. I leaned over and wiped her tears with my thumb.

We went into the house and had just taken off our jackets when the phone rang.

"Hello?... Yes, this is John Richards..."

Lydia must have read my face. She came up and put her hands on my shoulders, her head on my chest. And when I broke into tears, she clenched my shirt and wept with me.

"Thank you for calling," I was barely able to say over the phone. "We'll leave right away... Yes, I understand... Thank you..."

95

By the time we reached the room at the hospital, the bed was laid flat, the rail lowered. The IV was out of Heidi's arm, the machines and monitors turned off and pushed to the side.

Heidi looked like she had fallen asleep. Her eyes were closed, her hair neatly brushed behind her ears. Her mouth relaxed, slightly open.

Lydia and I stood at her side, one arm around each other's waist, looking down through silent tears, poring over precious memories of the one who lay before us, the one whose work and struggle had finally come to an end.

I brushed the back of my hand softly against her cheek as I had done less than three hours earlier.

Her skin was still warm.

So lost were we in our thoughts, neither Lydia nor I noticed the aide who slipped into the room, until she cleared her throat.

"Mr. and Mrs. Richards," she said. "My name is Georgia, I was here earlier tonight."

"Of course," Lydia said. "You came to bathe Heidi."

"Yes, Ma'am, I did. And me and your daughter got along right fine, too. We talked about The Good Book, and about the Lord. I'm sure she's walking with Jesus now."

Lydia let out a cry and sunk her face in my shoulder. Georgia excused herself and was about to leave, but Lydia turned and asked, "Were you here when she passed on?"

"Yes, Ma'am, I was."

"Did you notice what time she left?"

"No, Ma'am. I had no idea she was 'bout to go. We was talking and laughing ourselves a good time. I told her about a couple I worked for down in Miss'ippi. They had three young boys, barely a year apart. One day the misses calls and tells me to give those boys a scrubbing."

Georgia chuckled as she continued.

"I filled the tub and called their names. Ohhhh, they went a hiding! They knew what was comin'! I rounded 'em up and told 'em to get them clothes off and go jump in the tub. 'Hurry up now,' I said, 'I've seen naked little white boys before.'"

Georgia laughed and added, "I tell you, your daughter was laughing so hard, I thought she was gonna hurt herself."

Lydia and I chuckled through our tears as Georgia went on. "I kept sponging her down and she grew all quiet. Then I sang a song momma use to sing back home:

♫ *Sometimes I feel discouraged, And think my work's in vain,*
But then the Holy Spirit, Revives my soul again...

"I sang and washed all the way down to her toes, then I said, 'All clean, young lady. Now don't you go out running in the mud.' I waited for her to laugh, but she never did. And when I turned to her, she was lying there—not like you see her now, oh no—there was a *look* on her face, a look I ain't seen but once before, when my grandpappy died."

As Georgia looked at Heidi's face, she said in a sure and steady voice:

"Mr. and Mrs. Richards, the nurse told me your daughter was blind. But I tell you, her eyes was looking at something. Something no more than a few feet away. And there was joy and surprise shining out of her, like light from the sun. As if she was looking at Jesus himself."

96

When we got home that night, we went into Heidi's room to walk in her Gethsemane, where she prayed herself to sleep near her Bible and her stuffed animals and her life savings of photographs, each with its own story.

On the nightstand next to the bed, her diary was opened to the last entry:

> *You are my light, though my eyes are darkened.*
> *You are my power, though my strength is gone.*
> *I'll fall asleep, but death will not keep me.*
> *For the trumpet shall sound,*
> *and I will rise to meet Him in the air.*
> *Called up by your power to glory there.*
> *I will have a new body: Immortal,*
> *imperishable, no longer subject*
> *to sickness or mishap or torments of time.*
> *The surprises of heaven — at last, mine...*

Despite the numbing fog that rolled through my mind, I somehow remembered my promise to Heidi earlier that night.

And as I walked over to her board, I remembered her 13th birthday party: the girls doing *The Twist*, Matthew and I sneaking the board up to Heidi's room, and the look on her face when she saw it.

Now her board was filled with remembrances of what she had done. In the only space left, next to the words *Go Unto the Prisoners*, I wrote: *May 29, 1973. Delegated to John Richards.*

Heidi's board, as filled as it had become, was barely a footnote to the extent of her work.

Attendance at her funeral told more of the story.

Four hundred and fifty seats were not enough for all who gathered at that Monday morning service. Heidi's teachers were there, along with her helpers—Dorks, Doopers, and Zombies—some of whom flew across the country to see off their mentor and friend. There was a busload of residents from the retirement home, and medical staff from Loyola and Children's Memorial. The Friday night Bible study group sat near the front, along with dozens of kids from Scoville Park, and volunteers and staff from Trailside Museum. Hundreds more gathered from the community, people of all ages who came to say goodbye after the paper ran Heidi's story over the weekend.

Afterward, it took three police officers to guide all the traffic into the cemetery. More than two hundred attended the simple graveside service. Words were said. We placed roses on the casket. People left in silence.

I drove back to the cemetery a half-hour later, and joined Matthew and Martha in their tears.

The Adventure Goes On

97

Ten years have passed.

Martha writes every month from the mission fields of the Ivory Coast. Matthew has his own story, which I'll let him tell for himself. Katie is a single mom, living in Boston with fifteen-year-old Sarah.

Lydia and Katie are good friends now. They talk on the phone every week and the four of us spend every Christmas together, alternating between Chicago and the east coast.

There are still times I shudder when I think that Heidi is gone and that I'll never share another moment with her. What I'd give to relive even the most mundane day with her again. Just to see her smile, or hear her call me *Daddy*...

I often wonder what she'd be doing today if she hadn't died. Would she have made a believer out of me? Would she have married Matthew? Would she be a pastor's wife with two kids and a third on the way?

And what about her work? Would her zeal have waned over time, would it have worn away in the turbulence of life? I don't think so. Something tells me she'd be doing even more—and still be wondering if it were enough.

The last thing Heidi wrote on her board was a verse from the Bible:

Hope deferred makes the heart sick,
But when the longing comes, it is a tree of life.

Every time I see that, I think of Heidi's hope, and of how I've been carried through the sorrow of her death by *my hope* that her longing has been fulfilled.

Lydia and I are traveling to the Middle East next month to visit Bethlehem, Galilee, and Jerusalem. I have lived in the company of spiritual giants; I want to know more about this Jesus who reached through the centuries and touched their lives. I want to see where he lived, and walk where he walked.

Meanwhile, I walk the paths of one who knew him well.

I walk the path behind Trailside Museum, where Heidi walked in awe and quiet reflection during her brief sojourn on earth.

I walk in and around Scoville Park where she shared God's love with people on the street.

I visit the nursing homes and homeless shelters where Heidi got her deepest satisfaction helping those who couldn't pay her back.

And yes, I walk to the jail, and visit inmates in her stead.

Sometimes, in the late afternoon, I walk the empty halls of the high school with my eyes closed and arms stretched out, trying to touch the Spirit that touched Heidi on her prayer walks.

And once every year, I walk to the garage and sit in the back seat of the slightly-dented baby-blue Volkswagen that waits where Heidi last parked it in the summer of '72...

I close my eyes and the car ascends in a sea of light as Heidi drives along celestial streets of gold with the windows wide open and the wind dancing in her long, beautiful hair.

She can see again.

And as a child caught up in the endless surprise of heaven, she points out the mansions along the way, and gushes on and on about the saints who live there.

Her strength and confidence restored, she downshifts into second and spins around the corner into the exact center of her lane. And with a look of satisfaction and accomplishment, she turns and smiles at her Lord, riding beside her.

He nods with a chuckle, and assures her again:

"Well done, thou good and faithful servant."

And I whisper... *Amen.*

Please Help!

Greetings from Stephen Goss!

I'm an unknown author without an agent or publisher and if this story is to go anywhere, I'm going to need the help of enthusiastic readers—like **you**, I hope.

If you enjoyed *Heidi's Hope:*

Can you tell your friends about it?
Maybe drop a good word or two on your social network?
Or write an encouraging review on Amazon or Goodreads, or on your blog?

If you live in the States and you're enthusiastic enough to have friends come to your house to discuss the book, I'd be happy to join you over the phone—unless a miracle happens and I'm inundated with requests. In which case I might have to limit my thanks to the first 25 folks who contact me through my Facebook Page which hardly anyone knows about.

I hope you'll help me get others interested in my writing so I can publish more of the stories that are floating around in my head and on my hard-drive.

For a list of what I've written,
visit my Author Page on Amazon:
www.amazon.com/Stephen-Goss/e/B006FQIMB2

I'd like to read your comments
on Amazon, or on my "secret" Facebook Page:
www.facebook.com/AuthorStephenGoss

Thank You!

Q & A with the Author

Q: What did you study in school?

A: I hold degrees in engineering. I've worked at IBM, Bell Labs, and Lucent Technologies. While doing what engineers do, I also wrote on the side. I had seven unfinished novels spinning around my hard drive when I was offered a buyout during a parade of corporate downsizings. I took the *Buyout* in 2001 before they could give me the *Get Out*.

Q: So how did this story come to be?

A: My mom died later that year, and I don't know if that had anything to do with what I'm about to tell you. But one year after mom's death, I was standing at the stove fixing breakfast when the seeds of *Heidi's Hope* flew into my mind. I stood there and said, *No! Not another unfinished novel!* But within four months, I had an 80,000-word first draft.

I've been asked if the story is autobiographical. It is not. Nor is it about my mom. But it came at a time when my life was affected by change and death, two things we all face in life. I hope readers going through tough times now will find *Heidi's Hope* to be especially uplifting, even as I did when the story came to me during a season of loss.

Q: Did John become a believer at the end of the story?

A: Some people think so and some don't. Looking at the reviews, I think people are filling in the backstory from their own experiences, which seem to be mostly positive.

I know what happened to John because I have this big backstory in my head, only parts of which made it to the pages of *Heidi's Hope*. I have enough up there to write two more books, based on Matthew's and Lydia's perspectives.

With enough reader support—*hint, hint: tell your friends*—the two books will be called *Heidi's Love* and *Heidi's Faith*.

Here's what the overall backstory is telling me.

Heidi's Love picks up the story as Matthew remembers Heidi after her death. It also reveals a genetic anomaly which gave Matthew the ability to see the universe as few people can. It's an unusual love story—not only because of Matthew's remarkable life journey, but also because of what it says about the reality we live in, and the reality to come.

Heidi's Faith is narrated by Lydia and seasoned with snippets from Heidi's diary. It explores the inner thoughts of "the twins" and looks into the faith of "the triplets."

Here also, readers learn more about John and Katie.

Q: What else are you working on?
A: I have more novels, short stories, and non-fiction pieces in the hopper. Some of them are serious, others comedic. They all offer something to think about and/or laugh over. I hope to get more of the shorter pieces out by the end of 2013. Keep checking my Author Page at Amazon for a progress report.

I'm especially excited about two of the ***non-fiction*** pieces I'm working on:

Earth Is A Happening Place — a look at the astonishingly special role the earth and its inhabitants play in the universe.

The Not So Great Science / Faith Debate — a look at this distracting war of presumptions, and the toll it has had on our ability to understand reality.

Stay tuned!

About the Author

Stephen Goss holds degrees in engineering from the University of Illinois. He holds seven patents and has worked as an engineer, consultant, college instructor, videogame developer, certified technical trainer, real estate agent, and day trader.

He's given hundreds of technical presentations as an engineer, and has recited scripture in hundreds of churches as a grateful believer in God, who created all things.

Seven unfinished novels were spinning around his hard drive when the seeds of **Heidi's Hope** flew into his mind one day as he stood at the stove fixing breakfast. He's been mining reality, imagination, and his hard drive ever since.

He's a former resident of Oak Park.

Made in the USA
Columbia, SC
02 March 2019